FREAKY RITES

A MYSTIC CARAVAN MYSTERY BOOK SIX

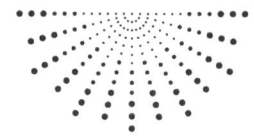

AMANDA M. LEE

WINCHESTERSHAW PUBLICATIONS

ONE

"Stop bouncing around."

"I'm not bouncing around."

"You are and it's driving me crazy."

"I don't think that's a very long trip for you."

"That did it!" Even though he was behind the wheel on a busy interstate, Kade Denton reached over the middle of the truck seat and made a grab for my best friend Luke Bishop.

I realized immediately this was a bad idea – and liable to end in disaster because we were in bumper-to-bumper traffic – so I slapped Kade's hand to keep him from wrapping it around Luke's throat and adopted my best "I'm in charge and you have to listen to me" voice.

"Focus on the road!"

Kade's irritation at being bossed around was obvious, but he did as I instructed, grabbing the steering wheel so tightly that his knuckles turned white, while focusing out the windshield and cursing under his breath as he regarded Route 101, a rather populated California highway that led to our destination.

"I'm going to kill him," Kade muttered under his breath. "I just want you to know that. You're fond of him and I find you adorable ...

and sweet ... and other things I can't talk about in mixed company. But I'm going to kill him. You should say your goodbyes now."

I ran my tongue over my teeth as I debated how to fix the situation. Generally I'm not much for mediating, but the trip between Portland and our new stop – a spot in the middle of nowhere that would serve as the circus hub for multiple northern California cities – had been one of the longest trips of my life.

Yes, that's right. Poet Parker – that's me, in case you're wondering – was officially at her limit.

"You guys both need to knock it off," I shot back, tugging on my limited patience as I rolled my neck and adjusted the vent in Kade's truck so the chilly air blasted directly at my face. "The last thing we need is a fight."

"Oh, now, don't be like that," Luke complained from the back seat. He was blond, handsome, utterly charming when he wanted to be ... and he knew exactly how to get under Kade's skin. Kade was my boyfriend and Luke was my best friend, so that made for some awkward encounters at times. Those encounters bothered Kade much more than they did Luke. Luke treated them as if they were games, which only added to his charm (although Kade would completely melt down if I ever pointed that out). "No one is fighting. We're having a simply lovely conversation about your new trailer, which will be waiting for you at the campground."

I flicked a glance over my shoulder and found Luke watching me with unreadable eyes. Ever since Kade and I made the decision to move in together he'd been oddly quiet. Sure, he teased me mercilessly at first – multiple digs about bedhead, shaving my legs in private and walking around in a face mask and ruining what he called my "sexual mystique" – but that was mild considering Luke's personality. I was still waiting for the big bomb to drop.

"Can you not irritate Kade when he's driving?" I asked after a beat.

"Because it's unsafe and you want to make sure we arrive at our next destination in one piece?"

I shook my head. "Because it's tacky. Think of it like a pink purse in a sea of red pumps."

Luke scowled. "Oh, great. You're going to give me nightmares."

I smirked as I slouched down in my seat and extended my legs to stretch. Despite the long drive – and even longer sniping fest – I was relatively relaxed. I was looking forward to getting my hands on the new trailer my boss Max Anderson – who also happened to be Kade's father – had secured for us. It was supposed to be waiting when we arrived, which meant we would officially begin sharing a roof. Unofficially we had been sharing a roof since we got together, because sleeping apart wasn't an option either of us wanted to explore.

"Somehow I think you'll survive," I said dryly, shrugging my shoulder against the seatbelt. "If those creepy dolls from last week didn't give you nightmares, I'm sure a pink purse won't."

I regretted the words the second they escaped my mouth. Bringing up the killer dolls was a bad idea, especially because some of the "dolls" were also people ... including the fourth person in our truck. Melissa Craft, my young sidekick, had been seduced by an evil entity that took over her mind and almost killed her. Melissa's recovery from that event had been slow, to say the least.

Melissa didn't respond to the statement, instead continuing to stare blankly out the truck window. She either didn't register my offhand comment or chose to ignore it.

Kade sensed my distress at opening my big mouth and inserting my foot, so he cleared his throat and tapped the steering wheel as he made an effort to change the subject. "What do you know about this area?"

I wasn't expecting the question but I was eager to focus on anything other than Melissa's morose countenance and the possibility that Kade and Luke might actually come to blows if this trip didn't end quickly.

"We're not staying in a town," I replied, anxiously rubbing my hands against my knees to shake off the sense of dread pervading the truck. We didn't often ride in a group like this. Melissa generally caught a ride with one of the other groups, but she was so despondent that no one wanted her. (Plus they weren't sure if she was completely over that whole "being possessed by a witch and trying to kill us" thing.) As for Luke, his truck was in for repairs. Max arranged for it to be delivered to the new campground the second it was finished. That meant Luke needed a ride. I was his best friend, so he immediately came to me to serve as his taxi service. Kade was still fuming about the development.

"If we're not staying in a town, where are we staying?" Kade asked.

"It's basically an open field between a lot of towns," I explained. "The biggest is Eureka, which happens to be close to the water if we get a chance to take a break one night. I know you like walking along the beach. Even though our last stop was close to a beach, we didn't really get a chance to enjoy it because of all the killing and bodies showing up."

I cringed again when I realized how irritating that must sound to Melissa.

As if reading my mind, Kade reached across the console and grabbed my hand to give it a good squeeze. He recognized I was struggling with Melissa – everyone in camp was having difficulty dealing with her – but he refused to let the conversation stall.

"What else can you tell us about the area?"

I smothered my worry for Melissa with attention to detail regarding our home for the next week. As a circus caravan, we hopped from location to location without calling any particular place "home." I was used to it. Kade was newer to Mystic Caravan Circus, so he was still coming to grips with the nature of his new world.

"Oh, well, there's a nature preserve not far away," I started. "There's also a few other small towns, which are supposed to be really cute." Something occurred to me. "Wait ... didn't you grow up in California?"

"I did, but not this part of the state. I was much farther south. I don't remember ever visiting this far north. It's a new adventure for me, too."

"Oh, well, I guess that makes sense." California was a huge state, after all. I grew up in Michigan and only saw small pockets of it before running away to join the circus, and Michigan was nowhere near the size of California. "Also, there's a reserve thing – um, I think it's called Headwaters Forest Reserve – and it's supposed to feature a lot of redwood trees. It's supposed to be really beautiful. I thought if we get set up in a reasonable time that maybe we could take a hike."

"I don't like hiking," Luke complained from the back seat.

Kade scowled. "I'm pretty sure she was talking to me."

Luke wrinkled his nose. "Why would she want to hike with you? I'm the fun one."

"I'll show you fun," Kade muttered.

I sensed the conversation getting off track and desperately tried to rein in my rambunctious best friend and easily irritated boyfriend. "I'm also looking forward to seeing Eureka," I added. "The name is cool – don't say anything obnoxious, Luke – and the entire city is a historical district."

"Wow," Kade intoned, his lips curving. "I didn't know you did so much research on this one. I'm impressed."

"We've never been here before. It's my job to conduct research in case ... well, in case things go south."

Kade tightened his grip on my hand but he kept his eyes focused on the road. He was ridiculously handsome, his dark hair cropped close to his eyes, and his jaw wide and strong. He was also sweet and loyal. He hadn't been part of the circus for long, but memories of life without him were already fading. It was as if he'd always belonged with us and seamlessly fit right away because he was always supposed to be with us.

It was a sobering thought.

"I believe it's my job to make sure our new locations are safe," Kade pointed out. "I'm the head of security. I didn't find anything in my research to worry me. You should relax and enjoy the trip. The view is spectacular – I mean, look at that water – and we'll be in our new trailer relatively quickly. After that I expect you to turn into a drill sergeant until we get the new place organized and set up exactly how you like it."

I was fairly certain that was a dig. "Are you suggesting I'm anal retentive?"

Kade immediately started shaking his head. "Absolutely not. You're not anal retentive. You're fussy."

Wait ... was that better? "I'm not fussy."

Luke snorted and even Melissa looked mildly amused by the statement. That didn't mean I would admit to being fussy. I mean ... what a stupid word. I'm extremely far from fussy.

"I'm not fussy," I repeated, hating the fact that my voice took on an edge and I sounded defensive. "I simply like things the way I like them."

"You're right, baby," Kade teased. "That doesn't make you fussy at all."

I jerked my hand away from him. "I am not fussy."

"Oh, you've lost her now, Kade," Luke teased from behind me. "You'll have to get on your knees and beg if you want her to forgive you."

"I plan to play that game later." Kade's grin was mischievous as he followed the highway. "We're looking for Elk River Road, by the way. "If anyone sees it, please call out. I think we're getting close."

"And we're out in the middle of nowhere?" Melissa asked, speaking for the first time since I insisted she ride with us to make sure there were no problems with some of the other workers.

"We are." Kade bobbed his head in confirmation. "There are towns within driving distance, including Eureka, but it's not like before. We're not part of a festival and we won't have other people on top of us."

Or breathing down our necks and poking their noses into our private business, I silently added.

"Good." Melissa's voice was small as she turned to stare out the window. She looked to be lost in her mind. Of course, in the week since we'd rescued her from a crazy woman and a life of possessed torment she often seemed lost. I didn't know what to do to make things better for her.

"Tell me more about the area," Kade instructed quickly. He was as uncomfortable with Melissa's reaction as I was. In fact, if I had to guess, he was even more uncomfortable. "I'm not really familiar with the history of Eureka ... or the set-up of the town."

"Oh, well, I have information here." I grabbed my phone so I could read the notes I'd typed. "The population of Eureka alone is more than twenty-seven thousand. When you add in the other nearby towns, I think that means we're going to have a busy week."

"That's good, right?" Kade was intent on keeping the conversation moving forward.

"No, it sucks," Luke deadpanned. "We prefer a dead stop so we don't make any money."

Kade growled low and deep, and I shot Luke a warning look before continuing.

"There's a healthy native population that still lives here," I read, determined to keep my focus on the area rather than Melissa's rather obvious internal upheaval. "It was part of the gold rush and has a rich history with loggers because of the redwoods. A lot of the homes are Victorian. I can't wait to see them. I love Victorian homes."

"Good to know." Kade winked at me. "What else?"

"Fishing, boating and shipping are big industries," I replied. "Um ... there're also a lot of earthquakes in the area, so we should prepare ourselves for the possibility of a rumble or two."

"That's normal for most of California," Kade pointed out. "I've survived more earthquakes than I can remember. That's not too bad."

"What about paranormal populations?" Luke asked, turning serious. "I would think – especially with the gold rush history and the wildlife preserve – that we're dealing with at least a few different populations."

"That is definitely true," I agreed. "There are two different shifter populations at opposite ends of the county – bears and wolves – and there's a coven working out of Eureka, although it appears small and not too powerful."

"You've obviously done your research," Kade said. "Is there any faction that worries you?"

"Not really." I knew what he was really asking. We'd been caught unaware when it came to Melissa's abduction and possession. I wasn't exactly sure what we could've done to avoid that. There was no way of ferreting out important information until we were well into the game. But that was not something to discuss now.

"There is one interesting tidbit," I added, hoping to engage Melissa in the conversation. She was a fan of old-fashioned ghost stories and the Eureka area had one of the best. "On the other side of the campsite – and I'm talking no more than two miles – we have a bona fide ghost town to tour."

Kade didn't look nearly as thrilled at the prospect as me, but I noticed Melissa perked up at the news. She didn't comment, but her eyes were keen.

"It's called Falk," I continued, eager to keep her engaged. "It was a booming lumber town for fifty years. It had four-hundred residents at one time, which was pretty impressive in the late-1800s. Back in those days it was an hour commute from Eureka by wagon, which wasn't convenient, so the town was built to be self-sufficient.

"Then, when the Great Depression hit in the 1930s, the mill had to be shut down," I continued. "A couple of families stayed until the 1940s, but it became a ghost town after that. Not a literal one, at least at that time. Because squatters wouldn't leave it alone, all the buildings were razed, but now they run tours and stuff there."

Kade furrowed his brow. "And we're interested in tours because?"

"Oh, we're not going on a tour. I wouldn't mind seeing the town, though."

"Why? If the buildings are gone, nothing is there."

"Some of the framework is still there," I argued. "Plus, I guess there are cool rosebushes and English ivy. There're also some foundation areas you can find and gardens that are supposed to be out of this world."

Kade blinked several times in rapid succession. "You want to go to a ghost town to see gardens?"

I shrugged. "I wouldn't mind seeing the ghosts, too."

"You just said it wasn't a literal ghost town."

"I said it wasn't a literal ghost town at the time it shut down," I clarified. "Because of the trees, the area is often foggy. People have claimed to see ghosts wandering the hills and trails ever since the town was razed."

"And you sound excited about that."

"I am excited about that."

"Poet likes ghosts," Luke supplied, his head resting against the window. "She's always been fascinated with them. While shifters, witches, vampires and all the other weird things we cross paths with can be dangerous, ghosts usually keep to themselves and don't offer much trouble. That's why she likes them."

"I guess that makes sense." Kade said the words, but I could tell he remained confused.

"You don't have to go with me," I offered. "I can take someone else or go on my own. I just want to see the town. It's supposed to be neat."

"But ... there are no buildings to look at."

Sometimes he's far too pragmatic for his own good. "I think there's like some sort of train barn or something at one end," I argued. "That's on top of the gardens."

"What is it with you and the gardens?"

That was a good question. "I don't know. I just think it's neat that the gardens somehow survived without tending. It's like nature always finds a way. There are fruit groves and flowering plants. I can't explain why I want to see it. Like I said, you don't have to come. I'll be perfectly safe taking a hike in the woods on my own."

"No, I want to go."

Luke snickered. "He doesn't want to go. He simply wants to make sure you don't find trouble with the ghosts and get hurt. You know that, right?"

I'd figured that out on my own. "We'll talk about it later," I said. "In fact ... I don't have to see the town. It was simply something I was thinking about. We can focus on Eureka and leave it at that."

"We'll talk about it later," Kade said, hitting his turn signal. "Here's the road. We're almost there."

"Great," Luke enthused. "I can't wait. This has been the longest drive ever."

"You should see it from my point of view," Kade groused.

"I have and you got the better end of the deal." Luke was blasé. "I happen to be a witty conversationalist. You're boring and ... um, what's worse than boring?" When I didn't answer, Luke barreled forward. "What are we going to have for dinner? I'm starving. How about steaks?"

And just like that we were almost to our new temporary home and everything was almost exactly the same as before ... except for Melissa. I had no idea when things were going to turn for her. I hoped it was soon, though. I couldn't take much more of the melancholy.

2
TWO

I was impressed with our site. The minute we stopped, I could do nothing but smile at the large trees buffering the location on three sides ... and the spanking new trailer located in the exact right spot to kick off entrance to what we affectionately referred to as trailer row.

"Do you see that?" Kade sidled up and slung an arm over my shoulders. "That's our new home."

He seemed so earnest, so content, all I could do was smile. Of course, the new recreational vehicle was beautiful. It was the fanciest trailer to date – including the one Max called home – and I couldn't help being a little proud ... and smug.

"Do you want to see it?" Kade asked.

I nodded. "Don't we need keys?"

Something jangled in Kade's hands and I smiled when I saw the keyring. "Where did you get that?"

"Max had them. The guys who dropped it off left a set next to the fence post."

I was beyond excited. "So ... let's check out our new digs."

"Definitely." Kade linked his fingers with mine as we tromped across the grassy ground. "Hey, Luke, I'll be back in a little bit if you need help unloading things. You're strapping and strong, though, so I'll bet you can do it yourself."

Luke, his arms laden with chairs for the common area, shot Kade a withering look. "Oh, no, let me do all the heavy lifting while you do my best friend."

Kade was unbothered by the snark. "That's the plan."

"Whatever."

I left Luke to his bad mood, sparing a quick glance for Melissa, who appeared to be helping the others without saying a word, and then pushed the worry out of my head ... at least for the time being. "Let's see it." I rubbed my hands together as Kade fit the key into the lock and pushed open the door. My breath all but whooshed out when I saw the clean interior, which was ten times nicer than my previous trailer. "Wow!"

"Yeah." Kade was equally impressed, running his hands over the granite countertops (Max spared no expense trying to woo his son into forging a new start) and letting loose a low whistle. "This is nice."

"For all the cooking we do inside the trailers," I teased, smiling as I bounced on the leather sofa. It sat across from two matching chairs, both of which were pointed at a flat-screen television. "This is like the queen of all trailers."

"King," Kade absently corrected. "The king of all trailers."

"Not in a matriarchal society, which is what we embrace at Mystic Caravan."

It took Kade a moment to realize what I was saying and he looked legitimately amused as he tore his gaze from the cupboards. "Good point."

"Your old trailer is being moved to the administration row, right?" As second in command to Max, I was the organized sort. I couldn't stop myself from focusing on logistics even though Kade clearly wanted to focus on something else. "We got everything cleaned out and it's just waiting for desks."

"It's taken care of. Your other trailer is going to Melissa, right?"

I stiffened at mention of her name. "It is. I thought she would like it because the old trailer she had was falling apart. The one she'll get isn't top of the line or anything, but it is a vast improvement."

"You don't think she'll like it?"

I shrugged. "I think she has other things on her mind."

"As do you." Kade folded his arms over his chest and leaned against the small row of cupboards. "Poet, you can't force her to talk about what happened. It's only been a few days."

"A week," I corrected. "It's been a week." We'd had a week off in our schedule, which we used to take a break and regroup in Oregon.

"And you think that's enough time for her to get over what happened?" Kade wasn't one to purposely pick fights, but he held his ground when he believed in something. "I'm not sure I think a month or even a year is enough time to get over what happened to her."

I furrowed my brow. "But we saved her. She's okay. Don't you think she should take the first step and start talking about what happened? She'll never get over it until she talks it out."

Kade exhaled heavily as he moved to the couch to sit with me. He lifted my hand, flipping it over so he could trace the lines on my palm, seemingly searching for the right thing to say. "I think there's more than one thing going on here. For starters, before it happened Melissa was being something of a pain. She was acting out and we were punishing her because of that."

I scowled. "Yes, it was more like we were parents than employers."

Kade chuckled. "You don't look old enough to have a child Melissa's age. Don't worry about that."

That honestly hadn't occurred to me. "I don't like being the mommy of the group," I countered. "I like being the cool and sexy ... cousin."

Kade laughed so hard I thought he would fall over. "You're definitely cool and sexy. I refuse to think of you as my cousin, though."

"That would be criminal."

"Definitely." Kade licked his lips as he stared at my hand. "Melissa is struggling with her attitude and what happened after that. She probably thinks that was another punishment. She'll come around on her own – you don't have to worry about that – but the more you hover the longer it'll take."

I balked. "I haven't been hovering."

"You have. Everyone recognizes it, including Melissa. I think most of our friends understand why you've been doing it. Melissa almost died, after all. You managed to keep that from happening."

"I had help."

"You did, but you were the one who kept things together," Kade pressed. "You're the reason we got her back safe, and I don't want to hear one second of arguing about it. You were the hero."

Under normal circumstances I would like being referred to as a hero. Given what happened in Seattle – the horror that almost occurred – I was keener to put the entire episode behind us. "I just want her to smile every now and then," I admitted. "She seems so despondent and she purposely keeps distance between herself and us. I don't know how to fix that."

"I think the problem is that you can't fix that," Kade countered. "Melissa has to come out of this on her own. It's not up to you."

He had a point. It wasn't one I liked, but I understood what he was saying. "I guess you're right."

"I'm always right." Kade poked my side to get me to look at him. "Now, how about checking out the bedroom and seeing how right I can be in there?"

I didn't want to smile. It would only encourage him, after all. But I couldn't stop myself. "Okay, but when Luke complains that we didn't help unpack I'll blame you."

"I'd expect nothing less."

"YOU TWO LOOK all flushed and happy."

Raven Marko, our resident lamia and pot stirrer, fixed Kade and me with a knowing look as she delivered a platter of grilled corn on the cob to the table.

Mystic Caravan essentially separates into three rows during setup. The midway workers take one, the clowns and others who don't fit in with either group (essentially the "irregular" workers) take another, and my outgoing performance-focused brotherhood take the third. The fourth side is always open and near the parking lot, and that's by design.

"We are happy," Kade said, smirking when my cheeks turned red as several pointed stares turned in our direction. "Only one of us is flushed."

I smacked his arm as he smoothly shifted to deflect the playful blow. "I'm not talking about this."

"Talk about your new trailer," Nellie instructed, hiking up his pink evening gown so he could get comfortable on the picnic table bench. "Everyone is drooling we're so jealous. Is it nice inside?"

"It's very nice," Kade replied. "The counters are granite and the cupboards aren't made of particle board. The bedroom is great. We have a queen-sized bed for a change."

"Nice." Raven winked at Kade before smirking at me. "Oh, look, Poet is so red I think we should chop her up for the salad. People will think she's a tomato."

"Leave her alone," Kade instructed, rubbing his hand over my back as he took a look around the fairgrounds. "Where are the rest of the tents and stuff?"

"Not arriving until tomorrow," Max announced, appearing out of the gloom and offering me a smile before sitting at the end of the table. "The fog came on when the trucks were still two hours away. It was thick enough that I told them to stop at a hotel for the night."

"Oh, well, that's convenient." Nellie made a face. The dwarf – the bearded variety from another plane of existence – had a ridiculously expressive face. "I can't believe they let a little fog stop them."

Now that they mentioned it, the grounds were quickly filling with a thick fog that I wasn't anticipating. "Is it normal to fog like this?" I rubbed my hands over my knees as I regarded the expansive grounds. "I mean … we won't be able to see from one end of the fairgrounds to the other once this fog settles."

"My understanding is that the fog is normal during the overnight hours," Max replied. "The ground gets warm during the day, but the nights are cooler. That creates the fog. Plus, well, there are so many trees in this area that they help keep the fog cover low."

"That sounds like something out of a horror movie," Luke complained, rubbing his neck as he stared toward the woods to the east. "I don't like it."

"That's because you're dramatic and tend to be a big baby when you want to be," Kade fired back. "A little fog never hurt anyone. In fact, it's kind of fun. It's atmospheric. I think, once we finish moving the rest of our stuff into the new trailer that we should celebrate with a horror movie or something, Poet. That sounds like the perfect evening to me."

"You just want to get her worked up so she'll give you a little grab when you're sharing a blanket," Luke shot back. "Just for the record, horror movies don't freak Poet out. She likes them well enough, but she's more horrified by chick flicks."

Kade cocked an eyebrow as he snagged my gaze. "Is that true?"

I nodded without hesitation. "*Dirty Dancing* gave me nightmares for weeks."

Luke extended a finger. "Nobody puts Baby in a corner!"

Most everyone grouped around the table burst out laughing. Melissa was the lone holdout. She sat at the opposite end and stared at the fog, seemingly oblivious to the conversation going on around her.

"It seems you like the new trailer." Max's smile was indulgent as he looked at Kade. Their relationship was something of a work in progress, mostly because Max was a magical mage who didn't have a hand in his son's upbringing. Kade had always thought his father died before he was born. When he found out his father was Max – a man he thought of as a funny uncle (not in a gross way) – things didn't go well. After several weeks of strain and fighting, Kade and Max were officially trying to forge a bond. It was slow going but entertaining to watch. "I'm glad it worked out."

"The new trailer is great. Thank you." Kade's smile was easy. "I think we'll be very happy there."

"We still have to get your trailer set up as an office," I reminded him.

"Yes, dear." Kade adopted a put-upon tone that caused more than a few snickers. "I figured we could focus on that tomorrow and the next day, before the circus opens, and we should have everything put together by opening night."

"That'll put a crimp in your exploration plans, Poet," Luke pointed out. "There won't be time to visit ghost towns if you're constantly working."

Max, his interest piqued, arched an eyebrow. "What ghost town?"

"Falk," I answered. "It was a former logging town. There are a lot of ghost sightings and it's within walking distance."

"I didn't know that." Max appeared more curious than concerned. "I'm sure we can find time for those interested in seeing the town to take a walk in that direction. We're organized in a way that we can run this place in our sleep. Even with the rest of the trucks arriving later than expected tomorrow morning, I have no doubt everything will work out."

"I'm sure it will, too," I agreed, inadvertently leaning closer to Kade when I realized the fog was thickening. "Wow. That is ... something."

"It is," Raven agreed, her tone somber. "I know we're in the middle of cooking dinner, but I almost think we should take a pause to erect the dreamcatcher. I'm worried that someone might end up lost in this if we're not careful."

That's not what she was worried about. She kept her true concerns to herself. It wasn't that she was afraid we would lose someone in the mist. It was far more likely we would pick up someone, and without the dreamcatcher in place we might not even pick up on the danger.

You see, in addition to being a source of entertainment for families, we're also monster hunters. Yeah, that's not an exaggeration. Most of us are paranormal beings with a sense of right and wrong and an innate desire to rid the world of legitimate threats. As part of our process, we created a magical dreamcatcher. Four of us – Raven, Nixie, Naida and myself – work together to erect the dreamcatcher, making sure it covers all four corners of whatever fairgrounds we happen to be calling home at any given time. The dreamcatcher alerts when an evil paranormal being crosses its boundaries. It also serves as a lure, calling to those creatures. Unfortunately for us, the magic is so strong it often calls to the occasional evil human as well. We dispatch them as quickly as we hit the actual monsters. We don't discriminate.

"I think we should definitely do that." I licked my lips as I got to my feet. Something about the fog set my teeth on edge. I couldn't explain it. "We should go in teams."

Kade must have sensed my unease because he remained close, his hand on my elbow to still me should I try to walk away. "I'm fine with going in teams. I'll be on your team."

"Who didn't see that coming?" Luke muttered, rolling his eyes.

"Because you want to be part of everything, you can be Nixie's partner," Kade instructed, his tone practically daring Luke to pick a fight. "Nellie, you should go with Raven." Kade was uncertain when he glanced at his father. "Do you want to help?"

Max nodded without blinking. "I think that's a good idea. I haven't participated in a good dreamcatcher ritual in some time. This fog really is ... something. I don't know what to make of it."

Max wasn't the worrying type, but I didn't miss the way his gaze briefly touched on Melissa before shifting to me. "Let's get the dream-catcher up as soon as possible. If it's not perfect because of the fog, it's still something. We'll test the lines when the sun comes out tomorrow. I think it would be wise if after dinner tonight everyone hits their trailers early."

Luke made a protesting sound in the back of his throat. "What about the bonfire? We always have a fire our first night in a new place."

"I think it's wiser for everyone to go to their trailers," Max replied, unruffled. "If you want to have a fire, I certainly won't stop you. I'm your boss, not your keeper."

"Good." Luke slid his eyes to me. "I think we should stick to our usual schedule."

Oh, now he was just messing with me. "You only want me to stick close to you so Kade and I can't enjoy our first night in the trailer."

"That is a vicious lie."

"It's not," Kade argued. "It doesn't matter, though. We're doing the dreamcatcher and then eating dinner. After that, we're going to bed. Alone. There will be no visitors this evening."

"Like I would want to visit you." Luke's tone was haughty as he turned to Nellie. "They're boring and old. Do you want to sit around the bonfire with me and hunt anything that might take advantage of the fog?"

Nellie shrugged, noncommittal.

"You can bring your ax."

"That's a given," Nellie shot back.

"We can have s'mores."

Nellie brightened. "You had me at hunting."

Luke made a face. "I had you at s'mores. Let's not stray too far from the truth, okay?"

"Fine." Nellie's eyes lit with mirth when he flicked them to me. "Let's handle the dreamcatcher. We'll need it if I'm going to chop off heads tonight."

Oh, well, at least he had constructive plans for his evening.

3
THREE

The fog was so thick it made me feel closed in. Here I was, outside and in the fresh air, yet I couldn't help feeling as if I were locked in a coffin.

"This is creepy," Kade commented. He remained close, the idea of me disappearing in the fog apparently too much for him to handle, and occasionally pressed himself to my side. "I don't like it."

"Do you want to hold my hand?" I teased, marking off the paces in my head as I moved across the north side of the fairgrounds. We all took a quadrant and placed magical markers before weaving the magic to build the dreamcatcher. Nixie, Naida and Raven provided most of the magic, which I formed into the right shape. We'd been doing it for years, so I had it down to a science. "I promise to protect you."

"Ha, ha." Kade faked an utterly humorless laugh. "Are you telling me this doesn't bother you?"

We'd made a pact to always tell each other the truth, so I couldn't exactly say that with a straight face. "No, it's definitely weird."

"You said you guys have never been here before, right?" Kade searched the murk for signs of a predator while continuously flicking his gaze back to me to make sure I remained close and hadn't inadvertently wandered away. "How did you end up here this year?"

"A lot of our stops are annual. A lot of them aren't, though. I would say it's about half and half. The ones that are standalones generally come through when a city or township has some special event planned. Only big cities can generally afford us. Occasionally smaller cities call for our services, but only after they've saved considerable money or held a series of fundraisers."

"And that's what this is?" Kade questioned. "This is a one-and-done deal?"

"Pretty much. The one we're going to next is even more unusual."

"I thought we were heading to Michigan next so we could finish out the summer in the Midwest before going south for autumn."

"We are, but our usual stop is in the suburbs of Detroit," I explained, dropping a bit of magic to mark a line and smiling when the entire stretch between my corner and Raven's corner of our new world illuminated. "We're still doing that, but it's after our stop in northern Lower Michigan. It's a place called Hemlock Cove. I just got the paperwork today so I haven't been able to do much research on it yet."

Kade wasn't nearly as interested in the addition to our schedule as I felt. "Michigan is nice in the summer. I've been there once or twice."

"I was raised there until ... well, until Max found me and I started my new life with Mystic Caravan."

Kade stilled, his eyes shifting to me. "I forgot about that. For some reason, when I think about it, I always picture you growing up with the circus."

"Like a well-trained monkey?" I teased.

"Like ... you."

I understood what he was saying and refused to get offended. "No, I was a regular kid for a bit."

"Then your parents died."

"And I was put in the system," I finished. I knew talk about the time I spent in foster care was hard for Kade to hear. He tried to perfect a balancing act, one in which he was the caring boyfriend who was curious but not overbearing. It wasn't always easy for him. "Does it upset you to go back to Detroit?"

I shook my head and smiled. "No. I have a few acquaintances left there. They always turn up. It's not the Detroit you see on television. The fairgrounds are on the city's northern border at Eight Mile and Woodward, but it's not a terrible area. It does make erecting the dreamcatcher difficult because it's so busy, but we always manage."

"And what kind of paranormals are running around Detroit?"

"Mostly wraiths. The northern locations in the state are inundated with wolves. Detroit, though, is something else entirely."

Kade's expression was contemplative. "And what's weird about the job we're going on after this, other than the fact that we get a whole week to drive there, that is?"

"Oh, it's set in a town full of witches."

Kade wrinkled his forehead as he followed me back down the line. I had to test the boundary before we ignited the entire thing. "I'm sorry but ... what?"

I was beyond amused at his reaction. "It's a tourist town that bills itself as a paranormal vacation destination. It's all humans pretending to be witches ... and the occasional tall tale of real witches infiltrating the fake witches. I'm sure there are shifters running around – and apparently there are people who claim to see Bigfoot all the time – but it's supposedly a kitschy town that hosts festivals every five minutes. I'm actually excited to see it."

Kade rolled his eyes. "That sounds like a nightmare."

"It sounds peaceful," I corrected. "The town isn't big enough to stir up a lot of trouble. It's supposed to be chockful of inns, and people travel from all over the country to visit. I think it sounds fascinating."

"I'll take your word for it," Kade said dryly. "As long as it doesn't have fog like this place, I'll consider it an improvement."

"Yeah. That would be nice, huh?"

We met Raven at her corner when we'd finished. She seemed to be agitated, although I couldn't put my finger on why.

"What's wrong with you?"

As if on cue, Luke came shuffling out of the nearby trees, his nose lifted to the sky as if he were scenting the air.

"I thought he was with Nixie," Kade complained.

"He was, but he came running this way about five minutes ago," Raven replied. Her relationship with Luke was one of siblings, and those siblings weren't all that fond of one another. "He barely said a word before barreling into the trees."

I didn't like the sound of that. "Why didn't you say anything?"

Raven shrugged. "It's not my day to watch him."

Come to think of it, my relationship with Raven wasn't warm and fuzzy either. We often irritated each other until magic and insults were flying freely. As of late, though, we'd managed a tolerable truce. I couldn't help but wonder if that was about to fall by the wayside.

"Did you ever think he went over there because of something important?" I challenged, pointing myself toward the trees in question as I fought the urge to throttle Raven. "He could've been hurt."

"If only." Raven sounded disinterested, but she followed as I closed the distance to Luke. He didn't bother looking in our direction, his eyes instead bouncing along the walls of wilderness.

"Do you smell something?" Kade asked.

Luke nodded. "Yes. You and Poet took a roll in the hay before dinner to christen your new camper. I can smell the sex all over both of you. Next time you should shower before dinner."

Kade scowled. "Must you always make things so difficult?"

"Yes."

"Why?"

"Because that's how I roll." Luke cocked his head to the side, as if listening for a sound only he could hear. "I don't think we're alone."

The way he said it, so simple and matter of fact, the hair on my arms stood at attention. "What do you mean? Are wolves close? Is something watching us in the woods?"

"Something is definitely watching us, but I don't think it's wolves," Luke replied. "Don't get me wrong, there are shifters close. I've scented at least two separate wolves, one bear and one llama."

Kade was flabbergasted. "There are llama shifters? That can't be right."

"There are, but they don't spend a lot of time around here," I replied. "They're mostly a thing in South America. You won't see many of them in the United States. If you do, they're not really a threat as long as they don't spit on you."

"They're one of the lesser shifters," Luke volunteered, puffing out his chest. "They're not top dogs like wolf shifters."

"I think that goes along with the name," Kade said. "Llamas don't exactly strike fear in the populace."

"They have venomous spit," I pointed out. "They're kind of nasty when they want to be."

"Ugh. I can't even talk about this." Kade slapped his hand to his forehead. "Are we really over here because we're living in fear of a llama shifter?"

"No." Luke immediately started shaking his head. "The shifter scents are low and buried. They're weak. That means shifters crossed the boundaries days ago. I haven't scented anything dangerous."

The way he phrased the statement caught me off guard. "If you haven't scented anything dangerous, why are you worked up?"

"Because I can hear something."

I chewed on my bottom lip and glanced at Raven to see what she made of the comment. She looked less than impressed, bored even. The way she stared at her nails told me she thought Luke was simply being his usual self and trying to gain attention he didn't necessarily deserve.

Kade asked the obvious question. "What did you hear?"

"Chanting."

My eyebrows migrated higher. "Chanting?"

"That's the only way I can think to describe it." Luke turned defensive. "I swear I heard it. It sounded like a bunch of people whispering all at once. It only happened for a second – and I swear it was in this direction – but I heard it."

He was so earnest I instinctively believed him. Still, Luke's ears were good – it was a wolf thing – but he was hardly the only animal shifter in our group with sensitive ears. If someone else heard the chanting, surely there would be more people looking around to find the source of the noise.

"Well, do you hear it now?" I asked finally.

"No."

"It just stopped?"

"Pretty much."

I looked at Kade. "What do you think?"

"Oh, what are you asking him for?" Luke complained. "He's going to say I'm crazy and imagining things."

"That's not what I'm going to say at all," Kade countered. "I think you probably did hear something. Most likely it's the fog making us all a little nervous. The voices probably came from clown row or where the midway crew is spread out. I doubt you heard it from the trees."

Luke was incensed. "I think I know where I heard the noise."

"And I think there's nothing out here." Kade extended his hands so he could gesture left and right. "It's just us. Raven and Poet would've sensed if something else was close. They didn't. That means there's nothing out here."

Luke is stubborn by nature, so his reaction didn't surprise me. "I don't happen to believe that's true." He folded his arms over his chest. "I think I'm right. Something is out here."

Kade turned to me for confirmation. "What do you think?"

I hated being put on the spot. "I think that I'm hungry and I want to finish the dreamcatcher. We can talk about this more at dinner."

"See, she agrees with me." Luke was haughty. "She doesn't want to come right out and say it because she thinks it will ruin your first night in your new digs, but she totally agrees with me."

Instead of disagreeing, Kade merely cuffed the back of Luke's head before falling into step with him for the trip back to the fairgrounds. "I think you're dreaming."

"And I think you're dreaming."

"I think you're both annoying," Raven snapped. "I mean ... what are you bickering about? Do you even know?"

Kade and Luke exchanged a look that made me smile.

"We always know what we're fighting about," Luke replied. "We're not idiots."

"No, of course not." Raven flicked her eyes to me. "How do you put up with this?"

I shrugged. "I'm getting kind of used to it."

"It's beyond annoying."

"Sometimes. Other times it's fun."

"I think you're all sick in the head."

I couldn't help but secretly agree with her.

IT WASN'T HARD TO leave the testosterone trio of Dolph (our strong man), Nellie and Luke to man the bonfire. They claimed they were watching the shadows for our safety, but I was fairly certain they were doing it for the s'mores, beer and chance to chest thump to their hearts' content.

Raven's irritation was evident when it came time to retire. Her boyfriend Percival, a man who spoke with a fake British accent and purposely dressed as a clown, offered to stay and be brave with the other three, but Raven was having none of that. She practically dragged him away, although it didn't look like much of a hardship on his part. He was practically drooling thanks to the sexy suggestions I was sure she whispered in his ear.

I didn't even have to bother with the suggestions. The second we finished dinner and dishes, Kade was on his feet and herding me toward the new trailer.

"We'll see everybody in the morning," he called out. "Don't bother knocking unless the world is coming to an end."

"Why would we come knocking?" Nellie asked, a marshmallow fork in his hand. "We've got everything under control. If something comes hunting we'll take care of it."

"I was saying it for Luke's benefit," Kade replied. "Luke, no visits tomorrow morning. I mean it. We'll come up with a visitation schedule for you, but it won't begin with a cameo appearance before breakfast on our first full day here."

"Oh, whatever." Luke's irritation was evident as he swung his marshmallow fork as if it were a sword. "Like I would waste my time visiting you guys in the morning. I'm going to be far too busy lording over my kill to worry about you two."

"That's fine." Kade practically lifted me off my feet when we hit the steps to our new home. "We will see everyone else in the morning."

"He's kind of like a high school kid, he's so eager," Nellie noted, not bothering to lower his voice. "I hope he has more staying power than a high schooler."

Kade scowled as he opened the door. "Don't make me come over there."

"Oh, I'm shaking in my Louis Vuitton first-lady pumps."

Kade's expression was hard to read. "Am I supposed to know what that means?"

I laughed as I pushed him inside. "No. Ignore him. He's just trying to get under your skin."

"He's doing a good job. So is Luke."

"Yeah, well ... ." I risked a glance outside, staring hard at a cavorting Luke before the door slammed shut.

"What are you thinking?" Kade asked, stripping out of his shirt. Apparently he was eager to check out the bed a second time.

"I'm thinking that Luke thought he heard something in the woods."

"So? You didn't hear anything."

"I'm not a wolf. He has better hearing than I do."

"Yes, and you have better senses than he does." Kade tipped me over into one of the leather chairs so he could remove my shoes. "Do you really think something is out there watching us?"

"I don't know. I think Luke believes it."

"Yes, but I'm more interested in what you believe," Kade drawled. "If you think something is out there I will believe you because you have a track record of being right about these things. Two weeks ago, Luke thought he saw the lady in white and it turned out to be a Chick-Fil-A sign."

He had a point. "I know. I just don't want to miss anything this time."

"You're missing the moves I want to put on you."

I barked out a laugh. "I'm sorry. My attention is completely on you."

"Good. That's just the way I like it."

AN HOUR LATER, MY body lax and my mind ready to drift off, I thought again about what Luke had said. Chanting. Witches chanted. Well, they chanted if they were working in a coven. The lone coven in this area was thought to be weak and disorganized, more yoga witches than evil witches.

Still, it bore looking into. A little more research never hurt anyone.

Kade was already asleep beside me. I could tell by his breathing. He was on his stomach, his fingers linked with mine. He was a heavy sleeper, although he often woke when I had a bad dream or something was about to happen. For now, he slept heavy.

That was a relief.

I believed that until the moment sleep finally claimed me. That's when the chanting started in my head. I initially blamed Luke in my subconscious and thought I was imagining it, that his freakout pushed the kernel into my mind and ultimately allowed it to germinate. Eventually, though, I came to feel the opposite was true.

I slept even as the chanting continued, although it was restless rather than restful. I couldn't make out the words, or even if the voices were male or female.

There was something off about the sound, though I couldn't quite put my finger on what.

4
FOUR

Kade was already awake and watching me when I woke the next morning. His smile was smug and sleepy, but a hint of worry flitted through his eyes before he shuttered it.

"Good morning."

"There's nothing good about a morning." I stretched my arms over my head and turned to look out the window. Unlike my previous bedroom, this one boasted clean blinds that blocked out much of the sun. Still, it was clear that the sun had officially risen and the fog was nothing but a memory. "Have you looked outside? Nellie didn't hack off a head or anything while we were asleep, did he?"

Kade snorted. "I haven't looked. I'm sure we would've heard if they'd been running around last night. I'm guessing they kept up their courage until the s'mores ran out and then retreated from the fog like everybody else."

"Probably." I ran my fingers through my hair, wrinkling my forehead when my fingers snagged. "How did you sleep?"

"Hard. I'm a big fan of the new bed."

"That's good."

"How did you sleep?"

"Fine." I kept my gaze on the window. "We should probably get up and start breakfast. We have a lot to do today because the trucks are coming in late."

"We'll get everything done. We always do."

"Yeah, well ... ."

Kade's fingers landed on my chin and forced my face to him. "You didn't sleep, did you?"

That wasn't entirely true. I'd slept. At times I'd slept hard. Other times, though, I could hear chanting. I tried to push it out of my head as best as possible, but the sound was always there, humming in the background. It didn't make for restful slumber.

"Do you not like the new bed?" Kade asked.

I immediately realized what he was worried about and wrapped my fingers around his wrist to reassure him. "I like the bed. I love the trailer. I happen to really like you in the bed and the trailer."

Kade's expression was plaintive. "So, what's the problem?"

I shifted my fingers to his stubbled jaw and pursed my lips. "I'm kind of afraid to tell you."

"Oh, something tells me I'm going to hate this."

I heaved out a sigh. Lying wasn't an option, for various reasons. I had to admit the truth no matter how crazy he thought I was being. "I heard chanting."

Kade didn't as much as blink. "What kind of chanting?"

"I have no idea. It was just chanting, and only when I was trying to sleep. It went on all night and kind of invaded my dreams."

"Huh." Kade was calm as he cupped my hand and pressed my palm tighter against his cheek. "What do you think it means?"

I expected him to laugh at me, or at least offer some teasing about letting Luke infiltrate my brain. Instead he was serious. "I don't know. It could be a variety of different things."

"For example?"

"Well, for starters, I could've dreamed the chanting because of what Luke said in the woods last night."

"Do you think that's the case?"

"Honestly? I wish that was true. I don't think that's it."

"So, basically you're saying something is out there and ready to attack," Kade mused. "That's essentially every other day for us, isn't it?"

I pressed my lips together to keep from laughing at his serious expression. "Kind of."

"Then don't sweat it." Kade released my hand and gave me a playful swat. "If something is out there, we'll figure it out. You said yourself that Luke could've planted the suggestion in your head. However unlikely that is, we can't rule it out. We also have nothing to rule in right now."

He had a point. Still ... . "What if something is out there watching us?"

"Then you'll figure it out."

"How can you be sure?"

"You haven't let me down yet," Kade pointed out. "We've been wandering through this wacky world together for months now and you always come through. I don't expect this situation to be any different."

"So ... you're really not worried?"

Kade shook his head. "We have a new home to share. We have a new office to share. I'm mildly worried that too much togetherness might make you cranky, but somehow I think we'll get through it."

I narrowed my eyes. "What makes you think I'm the one who will be cranky?"

"I've met you."

I was fairly certain I should be insulted. "You could be cranky."

"Never. I'm a dream to be around. Ask anybody." He tickled my ribs when I opened my mouth to argue. "A total dream," he repeated. "Now come over here and have fun with your dream. We don't have much time before breakfast."

Ah, well, I'd heard worse offers.

KADE HEADED STRAIGHT to Max's trailer once we moved outside to greet the day. He was determined to get the latest update on the location of the trucks, promising he would head back to help with breakfast as soon as possible. Unlike most of the Mystic Caravan men, Kade was always willing to pitch in and help when it came to "women's work." That was Nellie's term, by the way. He spent all his time in dresses but refused to do the dishes unless someone bribed him with new shoes.

My plan was to head toward the communal cooking area to offer help, but the woods to my left – the same group of trees Luke raced to the day before – called to me when I hit the bottom of the stairs. I spared a look for Raven, Nixie and Naida. They looked to have breakfast well in hand, which allowed me an opening to do a little investigating on my own.

With that in mind, I headed straight for the woods. I didn't look over my shoulder, instead acting as if I had a specific goal in mind. I figured my co-workers would be less likely to question me if they thought I was actually doing something of importance.

I stopped at the edge of the dreamcatcher long enough to test the strings. They had a healthy bounce, meaning they were whole and intact, but that didn't necessarily prove that nothing managed to cross over the previous evening. I'd heard chanting in my dreams. The dreamcatcher wasn't designed to keep out random chanting, but given how weary I felt I wasn't against seeing if that was something we could add to the design.

The woods were thick, the trees staggeringly tall. Growing up in Michigan I was used to trees, even though I'd lived in the suburbs. These trees were something else. They were so tall they completely blocked out the sun except for an errant glimpse here or there. Because of that, the invading fog from the previous night remained. It rested close to the ground, not as thick but giving the location an eerie feeling.

"What are you doing?"

I jumped at the sound of Kade's voice, wrinkling my nose as I swiveled to face him. My initial urge was to punch him in the face for frightening me, but that seemed a bit over the top, so I reined in the inclination. "Nothing. What are you doing?"

"Me? I'm following my girlfriend into the woods. She was

supposed to be making breakfast, but she ran off into a bunch of trees. I was naturally concerned because she had nightmares – the kind that will probably lead to danger or some sort of monster that I've never heard of – and I'm worried that she'll run off half-cocked because she can't seem to keep herself out of trouble."

Oh, well, crap. It's hard to take the moral high ground when he has a point. "I'm not half-cocked." Of course, nothing stops me from arguing when the mood hits.

"Does that mean you're fully cocked?" Kade asked.

He asked the question with a straight face. Of course that made me laugh. "Ha, ha." I lightly slapped his arm. "I only wanted to see if something was out here. It occurred to me that Luke was the only one to run around the woods last night. I wanted to make sure something dark and dank wasn't living in here."

"It's the woods, darling," Kade drawled. "There are all manner of dark and dank things that live in the woods."

"I know, but ... I just wanted to look around. Is that so awful?"

Kade stared into my eyes for a beat. "No, it's not awful," he said finally. "Having company while doing it isn't awful either."

"You were with Max."

"I was two minutes behind you," Kade corrected. "You could've waited. You didn't want to, which I get, but you still could've waited instead of running into the woods without anyone knowing where you were going."

"I'm sure someone would've missed me eventually," I muttered.

"Yes, well, I missed you and now we're going to look around together." Kade's tone promised I was in for an argument if I even thought about giving him guff. "Now that we're here, where do you want to start?"

That was a very good question. "I don't know." My gaze bounced around the trees as I gathered my senses. "Everything looks alike."

"Trees often do."

His blasé attitude was beginning to chafe. "Hey! You wanted to come with me. You said it was necessary. Now you're here, and I'm not a big fan of the whining."

Kade balked. "I'm not whining."

"It feels like whining."

"Someone is definitely cranky this morning." Kade moved closer to an odd-looking bush and gave it a long once-over. "What's this?"

"A bush."

"Oh, really?" Kade rolled his eyes. "I never would've guessed."

"Probably because you're not cranky."

Kade extended a warning finger. "Do you really want to start our first day of living together with a fight?"

"Technically yesterday was our first day of living together."

"Today is the first full day."

Ugh. I hate it when he has a point. "Fine. I don't want to fight." I meant it. "I also want to look around without getting a lot of grief. I'm honestly ... worried ... about what I heard last night. I couldn't push it out no matter how hard I tried. I think something abnormal is about to hit us over the head."

Kade's expression softened. "And I trust your instincts. No, seriously. If you think there's something out here we should investigate, I believe you. You have good instincts. That's one of the first things I noticed about you."

"Oh, and here I thought you noticed her butt first." Luke, a partially-eaten banana in his hand, appeared behind Kade. I had to bite the inside of my cheek to keep from laughing at the way Kade practically jumped out of his skin ... and then singed Luke with a hateful glare. "You don't have to be embarrassed. It's a nice butt. If I played for her team I would've totally went for that butt, too."

Kade made a face that was straight out of a sarcastic sitcom. "Oh, well, that's good to know."

"Isn't it?" Luke's eyes gleamed as he glanced between faces. "What are you guys doing out here?"

"Nothing," I answered automatically. I didn't want to get Luke worked up unless I had good reason.

"We're looking for anything and everything," Kade corrected. "Poet heard the chanting in her head when she was trying to sleep last night."

Luke's eyes widened to comical proportions. "You did? See, I wasn't imagining it." He poked Kade in the arm for emphasis as he passed. "What did you hear?"

I shot Kade a weighted look so he would know I wasn't happy and then shrugged. "I can't be sure. It was after I fell asleep. There's a chance I imagined all of it."

Luke's snort was disdainful. "Not likely. If you heard it there has to be a reason."

"Which is why we're out here looking around," Kade said. "Poet can't shake the feeling that either someone is watching or something is about to happen, so we're trying to head that off before something bad happens."

"I'm hip." Luke bit into his banana and smiled as he chewed. "Where do you want me to start looking?"

"Back at the grill so it's not only the women doing the cooking," Raven barked, appearing just behind Kade. She was close enough that he jumped again, and I almost felt sorry for him. The look on his face was so comical that it overrode the sympathy factor. This walk was turning out more enjoyable than I envisioned. "Why are you guys out here?"

"Why are you out here?" Luke challenged, wrinkling his nose. "I don't believe you were invited to the party."

"I don't believe you were invited to the party either," Kade pointed out.

I cleared my throat to get Kade's attention. "Technically it was a party of one when I set out."

Kade's scowl was so pronounced it caused Raven to giggle like a school girl as she brushed past him and moved closer to me. Her long silver hair was tied back in two ornate buns – a little more conical than Princess Leia, but close enough to make *Star Wars* fans everywhere hop to their feet and applaud – and she looked as if the last place she wanted to be was wandering the woods. "So, what are we looking for?"

"Poet heard the chanting in her dreams last night," Luke volunteered, finishing off his banana and tossing the peel into a nearby bush. "What? It's biodegradable. It's not like littering."

"Fine." I often got on him for littering, but he wasn't wrong in this particular case. "As for the chanting, I can't decide if it was real or imagined. I simply thought I'd take a look out here because that's where Luke heard the same noise. I didn't mean for it to turn into a group thing."

"Oh, well, I was looking for a reason to get out of cooking anyway," Raven said, turning her attention to some nearby foliage. "Wolf's Claw."

I tilted my head to the side as I regarded her. "Is that indigenous to this area?"

Raven shrugged. "I'm not sure. I'll have to do some research. I'm also not convinced it's important."

"What is Wolf's Claw?" Kade drifted closer to Raven so he could look over her shoulder. "That's called Club Moss. It's native to moist areas, and given the fog we saw last night I'd guess this place stays plenty moist."

"Now you're a student of plants and herbs?" Raven challenged.

Kade frowned. "I know what Club Moss is. It's not a big deal."

"In witch circles it's known as Wolf's Claw," I offered. "It's used for power and protection spells."

"And purification," Raven added. "It's ... interesting ... to find it here."

"And why do you think that?" Kade challenged.

"Because there's no sun," Luke automatically answered. "The trees get sun because they grow so tall. Nothing in here gets sun, though. That's why the fog hangs so late in the day when it's been burned off everywhere else."

"Whatever." Kade stared hard at the moss. "Is this a clue?"

"Probably not," Raven replied. "I simply found its presence interesting."

"You find weird things interesting."

Raven flicked her eyes to me and offered an evil grin. "I feel the same way about you at times."

"Let's not argue," Luke said hurriedly, perhaps sensing my irritation. "We're supposed to be a team."

I ignored his peacekeeping efforts and increased the distance between Raven and myself. Something on the ground, a flash of color that shouldn't have been there, caught my interest. I knelt when I got closer, knitting my eyebrows as I leaned over the noticeable stain on the ground.

"What are you looking at?" Kade asked, starting in my direction.

Luke beat him to my side. "It's blood."

"Human blood?" Kade asked, leaning over my shoulder.

"I don't know," I replied after a beat, looking to Luke for answers.

"I don't know either," Luke admitted. "Sometimes I can tell. This time I don't know. That probably means it's animal blood. There are probably all different types of furry fiends hanging around in here."

That was true. Of course, there was a chance it wasn't true, too. "What if it's not animal blood?"

"We could try to figure out a way to test it," Raven suggested. "I'm sure the pixie twins have something in their arsenal to do the job. We have to collect a sample first."

That sounded like more work than was necessary, especially because it was such a small stain of blood and we had no reason to think a human was in danger.

"It's probably nothing," I said finally, straightening. Something else directly under the nearby bush caught my attention and I swept my hand beneath the green bough, frowning when I came back with a twenty-dollar bill and a driver's license.

I held up the twenty, which was free of blood, and read the driver's license aloud. "Amanda Stevens."

"Do you know who that is?" Kade asked.

"No. You know as much as I do. She's twenty-four and a local."

"Do you think the blood is hers?"

I didn't have an answer. "Not necessarily. Even if it is, some kids or young people might've come out here partying and the stuff could've accidentally fallen out of her pocket. It could be innocent."

"And the blood?"

"It might belong to an animal." That was possible, I reminded myself. It could also be more than that. "I don't think it's something to panic about."

"We could call the police and alert them to it," Kade suggested.

"No." I shook my head, firm. "I don't think that's a good idea."

"Why not?"

"Because then the cops will be crawling through the woods right next to our campsite," Luke replied without hesitation. "They might want to see the animals or something, which means those of us who pretend to be animals for the show will have to shift and climb into cages."

"It will also bring unwanted attention," Raven added. "I don't think calling the police is a good idea when we have so little to point them toward. It's just a license and a little blood."

"Are you sure?" Kade focused on me. "I'll defer to you on this one."

I made up my mind on the spot. "We'll wait. We have no reason to believe something bad happened here. It very well could've been an animal. Maybe the animal caused Amanda Stevens to jump and drop what she was holding. There's no body or anything, no drag marks. I think it's probably nothing."

"And the chanting?"

I held my hands palms out and shrugged. "We'll have to wait and see if we hear it again."

Kade didn't look convinced, but he nodded. "Okay. Let's head back for breakfast." He held his hand out for me to take. "I'm hungry and these woods are officially giving me the heebie-jeebies."

I took his hand. "I'm sure it's nothing."

"That would be a nice change of pace."

5
FIVE

I kept telling myself through breakfast that the blood likely belonged to an animal. More importantly, I tried to convince myself that Amanda Stevens did not meet a dark end in the forest and that I wasn't complicit in her death for not calling the police because I had nothing concrete to point them to. Then I internally repeated that refrain over and over (and over and over and over) as Kade and I debated how to set up our new office camper. The whole point of separating our work area from our play area was that we were afraid that being on top of one another twenty-four hours a day would make for frequent arguments. We were barely inside our new office digs – Kade's old living quarters – when he decided to take control and start moving furniture.

I was in no mood to move furniture even though the sight of Kade shirtless and straining enticed, so I begged off and told him he could do whatever he wanted with our office space. I had things to do around the circus grounds, after all, and that included making sure the late trucks dropped their cargo in the right places. Kade was so enthralled with being Mr. Organized that he basically waved me off without a backward glance. That was best for what I had planned.

I stopped in the heart of the circus long enough to make sure the big tent was on its way up – it is the main draw, after all – but Dolph was in charge today and I needn't have worried. He wasn't messing around as he barked orders (some in a language I didn't understand) and he didn't so much as spare me a glance when I happened by.

Things were running well so I decided to investigate the area surrounding our current home. Even though I found it rational to believe I was overreacting, that in fact the blood belonged to an animal, I couldn't shake the idea that I was making a big mistake. Very few times over the course of my history with Mystic Caravan could I actually say that the scariest outcome wasn't the one we found ourselves mired in at the end. That's what fueled me now.

"Do you want to take a walk with me?"

I cozied up to Luke's back as he watched the animal tent being erected. The tent was almost always empty unless we had to pretend we had animals in the cages. I was trying to be nonchalant, but the way Luke arched an eyebrow told me he was in the mood to be the exact opposite.

"And why would I want to take a walk with you?"

"Why wouldn't you want to take a walk with me?"

"I'm angry with you."

"Why?"

"Because you always take Kade's side over mine."

"I think that's a gross exaggeration."

"And I think I'm losing interest in this conversation." Luke was nothing if not full of himself, so I was resigned to begging when he folded his arms across his chest and fixed me with his most obstinate look.

"Fine." I blew out a sigh. "I'm sorry about always taking Kade's side instead of yours. I will make it a point to take your side whenever the next fight arises, even if I think you're being a complete and total tool. You are a wonderful best friend and handsome man. I am sorry to have offended you."

Luke rolled his eyes. "And?"

I ran the apology through my head. "And you're the best dresser in all the land," I automatically added. "You're so good you should have your own clothing line and people everywhere should let you dress them."

"Much better." Luke brightened considerably. "Where are we going?"

"For a walk in the woods."

Luke's happiness hissed out of him like a balloon slowly losing air. "Why? I don't want to hang around the woods. It's creepy ... and dirty ... and there might be crazy people walking around while chanting. You know no good ever comes of chanting."

"I do know that," I confirmed. "That doesn't change the fact that I want to take a look."

"Why not take your boy toy?"

"He's otherwise engaged."

"Meaning he's being anal retentive while setting up your office," Luke translated, letting loose a sigh as he dragged a hand through his hair. "Why me?"

"You're my best friend and there's no one I would rather have at my side."

Luke narrowed his eyes. "Why really?"

I knew I was a little too perfunctory with my answer. If I wanted him to believe me, I should've paused and acted as if I was really trying to come up with the correct answer. "You can scent things and we might run into other shifters. I need appropriate backup for my quest."

Luke groaned. "You know I hate it when you use that word."

I was confused. "Backup?"

"Quest," Luke barked. "A quest sounds fun. I've always wanted to go on a quest."

Actually, I knew that. "So, let's go on a quest."

"Fine." Luke was resigned as he straightened. "I think we should bring someone else along for the ride."

"Who?"

"Take a wild guess."

"WHERE ARE WE GOING?"

Melissa wasn't exactly excited about being dragged into the woods, but she looked perkier than she had in almost ten days so I took it as a win.

"I simply want to look around," I replied, keeping my eyes on the ground as we picked our way through the woods. There was always a chance more items from Amanda Stevens' purse would appear, and that would be enough evidence to prod me to call the police. Once clear of the fairgrounds and initial stand of trees, we discovered a well-worn path that seemingly led into the woods. We had no idea where we were headed, and it appeared someone else most likely did know where he or she was going, so we decided to follow the path.

"What are we looking for?" Melissa's voice was soft.

"Poet is convinced something is out here and it wants to chant us to death," Luke replied. "I remain skeptical, but she appealed to my ego, so I had to come."

Melissa pressed her lips together as she regarded Luke. "Oh, well ... that sounds fairly normal."

I was worried about her. I wasn't sure how to broach the obvious topic. Instead I cleared my throat and opened my mouth. Nothing came out.

"I'm totally excited about looking for the mad chanters," Melissa said hurriedly. "It sounds like fun."

"Not fun but better than work," Luke corrected, smirking as he bumped his shoulder into Melissa's and caused her to almost lose her footing. "Pay attention. You don't want to fall out here. If the chanters show up, we might have to leave you. I don't think you want that."

Annoyance washed over me. "Luke! Don't say things like that to her."

"It's okay." Melissa flashed a wan smile. "I prefer he treats me as he's always treated me rather than acting as if I'm going to fall apart at any moment. The former is definitely better than the latter."

I tugged on my bottom lip as I trailed behind them. I hadn't given Melissa's predicament much thought ... or at least the type of thought that was necessary. I recognized she was struggling – so much had happened in Seattle that we couldn't touch on everything if we had an entire week to talk – but now I realized she was feeling ostracized because no one was bringing up the actions that led to her possession by a crazy woman.

"It's not that people don't want to treat you normally," I offered, my eyes landing on an extensive stretch of fog that pooled in a small depression to my right. The sun apparently never managed to show its face here, which allowed the fog to get a stronghold and never give it up. "It was my idea to let things rest for a bit because ... well, just because."

"Because you thought I couldn't handle it," Melissa finished. "You thought I was going to start crying or kill myself or something. Admit it."

"I never thought that." I opted for honesty. "I did think you needed some quiet time, so I ordered everyone to take it easy around you."

"Even though I'm often amused by Luke?"

"I wasn't particularly worried about Luke." I was mildly worried about Luke letting his mouth get ahead of his brain because that often happens, but he was hardly the one I wanted to behave when I issued the edict. "I was more worried about Nixie and Naida saying something inappropriate simply because they didn't understand what you went through. I was also convinced Raven might say something simply out of meanness."

Melissa was taken aback. "Oh, well, I didn't consider that."

I smiled. "It's okay. I'm glad you brought it up. If you want people to start treating you normally, I can release the muzzle."

"I'm ready to try to go back to normal." Melissa was earnest. "I know it will take time, but I would rather be treated normally."

I understood. "I will make sure everybody knows."

"Great."

We lapsed into silence, walking a good five minutes without a word. I was about to suggest turning around – it didn't seem as if we were going to find anything of interest – when Luke extended his hand to cause me to slow.

"What is it?" I whispered, instantly on alert. "Do you see something?"

"Do you smell something?" Melissa added, her voice low.

"It's more that ... there." Luke pointed and I followed his finger, frowning when I made out what looked to be an older home set against a wall of tall trees. It was so old I almost didn't see it because of the natural camouflage.

"Huh. Did you know that was there?"

Luke made an exaggerated face. "How would I possibly know that was there?"

I held my hands palms out. "I don't know. I thought maybe you sensed it or something."

"Maybe he smelled it," Melissa added. "That house definitely looks as if it smells."

"Scented," Luke corrected. "I don't smell things ... except, well, Poet's cooking. When in hunting mode, I scent things."

Melissa's face was blank. "Why is that important?"

"It's more manly," Luke answered. "As for the house, I have no idea. The only reason I even noticed it is because something about the roof line stood out. I couldn't figure out what I was looking at right away and then, somehow, it turned into a house."

That was odd ... and disconcerting. "Well, I ... ." I didn't finish what I was about to say, instead swiveling to the left when I felt a presence move in. I was ready to lash out with a bit of magic in case we needed to run, but the woman standing close to the tree line – who happened to have a goat tethered to a leash – looked relatively harmless. "Um ... hello."

The woman, her long silver hair pulled back in a loose bun, appeared amused by my reaction. When Luke jumped at her presence, she actually belted out a jaunty laugh. "Hello."

"Where did you come from?" Melissa asked as she instinctively moved closer to Luke. "I ... you weren't there a second ago."

"Probably not," the woman conceded. "Wasn't far, though. You guys were so loud I heard you coming from a half mile away. Wasn't sure what to expect."

I figured that was probably a gross exaggeration, but I let it go. "Do you live out here?"

"I believe you're looking at my house."

"But ... you're out in the middle of nowhere," I pressed. "How can you live out here? I mean ... what about groceries and doctor visits?"

"Don't put much faith in doctors," the woman said, her gaze busy as it bounced between faces. "Never needed one and I've been around a good seventy years or so. Figure the odds are in my favor in that regard."

I figured the exact opposite, but kept my observation to myself. "And the food?"

"I have a garden around back. I have cows and goats for milk. I churn my own butter. I'm pretty good at taking care of myself."

Luke, utterly charmed by the woman's bluster, grinned. "You churn your own butter? I can't believe I actually met someone who does that. I've been looking for a very long time."

"Well, now you can tell your friends you met me." She returned the smile. "I'm Caroline Olsen. You folks tourists?"

I realized rather quickly that I'd been remiss when it came to my manners and shook my head. "We're with Mystic Caravan Circus." I introduced all three of us in turn. "We're staying at the fairgrounds about two miles that way." I pointed in the direction I believed we'd come from. "We were just out taking a hike to look around when we came across your place."

"We didn't even see it at first," Melissa added, apparently eager to contribute to the conversation. "We were talking about whether or not we should approach when we saw you."

"Approaching probably isn't a good idea," Caroline offered. "I'm not the friendliest sort. I don't entertain and I have a schedule I have to stick to if I expect to get all my work done by nightfall."

"You probably don't want to risk walking around in the fog," I noted.

"Fog is only one of my worries. Minor one, really. It's the shadow hunters I'm trying to avoid."

She said it in such a matter-of-fact manner I could do nothing but stare at her for a long beat. Finally, Luke was the one to ask the obvious question.

"I'm sorry, but ... what are the shadow hunters?"

Caroline shrugged, noncommittal. "That's the name I gave 'em. Don't know if that's what they really are."

I glanced around, uncertain. "Can you be more specific?"

"Not really."

"But we're staying close to this area," Melissa pressed. "If there's something wandering around out here, well, we would like to know what to be on the lookout for. If there's something dangerous we need to know what to fear."

"Long as you keep your activities to the day, there's nothing to fear," Caroline shot back. "I'm not the type to talk out of turn."

"But you must have meant something by that statement," I pressed. "That's not a normal thing to say. Shadow hunters, the term and the beings ... whatever they are, means something specific to you."

"They do and I'm in no mood to share that with you," Caroline argued. "You have bigger worries, including the fact that this girl recently had her soul fragmented." She extended a finger in Melissa's direction. "I'd be more worried about that if I were you."

That was interesting. I'd never heard of possession being described in that manner. A fragmented soul elicited images, and they weren't far from what really happened, but they were still darker than what I was comfortable focusing on. I couldn't figure out how Caroline knew that. She was clearly trying to deflect. The question was: Why?

"She's fine," I said automatically. "Her soul is full and devoid of cracks now."

"It's still cracked," Caroline countered. "The cracks are mending, sure, but it's not something that happens overnight."

"That's an interesting observation."

"I'm full of them." Caroline pursed her lips as she regarded Melissa. "You're more afraid of what happened than what's to come. You're looking at things the wrong way."

As if sensing her discomfort, Luke slung his arm around Melissa's shoulders and tugged her close. He was in protective big brother mode and he didn't care if he appeared standoffish to Caroline. "We'll take care of her," Luke admonished. "You don't have to go all *Friday the 13th* on her."

I made a face. "*Friday the 13th*? What does that have to do with anything?"

"She's the crazy person who shows up in the beginning of the movie to warn about imminent death," Luke replied. "She knows her role well, but we don't need anyone to tell us how to live our lives."

"Good point." I rolled my neck until it cracked. I wasn't quite ready to give up on the conversation. "What are the shadow hunters?"

"It doesn't matter." Caroline was adamant as she gripped the goat's leash tighter. "These woods belong to them. Stay out of the woods and you should be fine. Don't go anywhere after dark and you'll be safe. That's all I'm willing to say on the subject."

"But ... ."

"No." Caroline started walking toward her house. She was clearly dismissing us, whether we wanted to be tossed out with the compost or not. "Just stay out of the woods. It's not safe for you to be wandering around."

"But it's safe for you?" Luke challenged.

"I know the rules."

"And what are the rules?" I called out.

"Don't go into the woods," Caroline repeated.

"And don't go out after dark," I finished. "I heard that part. Anything else?"

"Yeah. Stay off my farm."

She didn't look back as she trudged toward the odd house in the woods. When I was sure she was out of earshot, I turned my attention to Luke. "What do you make of that?"

"She's the crazy person everyone runs into at the beginning of a horror movie," Luke answered without hesitation.

"Should we listen to her?"

Luke shrugged. "She'll probably die early now that she's served her purpose. That's how horror movies work."

"Yes, well, at least you're getting your information from a reliable source."

"You can always rely on me for that."

"Uh-huh." I made up my mind on the spot. "Let's go back. I want to see if I can dig up any information on these shadow hunters."

"I think you'll be woefully disappointed, because they only live in her head," Luke argued.

He was probably right, but I couldn't dislodge the memory of the chanting ... and the fear it instilled inside me. "I'm checking it out all the same. It couldn't hurt."

6
SIX

Kade dragged me into our newly-organized office upon return to the circus grounds. I made the appropriate "oohing" and "aahing" he expected, although my heart wasn't truly in it. I was much more excited about our new living arrangements. Our working arrangement was merely mildly interesting and occasionally bordered on dull.

"It's nice."

Kade made a face when I didn't react as he expected. "We each have our own desk and another room to spread out in if we need a break. I thought you'd like it."

"I do like it."

"So ... what's the problem?"

I told him about my walk in the woods and running into Caroline Olsen. When I was done, he was flabbergasted ... and not in a good way.

"Why didn't you ask me to walk with you?"

I balked at his tone. "Because you were busy with the office."

"I would've put that off."

"I didn't want you to have to put it off," I argued. "You were excited to organize. In fact, I've never seen a man – or woman, for that matter

– more excited to organize than you were today. I didn't want to drag you away from that because I had a hunch that turned out to be nothing."

Kade was hardly placated by my tone. "I still don't like the idea of you running around the woods by yourself."

"I had Luke and Melissa with me."

"Two people you would have to protect in case of attack."

"That's not true. Luke has fought by my side many times. He's good in a battle. You don't have to worry about that."

Even though I could tell he remained agitated, Kade grudgingly nodded in acceptance. "So this woman just lives out there all by herself, huh?"

"And warns about things like shadow hunters."

"Have you considered that she might be a little nutty because she's isolated from society and she's simply telling tall tales?"

"Yes."

"And?"

"And I'm still irritated ... and a little uneasy," I admitted. "She seemed to know things about Melissa."

"Or she picked up on the dynamic of the group and tried to use it to her advantage." Kade ran a hand over his short-cropped hair. "I agree it's weird. I'll see if I can run her information and find out anything. It will have to be after we go to town for supplies, though."

Right. Supplies. That was part of our normal ritual on the first day of set-up. "We should probably get going if we expect to get back at a decent time."

"You mean before the fog rolls in, right?"

He knew me too well ... especially for a guy who was relatively new to my life. "Let's just head to town." I opted not to dwell on my fog fear. It seemed ridiculous, especially with the sun so high in the sky. "I was thinking we might make barbecued chicken for dinner tonight."

"Yum."

I MADE SURE MELISSA was tucked up safe with Naida and Nixie, our resident pixie twins, before snagging Luke and dragging him with us to town. Even though Luke made a big show of appearing annoyed about shopping, I knew the opposite was true. He enjoyed shopping and would melt down if I didn't invite him.

Kade plugged the coordinates of the closest shopping center into his GPS, and when we arrived at the store I couldn't help being impressed at the rather large produce market on the sidewalk in front of the building. "That looks promising."

"There's nothing better than fresh fruit," Kade agreed. He waited for me to join him at the front of the truck and linked our fingers as we crossed the parking lot. Luke trailed behind, his eyes trained on the ground rather than the market. Kade didn't miss my best friend's rather obvious performance. "What's wrong with you?"

The question caught Luke off guard. "Nothing is wrong with me. Why do you think something is wrong with me?"

"Because you're quiet," Kade replied without hesitation. "The only time I remember you being quiet is when you caught that cold and went to bed for two days."

"That wasn't quiet from where I was sitting," I reminded him. "I had to act as his nurse, wear one of those masks so he didn't catch any additional germs, and make him chicken noodle soup."

"That's what best friends are for," Luke pointed out primly. "You're supposed to take care of your beloved when illness strikes."

"Technically I think I would be her beloved in that scenario," Kade argued.

"Oh, no." Luke was hearing none of that. "I'll always be her beloved. You're simply her love monkey. There's a difference."

Instead of being offended, Kade laughed. "That's good to know." He squeezed my hand once as we stepped up on the sidewalk in front of the store and then released it, arching his eyebrows as he surveyed the offerings. "I definitely think we should get our vegetables here. This stuff looks great."

It actually did look pretty good, although I couldn't figure out if the women in matching cargo pants and "Holy Eureka Organic

Market" T-shirts were associated with the store or a separate operation. It didn't make much sense for the store to allow competitors to sell wares in front of its entry.

"Are you with the store?" I asked one of the women, flicking a quick look to the nametag on her shirt. It read "Liz." She looked like a Liz, her short hair perfectly coiffed and smoothed to within an inch of its life. Her outfit was completely put together, not a stray wrinkle or errant pet hair in sight. She wore no makeup (or bra, for that matter), and her smile was a little too ready and fake for my liking.

"We have a co-op agreement with the store," Liz replied, her voice unnaturally perky. "We supply fresh, organic produce to them year-round, and twice a year they allow us to have a mini-event, so to speak."

That sounded reasonable. "Well, the stuff looks great."

"It is, and great for you." Liz was so prim and proper in her delivery she immediately got on my last nerve. "You should always eat organic when it's an option."

I managed to maintain my cool, but just barely. "I totally agree."

Perhaps sensing the tension rolling through me, Kade lightly ran his hand over my back and offered Liz his megawatt smile, the one that brought women everywhere to their knees. That's not an exaggeration, by the way. That smile has brought me to my knees a time or two ... not that I would ever admit it out loud or anything.

"We're with Mystic Caravan Circus," Kade volunteered. "We need a lot of produce. Do you have crates or boxes around that we can use to transport some of the goods?"

"You're with the circus?" Liz's lips curved down. "You don't look like you're with the circus."

Kade kept his smile in place. "And what do people with the circus look like?"

Liz extended her finger and pointed directly at me. "Her. She looks like the circus sort. You don't."

"That's possibly very flattering," Kade deadpanned, widening the soothing circles he traced on my back to keep me in check. "It just so happens we're both the circus sort."

Luke was annoyed at being cut out of the statement. "Me, too." He slapped Kade with a dark look before focusing on the tomato display. "This stuff does look really good."

Liz beamed as she wiggled her hips a bit and focused on Luke, pushing out her boobs so he could get a better look. She obviously hadn't figured out he was not her target audience for those particular melons. "Organic is best. You should definitely put non-pesticides to the test."

I touched the tip of my tongue to my top lip to keep from laughing and turned so I was facing a variety of artichokes, determined not to let Liz see my mirth. She didn't strike me as the type to simply accept being the butt of a joke.

"Do you see anything you like?" Another woman, this one a brunette with a more snarky demeanor, stood on the other side of the artichokes and gave me an amused look. Her nametag read "Jenn" and I immediately liked her more than Liz. That wasn't much of a scale, though.

I recovered from my mirth burst quickly and sobered. "It all looks good. Do you guys have a farm around here?"

Jenn nodded. I heard Kade and Luke talking to Liz behind me, but I did my best to tune them out. Liz was the sort of woman who set my teeth on edge, so it was best to give her a wide berth. "We're a little southeast of town. Only about fifteen minutes."

I pictured the area map in my head. "That puts you close to us."

Jenn furrowed her brow. "Where are you located?"

"The fairgrounds off Elk River Road."

"Oh." Jenn brightened. "Yeah. You're about five minutes from us. You're with the circus?"

"I would've thought you heard that." I glanced over my shoulder and found Liz still yapping away, Kade and Luke acting as something akin to conversational hostages. "Your buddy just told me that I look like I belong in the circus, but my friends don't."

Jenn barked out a laugh. "Yes, well, I wouldn't put much effort into getting offended by anything she says. She can't help herself from blurting out whatever comes to mind."

"I have that problem, too." That was the truth. "She seems somehow more annoying with her affliction than I picture myself, though."

Jenn's smile was quick and easy. It was also a little snarky. "Yes, well, she is what she is. Sometimes I admire her for it because she doesn't care. Other times I want to shove a dirty sock in her mouth to shut her up."

"I think the dirty sock idea is grand." I moved to the next display and grabbed a baggie so I could start shoving ears of corn inside. "Have you lived in this area your entire life?"

Jenn nodded as she watched me stow vegetables, her eyes widening when I reached for another bag. "How many people are you feeding?"

"Quite a few."

"Meaning?"

"Meaning it's quite a few," I said. "We have a rather large group that travels with us. We usually split into three factions for food."

"Do you have clowns?"

The way Jenn wrinkled her nose told me exactly what she thought about the prospect. "We do. I don't feed them, though. Er, well, technically I feed one of them, but only because he's dating the woman who runs the House of Mirrors. Otherwise he'd be banished to the other side of the grounds with the rest of the red-nose brigade."

Jenn's eyes sparked with humor as she choked out a laugh so raucous that it caused me to jolt. "Oh, that is the funniest thing I've heard all day." She swiped at her leaking eyes as she straightened. "The red-nose brigade. I'm not sure I'll ever look at clowns the same way."

"I try not to look at them at all." I moved to the next display and grabbed another baggie so I could start collecting oranges. "If you're local to the area, does that mean you know most of the people who live around here?"

"I guess." If Jenn was surprised by the question, she didn't show it. "Is there someone specific you want information about?"

"Actually, yes." I saw no reason to lie or attempt subterfuge. Jenn would either tell me what she knew or tell me to mind my own business. "What do you know about Caroline Olsen?"

Jenn's eyebrows migrated so far north they almost disappeared into her hairline. "Caroline Olsen? Are you talking about the nutty woman who lives out in the woods?"

"That would be the one."

"Why are you asking about her?"

"Because we went for a walk today and she surprised us," I replied, debating how much of the story I wanted to share. "She caught us off guard. She was also walking a goat on a leash."

Jenn snickered. "That sounds just like her. She has a reputation of sorts."

"I can see that. My friend Luke likened her to Crazy Ralph in the *Friday the 13th* movies. She said a few creepy things to us."

"Like what?"

"Like ... she said the woods belonged to the shadow hunters and we shouldn't risk going out after dark," I answered. "Now, I'm not the type to get worked up about something like that, but the fog that came through last night was completely creepy and it almost did feel like someone was watching us through the haze."

"Oh, I didn't think about that," Jenn said. "You're not familiar with the area, so the fog would've caught you off guard."

"Are you saying it doesn't catch you off guard?"

"I guess I'm just used to it. The entire area suffers from coastal fog, which is different than the fog people inland deal with."

I hadn't come for a weather lesson yet I was intrigued. "What does that mean?"

"Well, our temperature around here stays pretty consistent year-round," Jenn explained. "We get warm days, but on average it's always sixty-five degrees here. That's in the summer and winter.

"The Pacific breezes also keep Eureka cooler," she continued. "Only a few miles inland – and I'm not exaggerating – temperatures jump really high a lot of the time. It could be sixty degrees in Eureka and ninety degrees twenty miles east. I've seen it happen."

"How does that explain the fog?"

"Well, the proximity to the coast is the main reason for the fog."

I'd never lived on an ocean – or any body of water, for that matter – so I couldn't claim knowledge about coastal weather patterns. "So, basically you're saying that I'm overreacting about the fog," I mused. "You probably think I'm a big baby."

"On the contrary." Jenn grinned. "I think that the fog is probably jarring for people who aren't used to it. It's like one of those things you see in horror movies and naturally associate with killing and death."

She wasn't far off. "I'm not all that worried about killing and death." I'd seen more than my fair share of both and I didn't exactly live in fear. "It's just the fog last night seemed … like it actually had a mind of its own or something."

"Really?" Jenn's expression was hard to read.

"What are you two talking about?" Luke ambled to my side and slung his arm around my neck. "I had to get away from that other one. She refused to shut her mouth and it was getting absolutely ridiculous. I mean … who can come up with that many puns about organic fruit?"

Jenn chuckled. "Yes, well, Liz is a person all her own. She doesn't conform."

"I'm a big proponent of nonconformance," Luke said, "but she's weird."

"Speaking of weird, I asked Jenn about Caroline Olsen," I volunteered. "She thinks I'm being an alarmist and there's nothing wrong with her."

"Then you clearly didn't tell the story right," Luke argued. "That woman is ten sticks of gum short of a pack."

"I didn't say there was nothing wrong with her," Jenn clarified. "I don't remember saying anything either way on that topic. We discussed the fog, not Caroline."

To be fair, she wasn't wrong. "So what do you think about Caroline?" I asked.

"Wait … what do you know about the fog?" Luke challenged. "It's creepy and people have gone missing in it, right? It's like that Stephen

King movie where the creatures trapped everyone in the grocery store. That's going to happen to us, isn't it?"

I furrowed my brow. "We're not trapped in *The Mist*." I lightly smacked his arm. "As for the fog, it's normal. She says we have to stop being babies and suck it up."

"I don't believe I used those words," Jenn said dryly. "The fog is naturally occurring, and you're going to see a lot of it. It feels as if we see it almost every day in the summer."

"That's disappointing." Luke rolled his neck. "What about Caroline Olsen? She's probably an ax killer or something, isn't she? Have a lot of people gone missing in the woods by her house? I bet she's cooking and eating them."

"Hey!" I extended a warning finger. "Let's not take things too far."

"Caroline is mostly harmless," Jenn volunteered, seemingly eager to keep us from getting into an argument. "She's odd and isolated. She doesn't come into town much. She has a menagerie of animals out there and spends all her time with them. She's not dangerous."

I didn't bring up the fact that Caroline seemed to have a psychic flash in our presence because there was no way I could explain it. I remained convinced there was more to the woman than was readily apparent. "And the shadow hunters?"

Jenn held her hands palms out and shrugged. "Maybe she sees things in the mist that aren't really there. It wouldn't surprise me. She is alone a lot. Plus, well, you said it yourself, the fog is really thick. It unnerves people."

I couldn't argue with that. "I guess."

"Listen, I wouldn't worry too much about Caroline," Jenn said. "She really is harmless and I guarantee she's not eating people out there. As for you guys, I'm going to grab two crates from the truck because you're buying so much. Look around and grab what you want. I'll help you load it."

"Sure." I forced a smile as I watched her jog toward a truck in the parking lot, my heart momentarily clenching when I thought for sure there was a ghost hanging close to the vehicle and Jenn actually ran through it. I felt like an idiot for my reaction when I realized it was simply the way the sun was bouncing off the truck hood. A glare, not a ghost – or shadow hunter – waiting to take out the amiable vegetable seller.

"I think we should get stuff for pasta salad, too," Luke suggested, oblivious. "I want to take advantage of these vegetables while we can. They look amazing."

I dragged my eyes from the glare, which still looked like a woman in a floor-length skirt for some reason, and nodded. "That sounds like a plan. Let's get it done."

7
SEVEN

I eventually managed to drag my attention from the odd reflection and finish shopping. Kade had a harder time extricating himself from Liz – I think she developed something of a crush on him – but we managed to collect our supplies and load them without too much trouble.

"Now, if you need anything else, don't hesitate to give me a call and I'm sure I can work something out for delivery." Liz offered Kade a business card and a wink. "I would love to see the circus."

I stared at the back of her head for a long beat, debating whether I wanted to let the overture go or smack her around. Kade made the decision for me. Apparently he recognized my conundrum and didn't want to take any chances.

"I'll keep that in mind." Kade pocketed the business card with one hand while grabbing my elbow with the other. "Doesn't that sound good, sweetheart? Liz might deliver groceries to us."

Sweetheart? Since when did he call me that? "Um ... ."

"We're very excited that you've decided to stop by the circus once we open," Kade added. "It will be a fun event for everyone."

"Yes," I drawled, nodding. "Perhaps you can bring your husband ... or boyfriend."

Liz slowly dragged her eyes from Kade's face and focused on me. "It will just be me. I'm looking forward to the visit. I'll make sure to look you up." She met my gaze as she said the words, but it was obvious she was talking to Kade.

"We're really looking forward to it," I forced out, pasting a faux smile on my face. "Speaking of that, we have a lot of work to do. Set-up days are brutal. We should get going."

Liz didn't bother to hide her disappointment as Kade helped me into the truck. "Yes. I understand about work. We're all dedicated to certain tasks."

Luke climbed into the back seat, positioning himself behind me, and started cackling like a loon as Kade attempted to ditch Liz during his walk to the driver's side of the vehicle. "I think she wants your man."

I'd figured that out myself. "I think she's going to be disappointed."

"Definitely."

Kade finally managed to extricate himself from the overzealous grower, and when he slammed shut the truck door his eyes were wild. "You could've done something to scare her off."

I leaned forward so I could look around Kade and found Liz standing a good ten feet away, her eyes focused on him. "I think she's in love."

"That's not funny." Kade scowled. "She's an octopus or something. I swear there were times she had eight arms."

I arched an eyebrow, amused. "Does that mean she grabbed you in eight places?"

Kade's expression didn't shift. "I can't believe you find this funny. Just for the record, if some random vegetable dude grabbed you eight times I wouldn't take it well."

"Good to know."

Luke leaned forward from the back seat as Kade shoved his key in the ignition. "What kind of vegetable do you think this imaginary guy has in your boyfriend's head?"

That was a good question. "I have no idea."

"I can hear you guys giggling," Kade growled. "I'm not happy with you, so stop making that noise."

"Yes, sir!" Luke barked, offering a mock salute.

"I don't find that funny either."

Apparently Kade wasn't finding much of anything funny this afternoon. "Would you like me to use my two arms to make you forget about her eight arms later?"

Kade's lips curved even though I could tell he was trying hard not to smile. "I might be open for that."

Somehow I knew that.

WE SPENT THE REST OF the day working. It wasn't glamorous or exciting, but you don't join the circus unless you have an excellent work ethic. There's too much to do and limited time within which to do it. Those who can't meet the demands of the schedule wash out quickly. That wasn't me, and I was often happy doing the work associated with set-up.

I separated from Kade and Luke so I could organize my tent. Thanks to the fog delay, we were a bit behind our normal schedule.

Melissa showed up to help shortly after I started unpacking. She didn't say much, but she seemed happy to have something to focus on. I considered pushing her on what Caroline had said, but ultimately I opted to let it go. Melissa would come to me when she felt it was necessary. She wasn't quite there yet. I could wait.

After finishing with the tent, I took a tour of the circus layout, which was largely the same but often varied by tiny degrees given the space we were working with. We'd made up some ground during the long afternoon, but we had another long day ahead of us. Once I made my circuit, I headed back to the communal cooking area to help with dinner preparations. I found Nixie, Naida and Raven shucking corn.

"How are you guys doing?" I asked as I sat at the end of the table. "Are you behind or caught up?"

"We're caught up," Naida replied. She was a water nymph, a pixie from another plane, and she was much older than she looked. Fairies aged differently on the other side and she was considered young for her people, but would've been dead long ago if bound by the human aging process. "It wasn't hard for us. We pushed through to make sure that we got everything done."

"Is that because you want to go skinny-dipping in the Pacific later tonight?"

Naida shrugged, her smile sly. "Maybe. I hear the coastal fog is a thing to behold when you're swimming."

"Just be careful while you're out there," I warned. "I think there are killer whales and sharks in this area."

"I'm not afraid of whales and sharks. I can handle myself."

I had no doubt of that. Other than Max, Naida was probably the most powerful being in our troupe. "It was simply a friendly reminder."

"I'll be careful." Naida pursed her lips as she continued husking. "I heard about the woman in the woods. What did you think of her?"

"How did you hear about that?" I was understandably curious. "Has Luke been flapping his gums? I'm not sure that's wise. I don't want people going out there and bothering her simply because they want to get a look at her."

"We didn't hear it from Luke," Raven replied. "We heard it from Melissa."

"Oh." I wasn't sure what to make of that. "What did she say?"

Raven shrugged. "She said the woman claimed that she had a fractured soul. I think she was looking for us to say that wasn't true."

"It's not true," I argued. "Her soul is intact."

"Only because of what you did." Raven was pragmatic. "You saved her and she will heal, but she's hardly whole right now. She needs time for that."

The words grated. "So, we'll give her time."

"Oh, don't take that tone with me." Raven wasn't the type to step lightly when tackling a difficult situation. "I'm merely saying that Melissa isn't whole, which means that crazy woman in the woods is either psychic or has some other sort of sight."

"Meaning?"

"Meaning that we have someone potentially powerful in our backyard." Raven was matter of fact. "We must keep an eye on her in case she has more up her sleeve than just random observations."

Huh. That hadn't even occurred to me. That showed how far I was off my game. "I think she's just a little bit crazy from being isolated. If she was fully crazy I think I would've noticed."

"Let's hope that's true." Raven clearly wasn't convinced. "As for Melissa, she's getting stronger, but it won't happen overnight. I think the best we can do for her is to treat her as we used to."

"You just want an excuse to be mean to her," Naida muttered.

"I'm mean to everyone," Raven countered. "She shouldn't take it personally."

I wasn't in the mood to start a fight. "Whatever. Let's get dinner going. I think we'll be stuck eating earlier this week thanks to the fog. My understanding after talking to that vegetable woman is that the fog is a regular occurrence around here. It's coastal fog."

Raven's face was impassive. "Are you a meteorologist now?"

My lips curved down. "Are you trying to pick a fight with me?"

"I would be fine with that if you're in the mood."

Ugh. She knows exactly what button to push. She always has. It's a special gift. "Well, if that's the case ... ." I didn't get a chance to finish because an unearthly sound – a howl that was more than a normal canine noise – erupted from the trees to the far right of the grounds. I jerked my head in that direction, my eyes going wide. "What the ... ?"

"Shifter?" Nixie asked immediately, her shoulders straightening as she stared into the trees.

"That doesn't sound like a normal wolf shifter to me," Naida countered, shaking her head.

Another howl, this one closer, filled the air. The register was higher than a normal wolf shifter would boast, somehow more mournful. It sent chills down my spine and gooseflesh breaking out on my arms.

"That's not a wolf shifter," Raven said finally, her eyes narrowed. "That's something else."

I was almost afraid to ask the obvious question. "Do you know what?"

Raven bobbed her head. "A wendigo."

Oh, well, great. That was so not what I wanted to hear.

"WHAT'S A WENDIGO?"

We managed to keep the conversation light and pleasant through dinner, but the second the dishes were cleared and the bonfire roaring Kade needed answers.

Raven offered him a flirty smile that felt as if sandpaper was being ripped through my stomach. "I forget that you're not familiar with everything that's out there. You accepted what we were and what we could do without a lot of fuss, so I just assumed you'd done your homework."

"Why would he possibly research wendigos before coming across one?" I challenged.

"Calm down, tiger." Kade patted my knee. "Raven is just being Raven. There's no reason to get worked up."

"She's treating you like you're stupid," I grumbled.

"She's just being herself." Kade moved his hand to the back of my neck and softly began rubbing, the motion soothing even as I fought the urge to give Raven's silver hair a good tug. "I think I've heard you guys use that term before. I'm not sure what it is."

"A wendigo is basically a cannibal," Nellie supplied. "It's a monster that used to be human. It craves human flesh. Historically, people believe that murder and greed create wendigos."

"What does it look like?"

"It never looks exactly the same," I replied. "A wendigo is a reflection of the human it used to be. So whatever twisted that person helps decide what the creature turns out looking like."

"We fought one in Wisconsin." Nellie rubbed his hands together, clearly enjoying the memory. "It had antlers. No joke. When we killed it I wanted to hang the antlers on my wall, but no one would let me."

"That's because it also smelled like a city dump," Luke said. "It was gross. That whole takedown was gross."

I made a face at the memory. "That was really gross. The smell kept making everyone gag."

"That sounds lovely," Kade drawled. "If wendigos don't all look the same, how can you be sure the howling you heard in the woods was a wendigo?"

"Because it certainly wasn't a shifter," Raven answered. "Wendigo cries are ... different. I can feel them inside. There's a certain anguish associated with them. I don't know how to explain it."

"I can feel them, too," I admitted. "I'm pretty sure that was a wendigo."

"Do they run in packs?" Kade asked. I could practically see his mind working. He was trying to figure out how we were going to fight the latest threat.

"Not generally, but it has been known to happen," Nellie replied. "Most likely we're only dealing with one of them."

"So ... how do you kill it?"

"I generally find an ax to the neck is the quickest route." Nellie's eyes gleamed at the prospect. "But most of the normal stuff works. They die like humans."

"Then why are you guys so afraid of it?" Kade's eyes landed on me. "You seem uncomfortable with the idea of a wendigo running around."

"It's not that I'm afraid of it," I clarified, "but to be fair, I'm never okay with the idea of being eaten. Wendigos are supposed to be insatiable. They're like sharks. They spend most of their lives either eating or hunting for food. They're relentless."

"And they eat people?"

I nodded. "They do. They can't be saved. Once you're a wendigo there's no going back."

"There's no salvation for a wendigo," Naida added. "They fracture their souls when they make the choice that transforms them. There's no putting a shattered soul like that back together."

Something occurred to me and I scanned the faces around the fire.

The fog was already rolling in and it wouldn't be long before we were enveloped. "Where is Melissa?"

"She went back to her trailer," Nixie answered. "Don't worry. I saw her go inside."

That was a relief. Talk of fractured souls would likely put her on edge, the last thing I wanted. "Caroline, the woman in the woods, recognized that Melissa's soul was cracked. That's not the same thing that happens to a wendigo, but I thought it was suspicious that she could so clearly see that."

"What do you think that means?" Kade's handsome face was creased with concern. "Do you think she's a wendigo?"

"No. She was a normal woman."

"She was flakier than a croissant," Luke argued. "She wasn't normal."

"She was human, though," I argued. "If she wasn't human I would've sensed it."

"She was definitely human," Luke conceded. "She was also crazy."

"Maybe that's because she's been hanging around a wendigo," Nixie suggested. "Maybe she's friends with it or something."

"I've never heard of a human and wendigo being friends," Raven argued. "I think it's impossible. Why be friends with her when she would make a nice meal?"

"She's old, though," Luke pointed out. "Maybe the wendigo doesn't think she will taste good. Old meat is chewy. Maybe the wendigo doesn't like chewy meat."

"Or maybe something else is going on." I slowly got to my feet, my eyes scanning the pooling fog. "I think we need to strengthen the dreamcatcher."

The change in subject surprised everyone.

"Why?" Kade asked as he moved closer. "Do you sense something?"

"No, but we clearly don't know everything that's going on, and I think we should play this the smart way."

"Meaning?"

"Meaning we prepare for the worst."

"Which is?"

"Multiple wendigos that might attack," Luke answered for me. "We heard only one, but that doesn't mean there aren't more out there. The dreamcatcher needs to be tested so we can be sure.

"Caroline mentioned shadow hunters," he continued. "She was obviously talking about the wendigo. She said it in plural form, as though there was more than one out there hunting."

"So we'll strengthen the dreamcatcher," Kade said decisively. "We'll break into groups and do it right now."

"I think that's the best plan we have," I agreed. "We'll conduct more research about the area tomorrow. I think we're missing something."

"Let's get to it." Raven was resigned as she stood. "I have plans with a certain clown tonight. I don't want to make him wait."

"Yes, that would be a travesty," Luke intoned. "There's nothing worse than an annoyed clown watching a clock."

Raven's glare was harsh. "Don't make me smack you around, dog boy."

"I love it when you get riled up." Luke beamed. "It makes a bad day good and a good day great."

"Keep it up. You won't like how I punish you if you push things too far."

"Now I'm definitely excited."

8
EIGHT

Everyone separated into teams again, Kade making it obvious that he had every intention to be my partner when Luke made noises about claiming me for his own. I knew Luke was simply messing with Kade's head, so I merely shot him a warning look to quiet him. At that point he joined forces with Nixie, and everyone broke up to tackle the dreamcatcher from four different angles.

"You seem more worried about this than I would've expected," Kade said, linking his fingers with mine as the fog rolled through the fairgrounds. "Is there something you're not telling me?"

"No." That was true, and yet I couldn't stop myself from slowing in front of the main circus aisle and staring at the big tent. "I don't know what else you want me to say."

"I want you to tell me what you're worried about."

The fog was so thick that it was hard to see through. It was almost as if clouds were rolling through the area because the fog shifted so quickly. It was wreaking havoc on my inner danger alarm because it constantly looked as if someone was moving through the shadows of the circus tents.

"Poet." Kade was directly behind me, his mouth close to my ear.

"Do you see something down there? Are we about to get attacked by a wendigo?"

I realized quickly that Kade was preparing for a battle that wouldn't come. Well, at least it wouldn't come right now. It would most likely become a reality in the coming days. For now, though, we were relatively safe.

"I'm sorry." I put my hand on his forearm to soothe him. "If a wendigo crossed into our territory we'd know it. The dreamcatcher would alert."

Kade didn't relax his stance. "You just said we need to strengthen the dreamcatcher. I'm guessing you have a reason for that."

I definitely had a reason. "The wendigo isn't here," I promised. "It might be close, but it hasn't crossed the dreamcatcher. I promise." I slid my fingers around his wrist and squeezed. "I didn't mean to frighten you."

Kade relaxed, though only marginally. "Then what were you looking at? I thought for sure you saw – or at least sensed – something down there."

"It wasn't that. It's the fog. It always looks as if something is moving because the fog is moving and playing with my inner senses, making me jumpy. It's a bit embarrassing when I say it like that, but there you go. I'm literally jumping at shadows."

"Oh." Kade let loose a low chuckle. "It's making me jumpy, too. I know exactly what you're talking about."

We resumed walking to our sector, our hands automatically joining. The silence that fell over us was amiable enough, but I could tell Kade had something on his mind. Instead of pressing him, I let him find the appropriate question on his own.

"Have you ever fought a wendigo?"

I automatically nodded. "I've fought six or seven of them. As far as paranormal creatures go, they're fairly common and easy to kill."

"That's good. I thought by the way Nellie talked that maybe they were hulking beasts that could kill us all."

"The true danger of a wendigo is its claws ... and cruelty." I thought back to a particular encounter I'd had three years before.

"They're mostly solitary creatures. Only once have we ever discovered a nest."

"How many were in the nest?"

"Fifteen."

Obviously stunned, Kade's eyebrows flew up his forehead. "Fifteen? That can't be right."

"Well, we didn't take the time to conduct an inventory with the body parts when we were finished, but I'm pretty sure Nellie counted fifteen."

"But ... how?"

"It was in Wisconsin. They're extremely prevalent in the Great Lakes region. They like the northwest and Canada, too. It's the trees that call to them ... and make it easier to survive. Whenever anyone sees a monster in the inner city they shoot first and ask questions later. That's why wendigos flee to the forest."

"And you found fifteen of them living together in Wisconsin?" Kade was fascinated by the story. "Were they Packers fans?"

The question was so surreal I could do nothing but bark out a laugh. "I don't remember asking. None of them were wearing those cheese-head hats that are so prevalent there, but I hate to burst your bubble. Why do you think that's important?"

Kade shrugged. "Maybe the Packers were having a bad year or something."

"Maybe. It puts a whole new spin on the story." I grinned as I scuffed my feet against the ground. We were close to the line and I was feeling better about our situation despite the fact that I was in the middle of telling a truly awful tale. "They were holed up in an abandoned building in a bad part of town. It was scheduled for demolition three months out, so it must've only been a temporary base. We were in Milwaukee for a stop – it had been quiet the whole week, something we weren't used to – and then Dolph practically tripped over a wendigo attacking a woman in the parking lot.

"He dispatched it quickly, basically ripped off its head with his bare hands, and we burned the body in a fire," I continued. "The woman was so confused and shaken she was happy to get away from us and pretended she hadn't seen anything. I could see in her mind and knew she would never tell the story, so we let her be.

"Anyway, we thought it was only the one wendigo and carried on with what we were doing," I said. "Saturday rolled around and another wendigo showed up. It scented the parking lot, obviously realized we'd killed his friend, and took off. Nellie and Dolph gave chase. They discovered the nest and returned for backup. Once the circus closed for the night, we moved on the nest."

Kade blinked several times in rapid succession. "That's it? Come on. There must be more to the story than that."

I chewed the inside of my cheek as I began magically tugging on the threads of the dreamcatcher to test for weaknesses. This was the second time I'd done something similar, but I wanted to be sure before I started fortifying the security system with magic. "It's not that interesting of a story," I said finally.

"I don't believe you." Kade folded his arms across his chest as he glared with slit-eyed suspicion. "You're not telling me the whole story."

"Are you calling me a liar?"

"I'm saying that you're keeping something to yourself." The fact that Kade looked more disappointed than anything else tugged on my heartstrings. "If you don't want to tell me, I can't make you. Let's just fortify the dreamcatcher and get out of here. You're right about the fog being creepy. It makes me tense, too."

I ran my tongue over my teeth as I regarded him. He was being combative, which I didn't appreciate. Still, I understood his frustration. "It's not that I don't want to tell you."

"It's that you don't think I can handle it, right?"

Ugh. He was purposely being difficult now. Irritation fueled me as I viciously tugged on one of the dreamcatcher strands. It showed signs of give, so I immediately funneled power into it. "I think you can handle it. I simply don't like remembering it."

"Why? Did someone almost die? Did you almost die?"

"No." That was true. I was never in any physical danger. Still, I didn't celebrate the nest eradication like others in our group. "You probably won't get this, but I'm going to tell you because I'm not in the mood to argue."

Kade remained quiet, his eyes sober as they followed me.

"There was one other thing about the nest," I explained. "For education purposes, it's important to note that wendigos don't often mate. It's usually a solitary activity. The Wisconsin nest was different from the start. All the wendigos were living together and formed something of a community."

"Okay." Kade remained calm. "Are you saying these wendigos mated or something?"

"That would be my guess ... unless they somehow convinced a human child to blacken her soul in such a way that it fractured and she willingly became a wendigo."

It took Kade a few moments to understand what I was saying. "Oh, geez."

I nodded in confirmation. "I think she was about six. It was obviously difficult to gauge age because she looked like a small monster. No one wanted to kill her. Killing children – even if they're part of an evil species – is never easy. But we couldn't simply leave her behind."

"Because she would eat people?"

"That and the fact that she was obviously too young to care for herself. Leaving her would've meant a much crueler death than the one we meted out."

"What happened?" Kade's voice was gentle.

"The mother was desperate to protect the child, but Raven wrestled her down with magic and killed her even as she howled and tried to get to the little one," I replied. "The kid was the last one left. No one wanted to take her out."

"Even Nellie?"

I forced a smile. "Even he has limits."

"I've never seen Nellie acknowledge limits, so I'll have to take your word for it."

"I knew what would happen to her if we simply left her behind," I supplied. "She would starve and then die. We couldn't risk leaving her anyway, but it was difficult. Eventually I basically put her to sleep with my mind and Nixie used some of her pixie dust and helped her slip away. It was the most humane death we could think of."

Kade turned pragmatic. "Well, as hard as it may have been to kill a child, I have to point out that it was a child with a propensity to eat human flesh. What else could you have done?"

"Nothing. That's not what's bothering me."

Kade was taken aback. "Okay. What's bothering you about the story?"

"The part where the wendigos formed human connections," I answered. "If wendigos have fractured souls, which in turn makes them monsters, how could that mother love the kid? How could she bond with a male long enough to get pregnant with the kid, for that matter?"

"The mating part could've been a physical reaction that she had no control over."

"Fair enough. That still doesn't explain her obviously desperate need to get to the kid."

"What are you really worried about?"

That was a good question. "I don't know. For some reason that old woman acting crazy in the woods has me all messed up. The fact that she recognized how Melissa was struggling and what almost happened makes me think that she's seen a soulless creature a time or two."

"The wendigo," Kade surmised. "I get that. You're wondering why the wendigo hasn't killed her because she's isolated and without backup out here."

"I'm wondering more than that. I'm wondering how she can recognize soul injuries. If she learned to do it because of the wendigo, that means they've been communicating on some level. For that to happen, the wendigo has to purposely shelve his need to feed. I don't think that's something that happens easily."

"You're wondering if the wendigo had ties to Caroline Olsen in life, aren't you?"

"Yes."

"Well ... I guess we could run a few searches and find out." He didn't look thrilled at the prospect, but I smiled anyway. "Not tonight," Kade added. "Tonight, once you're finished with this, it's just you and me. We can run searches tomorrow."

"Deal." I felt as if a weight had been lifted from my shoulders as I briefly closed my eyes and directed the magic I felt pulsing through the dreamcatcher. I recognized Raven and Naida's energy right away, and was lost in the process for several minutes.

Kade wisely kept quiet, keeping close to my side but letting me do my thing without interruption. When I finished, I felt markedly better. The feeling lasted only until I straightened and realized Kade had gone rigid as he stared at the trees on the other side of the dreamcatcher.

"What's going on?" I jerked my head to see what he was looking at, frowning at the way the fog seemed to shape and reshape itself into hints of human vestiges. "That's creepy, huh?"

Kade didn't immediately answer, instead swallowing hard. I instinctively moved closer to him and grabbed his hand. "Kade?"

Slowly, he turned to gaze into my eyes. "Something is out there." His voice was barely a whisper.

"How can you be sure?"

"I don't know." His face was white and I could practically feel the terror pulsing through him. "I just know."

I didn't know what to make of the utterance. Kade had never displayed a psychic streak, but that didn't mean what he was feeling wasn't real. He was the son of a mage, after all. Max was the strongest being I had ever come into contact with. It would only make sense for Kade to inherit something from his father. Of course, the odds of his powers suddenly flaring to life right now seemed long.

"Tell me exactly what you feel," I prodded.

"I can't explain it." Kade's frustration was palpable. "I don't know how to explain it. Something is out there. It's watching us."

I didn't doubt he believed what he was saying. I worried my tale about the wendigo mother triggered something, but that was for later contemplation. For now I simply needed to soothe him. "I don't see anything. Maybe ... ." I drifted off, my eyes narrowing when I caught a hint of movement between two tall trees. "What the ... ?"

"Do you see it?" Kade was beside himself.

"I saw something," I replied after a beat. "I'm not sure what it was." I squinted as hard as I could and stared at the spot where I'd seen the movement. A few moments later what I was sure was a face appeared in the darkness. It was hard to see – and even harder to make out features – but I was almost positive it was a face. "Holy ... !"

"What do you see?" Kade was practically breathless. "I think I see a man in a hat."

That was surprising because I thought I saw the opposite. "It's a little girl." My heart rolled. "She's in a dress ... like a *Little House on the Prairie* dress. I think she's smiling at me."

Kade balked. "It's not a little girl. It's a man." He pointed for emphasis, making me realize we were looking in two entirely different spots. "That's definitely a man."

I stared at the place he indicated for a long time, letting my eyes adjust as if I were looking at one of those mosaic posters that were all the rage when I was a kid. After a few seconds I saw what he was talking about. The figure standing in front of him was definitely a man ... and he looked demented. His features were impossible to make out because they were muted and flat, but his gestures were obvious ... as was the way he bobbed his head.

"That's a little creepy," I muttered, shaking my head. "He looks like a character in every bad horror movie I've ever seen."

"He's most definitely not a little girl."

"No, but she is." I forced Kade's chin to the right so he could see the girl in the trees. She looked amused and offered up a cheeky wave. There was nothing corporeal about her. She was very clearly a ghost or manifestation of the fog. She was there, though. "This is so weird."

Kade widened his eyes. "Oh, no, don't say that. This is completely normal."

He sounded as if he was about to lose it. "It's going to be okay."

"Really?" Kade flicked his eyes to me and I cringed at the fear and discomfort I saw there. "I don't see how this will be okay."

I swallowed hard and forced myself to remain calm. "We'll figure it out."

"How? There are weird ghost things in the woods and possibly a wendigo running loose. How will you figure it out?"

"The same way I usually do. We'll research it and come up with a plan."

"Well, great." Kade focused on the filmy man again, grimacing when the ethereal figure smiled. He looked more like a ghostly skull with mayhem on the brain than a despondent spirit who needed help. I had no idea what to make of the phenomenon.

"We'll figure it out," I repeated. "I promise. Just ... don't panic."

"Do I look like I'm going to panic?"

He definitely looked like he was going to at the very least freak out. "Of course not."

"Good. I'm not going to panic."

"Great."

"Really. I'm fine."

"Good to know."

Kade was silent for about ten seconds. "We need to get out of here. I can't keep looking at this. It's too freaky."

"I'm right there with you."

9
NINE

Calming Kade wasn't easy. I readied for bed, pulling on simple cotton shorts and a T-shirt, and found him standing in front of the bedroom window in nothing but his boxer shorts. He seemed intense.

"Do you see something?"

He jumped when I moved closer to his side, my presence clearly catching him off guard. "Just the fog."

"Okay, well ... ." I ran my hand up and down his strong back as I debated how to soothe him. "Do you want to christen the new bed with me again? I know we already did it once, but it can't hurt to make sure we did it properly."

Whatever he was expecting, that wasn't it. He barked out a laugh, his face lighting with mirth as he shook his head. "That's possibly the bluntest invitation I've had all day."

"I certainly hope it's also the best invitation you've had."

"It is." Kade shifted to slide his arm around my waist, his eyes drifting back to the fog. "I'm not sure I'll be able to sleep knowing those things are watching us."

"You don't know that they're watching us."

"You saw them by the woods."

"I did. I don't know what we're dealing with, though. They might not be real."

Kade furrowed his brow, confusion evident. "I don't know what that means. How can they not be real?"

"They could merely be figments of our imagination," I offered, although I didn't truly believe that. "They could've been created by another creature to distract us."

"The wendigo?"

"We don't have conclusive proof that we're dealing with a wendigo yet," I cautioned. "It's dangerous to assume one thing and find we're dealing with another. All we have by way of proof that it's a wendigo is Raven's assumption that what she heard was a wendigo howl. Don't get ahead of yourself."

"So ... what do you think it is?"

I hated being put on the spot but it was clear Kade needed answers. "I don't know." I exhaled heavily as I sat on the bed. "There are a lot of possibilities."

"Like what?" Kade joined me in sitting, but his eyes kept drifting toward the window.

"Like maybe Caroline is a witch and I somehow missed the signs when we met. She might not like us being so close to her place, so maybe she cast a spell to make the fog look like ghosts to keep us away. Maybe she's trying to scare us off with tales of shadow hunters and this is how she plans to do it."

Kade looked intrigued by the suggestion. "Do you really think that's possible?"

"Honestly? Yeah. I don't know if it's probable, but we need more information before we assume we're dealing with a wendigo."

"Fair enough. How do we get that information?"

"Well, for starters, we need to get access to the missing persons reports for this area," I answered. "If people are going missing, that might indicate there's a predator running loose. We might especially want to see if there are any reports about Amanda Stevens, for example. She would be a good place to start. A wendigo can't go for more than a week without a meal. That means there's no reason to stay here if it doesn't have ready access to food."

Kade's lips twisted. "And that means humans, right? I mean ... you've never heard of a wendigo opting to be a vegetarian, have you? Or what about a wendigo that eats animals instead of humans? You said that crazy lady had a goat. Maybe she was taking it into the woods to feed the wendigo. Maybe they've come to an agreement of sorts."

That was an interesting hypothesis, although I had trouble putting much stock in it. "I guess it's possible in theory, but the main reason a human turns into a wendigo is cannibalism. I can't see a wendigo suddenly turning vegetarian."

"That doesn't mean our wendigo isn't an anomaly."

"No." That was absolutely true. "Like I said before, though, we might not be dealing with a wendigo. We might be dealing with something else."

"Like what?"

"I don't know."

"You must have an idea."

His determination to pin me down to a specific ideology was frustrating. "Kade, I don't know. We'll do some research tomorrow and see what we can come up with. That's the best I can offer."

"Fine." Kade made a face as he flopped back on the bed and stared at the ceiling. "I thought you knew everything. I guess I was wrong."

He was very obviously teasing, so I didn't lash out. "I'll go back to my genius status tomorrow. I'm too tired to claim the title tonight."

"I thought you wanted to christen the new bed again?"

"That's all I have energy for."

"Me, too." Kade's smile was sly as I caught his gaze. "Let's put our energy together and see what we come up with."

"That's the best offer I've had all day."

SLEEP CAME FAST and hard, but it wasn't easy. I immediately slipped into a dream that caused my anxiety to spike and my heart to pound.

"What is this place?"

I glanced around, frowning at the fog as it rolled around me. It was so thick I could barely make out the silhouettes of people only ten feet away. The only reason I was absolutely certain they were there is because I heard them whispering ... and chanting.

I moved to head toward them, intent on a heavy conversation and explanations for exactly what was going on, but I found I was tied to a wooden stake of some sort in the middle of what looked to be a small town square.

"Oh, you've got to be kidding." My heart pounded harder. "What is going on here?" I tugged on my arms, hating the way the rope dug into my wrists and caused actual discomfort. I turned to my right to study the knots. They were tight enough, the rope thick enough, that I recognized I wouldn't be able to break free without magic. This was a dream – I had no problem understanding that – so the odds of my magic working correctly were slim to none. "I think we should have a discussion."

"The time for words is over," a ruggedly masculine voice intoned from the fog, causing me to snap my head back to the space I'd watched only moments before. I still couldn't make out any features, but I was almost positive I could see the outline of a hat ... and I was certain it was the same hat Kade became fixated on while strengthening the dreamcatcher.

"How can the time for words be over when we haven't exchanged any?" I challenged, my temper fraying. "I think we should talk before we declare a moratorium on talking. That only seems fair."

"You had a chance to speak at your trial, Gilly," the man supplied. "You said nothing of interest. You can't change your mind now."

Oh, well, great. "Who is Gilly?"

"That will not work with us." This time a woman spoke. She was to my right, but I couldn't make out anything in that direction because the fog only billowed stronger when I tried. She sounded downright evil, though, like an extra in *The Scarlet Letter* was going to get puritanical on my ass. "We know what you are. We know what you've done."

"Well, at least you seem to know what's going on." I fruitlessly struggled with my restraints. "What is this? Are you going to burn me at the stake or something?" I meant the question in jest, but once it escaped and I thought better about my circumstances, I cringed. "That wasn't a suggestion, by the way."

"Why would we burn you?" the man asked.

"I ... don't know. I think not burning me is a good idea."

"Your fate will be much worse," he said. "We have to purify you. Burning is not the purification we seek."

That sounded ominous. "Well, as lovely as that sounds, I think I'm going to pass. How about you let me loose and I promise to leave this place and never return? I think that's a good compromise for all of us."

"That is not what we're going to do."

"Yes, but ... ." I didn't get a chance to finish. Instead of furthering the argument, the man started chanting. They were words I didn't recognize, a language I didn't understand, but he was fervent and determined.

"Knock that off," I warned, my cheeks flushing with color. It was an involuntary response, as if my body was somehow reacting to the chant even though I had no idea why. It wasn't as if I understood the words. "I don't know who you think I am, but you're mistaken."

"Shut up, Gilly." Someone smacked me across the face, although all I saw was a hand right before it connected. I recognized the voice as belonging to the woman who previously spoke. Her hand shot out from the fog and caused me to offer a muffled cry as ragged fingernails raked against my skin. The pain was real. More real than it should be in a dream. I had no idea what to make of it, but I could swear I felt blood running down my cheek. "You are guilty and there is no escaping your fate."

I was starting to believe that was true ... and it terrified me. "I'm not who you think I am."

"You are evil and must be cleansed," the man said. "It is too late to repent. You must be cleaned out until you are hollow and then the goodness and light will find a way back inside. That is our purpose here. Nothing more."

"But ...."

The woman smacked me again, this time from the other side. Even as my fear grew, so did my temper.

"You're going to wish you'd never done that."

"And here is the devil we expected to find," the man intoned. "It is finally coming forth."

"Oh, you have no idea how devilish I can be." I yanked hard at my restraints, hoping against hope I would feel some give. There was nothing. My only option was to let loose some magic, which I did.

Unlike Naida and Raven, my magic is more restrained. I'm Romani by birth, but was never trained properly. Max once suggested that he might train me, but I wasn't keen on the idea – my parents were insistent that I hide my gifts as a child – so I shelved his offer after a polite "thank you, but I'm good." I was really starting to regret that now, because my magic fizzled almost instantly.

"Crap! This isn't real. I know it's not real." I put my head down and struggled harder. "Son of a ... !"

The chanting continued, increasing in volume and speed. The words rolled off me now. I couldn't understand them, yet I seemed to know what was coming next. A burst of pain opened in my chest, momentarily making me wonder if I had a creature inside that managed to crawl through my skin for escape. It was agony to stand there, tied to a stake in the ground with no recourse as something tore at my skin.

I wanted to cry but couldn't find the tears. I wanted to die but had no way to make it happen. The pain was all consuming, to the point where I thought my mind might implode.

Then I heard something else. I wasn't sure what it was at first, but then I realized it was Kade. He was crying, screaming for me to come back. His voice was close and yet far away at the same time. He wasn't alone. I heard another voice.

Whatever happened was quick. It was as if a set of hands grabbed me on either side of my head and barked a command. In the back of my mind I recognized the voice. I also understood that I was drifting higher, my consciousness escaping from the body on the stake.

The chanting was harder to hear now thanks to Kade's anguish. He was begging me to come back ... so that's what I did.

I BOLTED TO A sitting position in my bed, gasping for breath as I slapped at the hands on my head.

Raven, her silver eyes full of worry, stood over me. She was dressed in a slinky negligee, her assets on full display, and she didn't seem embarrassed in the least at being practically naked in my bedroom.

"Poet." Kade put his hand to my back, tears coursing down his cheeks. "Are you okay? What happened?"

That was a very good question. "I don't know." My voice sounded raspy and I couldn't help but wonder if it was because of all the screaming I did in my dream. Perhaps that carried over to the real world, which would explain Raven's presence and Kade's shaken countenance. "What happened?"

"You were having a nightmare," Kade replied, smoothing my hair with trembling fingers. "I couldn't wake you even though you were ... um ... ." He was clearly uncomfortable saying it.

"You were screaming," Raven finished. "It sounded as if you were dying."

"I think I might have been." I rubbed my cheek as I stared at her. "Did you hear the screaming? Is that what brought you here?"

"No." Raven seemed weary, as if whatever she did to wake me took a lot out of her. "I sensed you were in trouble from my trailer. That was before you started screaming. I was almost here when that infernal racket started."

"It's lovely to spend time with you, too," I drawled.

Instead of being offended, Raven smiled. "I'm glad to see you're getting your sassy attitude back. As for the dream, what can you tell me?"

I related everything that happened, leaving nothing out. When I got to the part about the man in the hat I felt Kade tense. He didn't speak. He didn't blurt out "I told you so" and start to swagger around the room. He merely kept his arm tight around my back as he lent me a bit of his warmth.

"That's odd," Raven murmured when I was done. "You're sure they called it a cleansing ritual?"

I nodded. "I have no idea what they were cleansing for, though. Whatever it was, it hurt. It felt as if something was bursting out of my chest."

"What happened here?" Kade asked, lifting my arm. "What did this?" He pointed to what looked like rope burn on my wrist. When I checked, I found I had marks on both wrists.

"That's where I fought being tied to the stake."

"You brought injuries out of your dream with you?" Kade was furious. "That can't be right."

"It's not right, but it is real," Raven countered, running her tongue over her teeth as she tilted her head to the side. "I have no idea what we're dealing with, but we need to add some individual charms to the dreamcatcher tomorrow."

"What's wrong with tonight?" Kade challenged. "She needs to be kept safe tonight."

"I don't have everything ready to do it tonight." Raven was clearly tense as she fought the urge to slap Kade back. "Tomorrow is the soonest we can do it."

"She won't be safe tonight then," Kade persisted. "She can't go back to sleep. If she does ... well ... she'll die."

"That's not entirely true." Raven stood. "Do you have any of the pixie sleeping draughts in your medicine cabinet?"

I understood what she was planning and nodded. "Yeah."

"I'll charm one so you don't dream." Raven was matter of fact. "I'll also have Dolph and Nellie watch the perimeter until dawn. I doubt those things can cross the dreamcatcher. But if they have found a way to invade our minds, we need to adjust the frequency of the dreamcatcher to stop that from happening."

Raven disappeared into the bathroom, giving Kade and me a moment of solitude.

"I'm sorry for frightening you. I ... am so sorry."

"Stop that." Kade's tone was harsh. "I just want you to be okay. I ... couldn't wake you. I was scared out of my mind."

He wasn't the only one. I decided to keep that tidbit to myself, though, at least until I was more settled. "I'm okay. I'm already feeling better."

"And this will take care of the rest of it." Raven strode back into the room, a small vial in her hand. "I charmed it so you won't dream. We'll deal with the dreamcatcher in the morning."

"What about everyone else?" I asked. "If they can't get in my dreams, what makes you think they'll stay away from everyone else?"

"I think they went after you for a reason," Raven replied simply. "You're more in tune with your psychic senses. It will take them – whoever they are – longer to infiltrate everyone else's minds. That means the dreamcatcher is our number one priority tomorrow."

I really had no choice but to acquiesce. "Okay."

Raven flicked her eyes to Kade. "I know that you won't willingly go to sleep because you'll be watching her, but she really will be okay. Don't work yourself into a frenzy over this. We're going to need you tomorrow to check on a few things. It would be better if you were fresh and at full strength."

Kade made a face. "Don't worry about me. I'll do my job."

"Yes, well ... ." Raven spared me a glance. "Try to make him sleep. Watching you won't do him any good."

"I'll do my best." I offered her a salute before downing the sleeping draught. "Thanks for yanking me out of the pits of Hell, by the way. I appreciate it."

"Yes, well, I wasn't doing anything else of note at the time."

Her outfit told me otherwise, but I knew better than to press her on it. "Thanks anyway."

"Don't mention it."

10

TEN

Thankfully Kade managed to get some sleep. I was fairly certain he sat watch over me long after I slipped into slumber, but his eyes were closed and he was breathing evenly when I woke.

Despite the terror of the dream, I felt fairly well rested. I did my best to remain immobile to give Kade more time to recharge, which allowed me to look back on the dream with something of a detached eye.

"I can feel your mind working from here," Kade murmured, his eyes still closed. "Are you okay?"

"I'm fine." I pressed my fingertips to his stubbled cheek. "I'm sorry for freaking you out."

"Don't apologize for something you couldn't control," Kade growled, finally opening one eye and fixing me with a stern look. "You're okay. That's the most important thing."

"It is." I stretched my arms over my head and heaved a sigh when I saw the marks on my wrists. "This sucks. I need to get some ointment from Nixie and Naida. People will think we've been playing some rather rough games."

Kade poked my side. "I don't find that funny."

No, from his point of view, probably not. "It was a bad joke."

"Let's not make it again."

"Sure." I briefly pressed my eyes shut before turning my head to the window. The sun was shining, the fog long since dissipated. It looked like a beautiful day. "We should probably get moving. Raven and I will be busy casting charms most of the morning."

"Are you strong enough for that?"

"I'm okay. It was just a dream."

Kade gently grabbed my arm and held it up so I could see the raw injuries around my wrist. "This is more than just a dream."

"I know, but I'm okay. You don't need to worry."

"I'm pretty sure that worrying is part of the job description. It says so right in the Boyfriend Handbook."

"I'm guessing you got all As in school," I teased, going for levity.

"I want to ace my class in Poet-ry."

I groaned at the pun. "Nice."

"It just came to me." He rolled and gave me a soft kiss, lingering for an extra moment. "Let's get your wrists patched up and head outside. You need food, and then we have to see what we can do about the dreamcatcher. Just for the record, I'm going to stick close to you. I know that will probably annoy you, but I believe it says right in the Girlfriend Handbook that you have no choice but to put up with it."

"Smooth."

"I do my best."

I WAS RAVENOUS WHEN it came time for breakfast. Nixie and Naida insisted I sit rather than help. Raven rolled her eyes but didn't argue the point, instead instructing Naida to fetch the ointment for my wrists and ordering Percival to lend a hand with breakfast preparations even though the men rarely helped with when it came to cooking.

The gender roles were somewhat antiquated at Mystic Caravan, but because the women were stronger on the battlefield it somehow managed to even out.

"That sounds all kinds of creepy," Nellie complained as he watched me shovel heaping forkfuls of eggs and hash browns into my mouth. "You knew it was a dream and yet couldn't get out?"

I swallowed, not bothering to wipe the corners of my mouth despite the food I knew to be clinging there. "I was definitely stuck. I kept telling them they had the wrong person but I don't think they believed me."

"The only name you heard was Gilly?" Percival asked, his fake British accent on full display. Not long after joining our group he let slip that he wasn't really British while screaming like a teenager at a boy band concert in the face of mortal peril. The next day he was back to being his usual self – clown shoes and all – and we'd barely mentioned it since. Yeah, it's totally odd. I can't explain it.

"Yes. No last name."

"We might be able to track the name down, but it won't be easy." Percival daintily wiped his mouth. "I'll see what I can dig up."

"That's a start, but I'm not sure Gilly is where we should focus our efforts," Raven said as she took her spot next to Percival. "I think we need to focus on the guy with the hat."

"Why do you say that?" Kade asked, alarmed. "Why do you think he's key?"

"I didn't say I thought he was key. I said that I thought we should focus on him. He was the ringleader in the dream. He clearly unnerved you out by the trees."

I ate as I considered Raven's statement.

"Poet says there's a chance that those things we saw weren't real," Kade argued. "She says that something else might be going on."

Raven exchanged a weighted look with me. "Do you believe that?"

I shook my head, hating the way Kade cringed. "I thought it might be a remote possibility before the dream. I believed that perhaps Caroline was a witch and I didn't pick up on it, that she created the shadow hunters to keep people away from her property."

"Oh, like maybe she's out there growing pot and doesn't want anyone to stumble over her stash," Nellie said knowingly. "That's a good possibility."

"Not after the dream," I countered. "I think we're definitely dealing with something that is rooted in history. Something bad happened – and it happened close to here – and I think whatever is lurking in the fog is somehow tied to that."

"Well, there goes the pot theory." Nellie made a face. "I was totally looking forward to pinching some, too."

"How does the wendigo fit into all this?" Nixie asked, her eyes bright and keen. "I mean … that's definitely what Raven heard howling last night, right?"

"I'm sure that was a wendigo," Raven acknowledged as she rubbed the back of her neck. "I can't be sure it was a real wendigo, though, or something cooked up by whatever faction is haunting us. Until we know if people have been going missing, I don't feel comfortable settling on the wendigo as a culprit."

"Besides that, I've never heard of a wendigo managing to pull off something on this grand of a scale," I added. "I think the most important thing for us to do is focus on the dreamcatcher. We need to be able to keep out whatever is haunting us."

"I have charms and potions ready," Raven offered. "I think we should make that our priority. We'll conduct research like we normally do, but the dreamcatcher charms are our biggest priority."

"Okay." I forced a smile before looking over the assembled faces, something occurring to me. "Where is Luke?"

"Oh, he's pouting because he missed out on the action last night," Raven explained with an evil smile. "He's angry no one told him until after the fact. He's gearing up to be a big baby for the rest of the day."

I didn't like the sound of that. "I'll talk to him. He can be part of my team for the charms."

"That team includes me," Kade reminded me.

"Yes, well, I happen to enjoy threesomes."

Kade fought the urge to return my grin … and failed. "You're lucky you're cute."

"I thank my lucky stars every day … and night."

"Finish your breakfast." Kade tapped the side of my plate. "I want these charm things done right away. I don't want to risk a repeat of last night ever again."

He wasn't the only one.

"I'M NOT BLAMING YOU."

Luke was a complaining mess for the duration of the dreamcatcher charms. They didn't take long – fifteen minutes tops – but he didn't shut up the entire time.

"Did I say I blamed you?" Luke continued. "I mean ... why would I blame you? That's ridiculous. You were injured and upset. I can hardly blame you."

"That's never stopped you before," I pointed out, staring at the woods. I had an idea and it was something that Kade wasn't going to like. He'd remained largely silent while I worked – mostly because Luke wouldn't shut up long enough to allow him to speak – but I could feel the underlying tension rolling off him.

"I blame Kade," Luke blurted out. "He's at fault for this."

Kade finally found his voice. "Excuse me? How is this my fault?"

"You should've told me she was hurt," Luke replied without hesitation. "You should've called for me so I could have taken care of her."

"I took care of her."

"I didn't need taking care of," I reminded both of them. "I was fine. There's no reason to get your panties in a bunch, girls. I'm standing right here and clearly fine."

Kade scowled. "It's sexist for you to compare us to girls simply because we care about you."

"Totally sexist," Luke agreed. "And hurtful."

I didn't bother to hide my eye roll. "Oh, geez. You guys are a lot of work."

"And don't you forget it." Luke poked my side and smiled before sobering. "You still should've found a way for me to be with you. You're my sidekick. That means it's my job to fret when you're injured or ill."

"She's my girlfriend," Kade argued. "It's my job to take care of her now. Not yours."

"Oh, whatever."

"How am I your sidekick?" I questioned, irritation bubbling up despite my determination not to be dragged into one of Luke's wacky side conversations. "If anything, you're my sidekick."

Luke's eyes flared with annoyance. "You take that back. Everyone knows I'm the Batman to your Robin."

Now it was my turn to scoff. "Please. You're the Chewbacca to my Han Solo."

"Ugh!"

"And because you're my sidekick, you have to be at my side for our next little adventure." I grabbed Luke by the wrist before he could protest. "I insist in case I need you to protect me."

"And what adventure is that?" Kade asked, suspicion evident as it crawled across his handsome features. "You're not going on an adventure without me."

"That's a given." I beamed. "You're the Princess Leia in our little group."

"Oh, good grief." Kade flexed his arms and glowered. "Where do you think you're going?"

My answer was simple. "Falk."

Kade's eyebrows flew up his forehead. "The ghost town?"

"All legends start somewhere. It can't hurt to look."

"But ... what if the wendigo is out there?"

"We can handle one little wendigo."

"What if those shadow hunter things Caroline was talking about are out there?" Luke asked.

"Then at least we'll know what we're dealing with." I remained determined as I glanced between them. "I have to see. I'll go by myself if you force me, but I'm going."

Kade was resigned as he sighed. "There's no way that's happening. We'll go with you."

"Yes, we're looking forward to it," Luke drawled.

"Great." I stepped over the dreamcatcher line and headed for the trees. "Let's see if this place lives up to the hype, shall we?"

"THERE'S NOTHING HERE."

I couldn't help being disappointed when we finally arrived at our destination. There was very little to look at. The promised gardens were beautiful, but wild and overgrown. There were no buildings to speak of other than a rundown hovel that was basically devoid of walls and a roof.

"I thought you said that all the buildings were razed because of squatters," Kade pointed out. He'd been initially nervous to visit the town, but his agitation dissipated when we arrived. There was nothing to fear, so it was hard to get worked up about pretty flowers and the absence of buildings. "Did you think the information you pulled was inaccurate?"

I shrugged. "I don't know. I thought I would be able to find something, a landmark or … anything."

"There's something over here," Luke called out. He'd wandered about a hundred feet to our right and was busy kicking at something on the ground. "I think this is a brick foundation."

That was hardly something to get excited about, but I trudged over all the same. It took me a moment to see what he was pointing at, but when I recognized the square outline I dropped to my knee so I could touch the brick. "There was definitely a building here."

"Is it something you recognize?" Kade asked. "I mean … from the dream. Did you see this in your dream?"

"Did I see a foundation overgrown with several decades of foliage? Um, no."

Kade's expression turned rueful. "I didn't mean that. I just … I guess I don't know what I meant." He ran a hand over his short-cropped hair. "I was hoping you'd be able to tell if this was the spot from your dream."

"I couldn't see much in the dream," I explained. "It was fog. Just a lot of fog."

"There's still a lot of fog," Luke pointed out, shifting so he could look over the pretty expanse. "It's almost noon and this place is rolling in it. It's not as thick as it is at night, but it's still pretty thick for this time of day."

I lifted my eyes to stare at the tree canopy. "It's because the sun can't get through. I mean … it gets through in places … but it never gets warm enough in here to burn off the fog. I'll bet this place always felt haunted for that reason alone."

"How lovely," Kade deadpanned, linking his fingers with mine. "Okay. You've seen it. Let's turn around and head back to the circus."

I immediately started shaking my head. "We're out here and there's nothing threatening us. I would know if something or someone dangerous was approaching. There's no reason to get worked up."

Kade's lips turned down. "You're still recovering from last night."

"I'm fine. If you keep making a big deal out of it I'm going to get angry."

"You wouldn't like her when she's angry," Luke offered, flexing his muscles for effect. "Hulk angry."

Even though Luke often went out of his way to irritate him, Kade grinned. "Fine. We'll look around. But I don't want anyone wandering off."

"You're not the boss of me," Luke shot back.

"Technically I am," Kade argued.

"I'm the boss of both of you," I pointed out. "That means you have to follow my orders. We need to look around and see if there's anything worth investigating. It won't take long if you guys stop being pains in my behind."

Instead of responding with words, Luke gave me a loud slap on the butt.

"Hey!"

"I just want to make sure I get my money's worth if I'm going to be a pain in your behind," Luke said. "Come on. I want to see what's over there. Those flowers are pretty, and I'll bet that was the center of all the activity around here."

That was the location I wanted to investigate, so I opted to capitulate. "Fine."

We fell into step together, Kade and Luke taking up protective positions on either side of me. If they thought they were fooling anybody they were sadly mistaken. It wasn't worth getting into a fight about, though.

"What else do you know about Falk?" Kade asked to break the silence. "What about the ghosts people claim to see?"

I shrugged, noncommittal. "I'm not sure. Ghost stories in a place like this are normal. That doesn't mean they're real."

"You obviously believe they're real after last night."

He wasn't wrong. "Yeah, well, I don't know. I ... ." I broke off when I caught a hint of something on the wind. "Is something burning?"

"Not right now," Luke answered, striding forward when his keen eyes fell on something of interest. "Something was definitely burning last night, though."

I followed him to what looked like the remnants of a bonfire. It was a big one, the fire probably going for at least a good ten hours, and looked to have been doused roughly around dawn if the smoldering remnants were any indication.

"I wonder who left this," I mused, my mind kicking into overdrive "This doesn't seem like a good place for teenagers to have a bonfire if they're in the mood to drink." I searched the immediate area for confirmation. "This is the only spot where a fire was built, at least recently."

"There are a lot of footprints," Kade mused, kneeling for a closer look at what appeared to be a well-defined print. "No markings on the bottom of the shoes to tell me the brand."

"Why is that important?" Luke asked, legitimately curious.

"Because if we were dealing with a bunch of Converse or Nike logos I'd bet we were dealing with kids," Kade replied. "It's not an exact science, but usually a fair bet."

"Good point." Luke rolled his neck until it cracked. "What do these footprints tell you?"

"I have no idea." Kade shifted his eyes to me. "I don't like it, though.

It feels off. I don't think we should stay here when it's just the three of us. If you want to look around further, then we need to collect some backup."

I wanted to argue – I wasn't a wuss, after all – but I couldn't shake the feeling that he was right. "Okay. Let's head back. But first I want to take a few photographs to show the others. They might have some ideas."

"Make it quick. This place gives me the heebie-jeebies."

He wasn't the only one.

11

ELEVEN

Kade volunteered to take Nellie, Dolph and Raven back to Falk. He was convinced the fire and footprints meant something. I agreed, but figured my time would be better spent conducting research.

Even though he wasn't keen on me taking off on my own after the previous evening, Kade put up only minimal opposition when I said I wanted to hit up a local library. He tried to get Luke to go with me, but someone had to handle circus tasks, and that fell to Luke. I knew Luke hated visiting libraries, so I figured he was secretly relieved that I was fully capable of heading out on my own without melting down or screaming for a dashing hero to come to my rescue.

Finding the library wasn't easy – I had to check my GPS three times to make sure I was at the correct location – and when I entered I found a building that felt somehow older than it should be. Computer terminals were available in cubbies along the back wall, although they looked ancient, and the periodicals section actually looked dusty.

I was taken aback enough that I stood in the doorway for what felt like forever, wondering if stopping here was a waste of time. I had just about made up my mind to head back to the circus when a young woman exited the office behind the front desk and fixed me with a tepid smile.

"Hello."

I awkwardly shifted from one foot to the other. "Um ... hello."

The woman waited for a beat and when I didn't blurt out my intentions she filled the conversational gap. "Do you need something?"

"Oh, well ... I was actually hoping you might have some books on the history of the area."

"We have history books."

"I'm most interested in Falk."

"Oh, the ghost rumors." The woman smiled as she moved from behind the counter, allowing me to see her full outfit for the first time. She wore polyester pants that looked as if they originated in the seventies, a cardigan boasting what I assumed to be moth holes in the elbows, and shoes that seemed a little too orthopedic to entice a young twentysomething. "I'm guessing you're with the circus, right? You guys are staying close to Falk."

"Near enough to visit," I confirmed, frowning as I stared at her shoes. "Have you lived here your entire life?"

"Yes."

I was hoping she would expand on that, but apparently I was going to have to drag out the information another way. "My name is Poet. I'm the fortune teller for Mystic Caravan Circus."

"Oh, that sounds like a delightful job."

Still nothing. Either she was being purposely obtuse or playing a game. I was leaning toward the former. "And you are?"

"Oh, forgive my rudeness." The girl pushed her blond hair away from her face and grinned. "Everyone in this area knows everyone else. I sometimes forget my manners with visitors. I'm Remy Langstrom."

"It's nice to meet you." I extended my hand but Remy ignored it as she turned and pointed toward the back of the library. "The information you want is probably back here. I wish I could say all of our material is on the computers, but it's not. Most of it's still on microfiche. Sorry about that."

I shouldn't have been surprised – the library was old, after all – but I was mildly disheartened. "Well, I've researched on microfiche before. It's hardly the first time."

"It's dead around here, so I can help you a bit." Remy directed me toward two microfiche machines. They were located in the very back of the building, as if whoever put them there was ashamed to have them out in the open in case people pointed and laughed. "It must be exciting to travel with the circus."

"What? Oh, it has its moments." I took the chair on the left and immediately started the machine. "I like visiting different places, and this is a fun way to do it."

"Don't you miss your family?" Remy's face was full of innocence and excitement as she stared at me. "I know I would miss my family if I was traveling all over the place. I would probably cry so much the other circus folk would send me back."

"Oh, well ... I don't have a family." I opted for honesty. There was no reason to lie. "My parents died when I was a teenager."

"Is that why you joined the circus?"

"I joined the circus because I was looking for a new life. I haven't regretted my decision even once, so I think it worked out well for me. It's definitely not the life for everyone, though."

"No. Probably not." Remy made a clucking sound with her tongue before turning serious. "So, what do you want to know about Falk?"

"What do you have?"

"I have a lot of nothing or a little of something. Which do you prefer?"

She was an interesting woman, her face almost youthfully angelic. Her clothing was dated and ratty. Of course, she probably didn't have a choice in how she dressed. If she was struggling for money – and I couldn't imagine she was pulling down a full-time wage for running an empty library in this area – then it didn't seem fair to judge her by appearances. I hated it when people did that to me. I should know better than to do it to others.

"Well, let's start with the history," I suggested. "I don't know much about the city other than it boomed about the time lumber was a big commodity."

"That's a simple deduction really," Remy countered, her hands busy zooming through newspaper files. "Falk did start as a lumber camp. It was hardly the only one in this area, though. You have to remember, back when the camps were popping up the only way to travel between destinations was by horseback or wagon."

"I understand that. But Falk somehow went from a camp to a town. At least that's my understanding."

"Only some of the camps survived. There was no way of telling which ones would," Remy explained. "At the height of its existence, Falk boasted hundreds of workers from the Elk River Lumber Company. The population was actually higher than that, because many of those workers had wives and children.

"It was founded as a company mill town in 1884 by Noah Falk," she continued. "He was an East Coaster who headed west due with the gold rush but ended up working in the lumber field instead. He worked at various lumber mills for thirty years before Falk came into being.

"Because of the travel limitations, Eureka was too far away for a commute, so Falk realized he had no choice but to build a fully-functioning town," she said. "He built the mill in 1884, and a cookhouse, post office, general store, dance hall and houses soon followed."

"What was town life like?" I asked, my mind drifting to the dream. "I'm guessing it wasn't easy."

"Oh, not in the least." Remy turned grim. "The men worked twelve-hour days, six days a week. The lumber had to be loaded on a train, which made stops in Eureka, so transporting the lumber was difficult.

"As for the women, they were in charge of the gardens and livestock," she explained. "That was difficult work because the women were often watching children while all this was going on. Everyone was expected to pull their own weight."

"What about schools and other activities?" I asked. "I mean ... it couldn't have been all work."

"No, but times were different," Remy pointed out. "People didn't live as long, and life was simply harder. Now survival is a given if you stay out of trouble and avoid certain illnesses. That wasn't the case back then."

"There must have been town meetings or something," I pressed. "Maybe they had town fairs or something."

"My understanding is that they had dances every Saturday night. A band would travel from Eureka to entertain everyone. That was the limit of the excitement."

"A band, huh?" I wasn't sure exactly what I was digging for, but I was eager to bend Remy's ear as long as she wasn't inundated with questions from other library visitors. "What about alcohol? I think I read Falk was a dry town. Do you think that's true?"

Remy's smile was mischievous. "I see you've done a little research of your own."

"A bare minimum."

"Local legend says that while Falk was supposed to be dry there were quite a few stills hidden across the acreage," Remy supplied, her eyes sparkling. "Despite that, the residents didn't have much time to drink."

"I guess not." I shook my head. "The town closed in 1936, right?"

"The mill closed in 1936," Remy corrected. "The town lasted another year. Residents thought the mill would re-open, but it wasn't just the Great Depression that took it down."

Oh, well, now we were getting somewhere. "What happened?"

"The mill blade warped." Remy was clearly enjoying her moment as the center of attention. She rubbed her hands together and leaned closer. "No one could figure out how it happened. There were whispers the town had a witch hiding in plain sight because only a witch could be powerful enough to warp the blade."

I wasn't sure that was true – I mean, what sort of witch gets her jollies warping mill blades? – but the tale was still interesting. "So, the mill closed permanently in 1936. What happened after that?"

"After the initial closing, people remained behind and subsisted off their gardens and hunting game," Remy replied. "The hope that the mill would reopen fueled them."

"Did the mill ever reopen?"

"Yes, but only briefly."

"So, when it became apparent that the mill was done, what happened to the workers and their families?"

"They left, and quickly," Remy answered. "Almost everyone was gone from the town within a few weeks. Because the workers fled so quickly, many items were left behind … like beds, dishes and even clothes."

"Did most of the workers flee to Eureka?"

"I think some of them did. I don't know if I would say it was most of them."

"Hmm." I ran the story through my head. "Did anyone stay behind?"

"Yes, from the 1940s to the 1970s, Loleta and Charles Webb stayed behind as the caretakers and only residents," Remy said. "There are hilarious stories about Charles carrying around a rock salt-loaded shotgun and scaring off anybody who tried to stop by the town. They've become local legends."

"Was he was worried about looters?"

Remy shrugged. "I think he just liked shooting at people. I can't say. After that, though, government officials were too worried about people going into the town and trying to live there – it was a lawsuit waiting to happen, frankly – so they destroyed all the buildings except for the railroad depot and the Webb house, and called it a day."

"What do you know about the Webbs?" I asked, my mind drifting to Caroline. "Did they have any children?"

"I don't know. Is that important?"

"Probably not." I tapped my fingers on the microfiche dial as I tried to wrap my head around the story. It seemed simple enough – the witch warping the saw blade notwithstanding – but it didn't feel like a complete tale. "What about ghost sightings?" I asked finally. "The town got its reputation for being visited by spirits. Do you have any idea who these ghosts are supposed to be?"

"I can't say I've ever heard names," Remy replied. "I think the ghost stories come with the territory when an entire town is abandoned. If you think about it, the men who worked there lived hard lives. A lot of them died on the job. I guess their ghosts could be running around."

"Right. And what about Caroline Olsen?" I decided to go for it. The worst I could do was offend Remy by being an unapologetic gossip. I could live with that. "What can you tell me about her?"

Something flitted through Remy's eyes and I instinctively knew she was about to lie. She shuttered her emotions quickly, but not fast enough for me to miss the furtive quality of her expression. "I have no idea who that is."

I decided to press further. "She's the woman who lives out in the middle of nowhere," I offered. "She's essentially got a rundown house between the fairgrounds and Falk. There's a path that runs right past her house."

"Oh, well, I can't say that I know who that is." Remy's tone was dismissive, but I didn't believe her. She was hiding something.

"She told me some stories about this area," I volunteered. "About shadow hunters and possibly a wendigo for good measure." I added that last part because I wanted to see how Remy would react. I wasn't disappointed. She jolted hard as she immediately started shaking her head.

"I don't know what that is."

"I think you might. In fact ... ." I broke off when I heard a whisper in the back of my head, furrowing my brow when I realized it sounded like chanting. I was alarmed enough to raise my eyes and snag Remy's gaze. She was watching me intently, as if she expected something to happen. Her expression set off the alarm bells in my head.

"What are you doing?" Remy moved to stand as I struggled out of my chair, purposely pushing the piece of furniture between us to cut off Remy's avenue of approach.

"I'm leaving." I managed to keep my thoughts together, but just barely. "Stay there."

"You don't look so good." Remy's words were laced with concern, but her eyes flooded with mayhem. "You should let me help you." She reached out a second time, but I hopped away to avoid contact. For some reason – and I'm still not sure how – I recognized that might signify real trouble for me. "I think you need to lie down."

"I'm good." My tongue felt thick and it was hard to form words. The chanting continued, louder, and the threat seemed to be shrinking rather than growing. "I don't need your help."

"I think you do." Remy made a tsking sound with her tongue. "I would feel awful if I didn't help you. I'm a giver by nature. That's why I work in a library."

"You're ... something." I increased the distance between us, focusing on the exit door rather than Remy as I worked overtime to escape the building. I had no idea if that would solve the problem, but if I could make it to Kade's truck – lock the door and regroup – I knew things would be okay. "Don't follow me."

Remy's voice was a soft hiss, although she didn't sound as if she was close on my heels. "You should come back. I have more to tell you."

"I don't want to hear it. In fact ... ." Whatever I was going to say died on my lips when I risked a glance at the mirror next to the door and almost tripped over my own feet at the sight of the two reflections staring back. One was me. I was ashen and sweaty and looked ready to pass out. It wasn't a pretty picture. The other was Remy, although she looked nothing like when I was sitting beside her.

Instead of the young woman with the pretty skin and bright smile, I found an old woman watching me from the spot Remy stood in only moments before. Her hair was bottle blond and brittle, shorn close to her head, and she wore the outfit Remy was clad in only seconds before.

"What are you?" I gritted out.

Remy barked out a laugh. "More than you can handle. If you want answers, you have to come back."

"Oh, I don't think that's a good idea." I felt stronger the second my fingers wrapped around the door handle. "I'll figure out what you are on my own."

Remy's smile – the one in the mirror and the one I double-checked when glancing over my shoulder – was evil enough that my blood ran cold. "Good luck with that." She offered a taunting wave. "I'll see you soon."

"Not if I can help it."

"You won't have a choice in the matter."

I was feeling braver than before now that my head was starting to clear so, of course, I stuck my foot in my mouth and offered a ridiculous challenge. "I guess we'll have to see about that."

"I guess we will."

"By the way, the orthopedic shoes were a dead giveaway."

Remy sneered. "Thanks for the tip."

I didn't waste time sharing barbs with her, instead stalking out of the building. I didn't stop until I was in Kade's truck, the doors locked, the windows up, and could catch my breath.

"What the heck was that?"

12
TWELVE

Kade practically ripped the door off his truck when I hit the parking lot at the fairgrounds. He was waiting for me – pacing really – and he had his arms around my waist before my feet hit the ground.

"Are you okay?"

I awkwardly patted his back while accepting the hug and looked over his shoulder to where Luke and Raven stood. They didn't look as worried, but it was obvious they were also on edge. "I'm fine. What's going on? Did something happen in Falk?"

"Something happened to you," Kade fired back, pulling away so he could study my face. "Raven sensed something going on with you, and I couldn't get you on your phone. I was about to have a meltdown."

"About to?" Luke cocked a dubious eyebrow. "You passed 'about to' thirty minutes ago."

Kade held up his hand to silence my best friend. "Don't make me hurt you."

"Like you could."

"Just ... don't." Kade ran his hands over my hair and forced a tight-lipped smile that didn't make it to his eyes. "Are you okay?"

"You already asked that. I'm fine." In truth, once I took a single step outside the library my mind cleared and I could breathe again. I drove Kade's truck to the nearest fast-food restaurant and spent ten minutes there getting my head together, running the afternoon's events through my mind. It was surreal. I was fine, so I saw no reason to freak out. Apparently Kade felt differently.

"What happened?" Raven asked. She was calm yet curious.

"It's a long story." I grabbed Kade's hand and gave it a squeeze. "Let's head over to the table. I could use some lunch. And then I want to hear about your trip to Falk."

"I think our trip was fairly boring compared to what happened to you," Kade pointed out.

"Yes, well, we'll talk about all of it." I flicked my eyes to Luke and grinned. "Wait until I tell you about the orthopedic shoes. You'll want to track down my new friend just so you can torch her fashion choices."

Luke smiled as he slung an arm over my shoulders. "I'm hooked already. You know how much I like complaining about fashion."

"Yes, that's one of my favorite things about you."

"WAIT, BACK UP ... she turned into an old woman but only in the mirror?"

Nellie, a hot dog loaded with onions and ketchup in each hand, was enthralled with the story.

"Basically," I confirmed, bobbing my head. "I thought I might've been seeing things at first – I did the looking back and forth thing a couple of times – but that's definitely what happened."

"That explains that horrible outfit." Luke involuntarily shuddered. "Polyester and orthopedic shoes? Someone shoot me if I ever wear an outfit like that in public."

Raven raised her hand. "I volunteer for that task."

Luke stuck out his tongue. "Ha, ha. I'm just saying, why wasn't the outfit a dead giveaway, Poet? I would've run screaming from the building the second I saw that."

I shrugged. "In hindsight I did feel a bit stupid about my lack of suspicion where Remy was concerned. "I thought maybe she was poor and had no choice but to dress in hand-me-downs or something."

"There's always a better choice than orthopedic shoes."

"Crocs?"

"Oh, are you trying to give me nightmares?"

Luke's feigned outrage had the desired effect on me and I smiled as I briefly rested my head against his shoulder. Luke found the story entertaining – mostly because I escaped without something terrible happening to me – and I enjoyed his jocularity given the heavy atmosphere.

Kade, on the other hand, was a moody mess. I had no idea how to cajole him into calming down. As it stood, I was afraid he was going to utilize handcuffs (and not in a fun way) to keep me at his side.

I cleared my throat to get his attention, resting my hand on his thigh under the table to offer him contact and a momentary reprieve from whatever seemed to be worrying him. "I'm okay," I repeated, lowering my voice and shifting closer to him. "I know you're upset – maybe even blaming yourself – but I really am okay. There's no way we could've anticipated that was going to happen, so stop blaming yourself."

"I should've gone with you."

"I wouldn't have allowed that," I countered. "I need a little time to myself. I know you mean well with the hovering – and I know what happened last night terrified you, because it did the same to me – but I don't need constant supervision."

"That's not what this is about." Kade's eyes flashed hot. "I knew you were in a vulnerable position. I should've made you stay in bed all day."

"That would just serve to wear her out in a different way," Luke interjected, earning a scowl for his efforts. "What? I'm trying to be helpful."

"And you're doing a marvelous job," I teased. "But stay out of this conversation. It doesn't involve you."

"Oh, whatever." Luke rolled his eyes. "I don't know why I take this abuse."

"I'm sure Kade wonders that about you occasionally, too."

"You've got that right," Kade muttered.

I gave his leg a squeeze and forced his eyes to me. "I know you can't help worrying, but I can take care of myself. I thought you understood and agreed with that."

"I do. It's just ... you couldn't save yourself from that dream. Raven had to practically break through the front door to do the heavy lifting. If she hadn't reacted, I think you would've died right there. Next to me. And I wouldn't have been able to do anything to stop it."

Oh, that's what was bothering him. I should've figured that out. "Well, you're not all-powerful and can't stave off death, so I don't see why you're so down on yourself. We didn't know it was going to happen. I'm fine. We've strengthened the dreamcatcher. I doubt very much it will happen again."

"You can't guarantee it won't happen again."

"That's true."

"Then I reserve the right to worry until we're sure you're safe." Kade grabbed the hot dog from my plate and waved it in front of my face. "Now eat and build up your strength while we discuss the fact that you keep stumbling across crazy old ladies."

I accepted the hot dog, but only because I was hungry. "It's not my fault crazy people are attracted to me."

"It is a rare and valuable gift," Luke teased. "Screw that thing you do where you crawl inside people's brains and make them do what you want, this is the gift you should list on your résumé."

I didn't bother to hide my glare. "Mmph ... mmph ... mmph."

"Don't talk with your mouth full. It's unattractive, and you're far too good for that." Luke amiably patted the top of my head. "I know what you were going to say anyway. You love me more than life itself and think I'm wiser than any man you've ever met."

That was so not what I was going to say.

"Let's focus on the problem at hand," Kade insisted, his temper flaring. "How did that woman know Poet was going to be at the library?"

That was a very good question.

"Maybe she didn't," Nellie suggested, his mouth full of food. I couldn't help but notice Luke didn't admonish him. "Maybe it was just coincidence."

"How could that be?" Raven challenged. "I doubt very much that there are magical people planted all over Eureka just waiting for Poet to venture out on her own."

"What did it seem like to you?" Naida asked, her expression thoughtful as she tapped her fingers on the tabletop. "Do you think she was waiting for you?"

"I ... don't ... know." I thought hard about the events and how they transpired. "The library was empty when I first entered. I didn't see anyone. I was focused on the fact that it was old, rather than anything else."

"You said the technology was outdated," Percival noted. "Did you get the feeling that people were often in the building?"

"No, but that's not unusual. It seems we visit libraries every other stop for research purposes. There are very rarely people in them ... or at least not many people."

"I shudder at what's to come for our society." Percival said it with a straight face, his pomposity on full display.

"Me, too," Nellie drawled, grabbing a handful of chopped onions from the central bowl and popping them into his mouth. He didn't so much as grimace as he chewed. "Society is ready to go down the toilet with the rest of life's crap."

I pressed my lips together to keep from laughing and slid a sidelong look to Kade. I found his mouth curving as well, although he was clearly fighting the effort. He wasn't ready to cede his bad mood.

"There was no one in the library," I repeated. "No one came in and, now that I think back on it, Remy didn't act as if she was expecting anyone to come in. She seemed fine helping me with my research."

"Did she tell you the truth?" Raven asked.

That was another good question. "I think so. I mean ... I didn't get the feeling that she was lying or anything. What would be the point? The history of Falk isn't exactly a secret. Most of it I already knew. She did throw in a few interesting tidbits."

"Like what?"

"Well, for starters, she mentioned that the mill didn't simply shut down because of the Great Depression," I supplied. "That's in all the history books – and it was certainly part of it – but there was also an incident with the primary saw blade at the mill becoming warped."

"I have no idea what that means," Luke said after a beat.

"I guess it was bent." I waved my hand for emphasis. "Apparently that's not supposed to happen, so the townsfolk believed they had a witch in their midst."

Kade jerked his shoulders. "Do you think that's possible? Do you think a witch was responsible for the downfall of Falk and she somehow carried through until we got here and now she wants to make Poet pay for ... um ... her lot in life?"

That sounded like one of the most ridiculous theories I'd ever heard. "Well, probably not." I was trying to be diplomatic, but Luke and Nellie were having none of it.

"You think she wanted Poet to pay for her lot in life?" Luke snickered. "Why would she wait around for fifty years and then go after Poet?"

"Longer than that," Nellie corrected. "The mill shut down in the thirties. It's more like eighty years."

"The mill shut down in the thirties, but I thought the town was standing until the seventies," Luke countered. "I'm guessing the witch didn't really get upset with her lot in life until all the buildings were torn down."

"I don't care if you think I'm being stupid," Kade challenged. "I want to know exactly what is happening and why Poet is being targeted. That's all I care about."

Raven snorted. "I hardly think she's being targeted."

"Really?" Kade refused to back down. "She's the one who first saw Caroline Olsen in the woods. She's the one who heard the chanting."

"Hey, wait." Luke made a face. "I heard the chanting first. Maybe I'm being targeted. I don't see you freaking out about protecting me."

Kade quieted him with a stern look. "Poet insisted on going into the woods the day we found the blood," he continued. "Poet was with me when I saw the dancing ghost things on the other side of the dreamcatcher."

"We all saw those," Raven pointed out.

Kade barreled forward as if she hadn't said a word. "Poet almost got killed in her sleep last night. Poet was attacked at the library today. The common thread in all of this is Poet."

His anxiety was so high I thought he might legitimately suffer some sort of heart malady if he didn't calm himself. "Kade, look at me." I stared hard until he reluctantly turned in my direction. "There is no reason to freak out. This is hardly the worst thing we've ever faced."

"I get that, but … I have this fear in my heart and I can't seem to shake it." He rubbed his temple, as if warding off a headache. "It's as if it's taking me over. I don't know how to explain it."

He seemed so lost I couldn't stop myself from going into a sort of protective mode of my own. "We'll figure it out." I patted his hand as I exchanged a quick look with Raven. I could practically see the gears in her mind working. "I think we should bring Max in on this as well," I added after a beat. "We haven't kept him in the loop on this one. He might have some ideas we haven't yet considered."

"That's a great idea," Raven said hurriedly. "You should pin him down now so he can enjoy dinner with us."

"Great idea." I slowly got to my feet. "I'll be right back, Kade. I won't be far."

"I can go with you." Kade continued rubbing his forehead, serving to increase my worry.

"No, I'll handle it. I won't be gone long."

"YOU HAVE TO JOIN us tonight."

I thought about asking Max to participate in the evening's festivities, using my nicest and sweetest voice and wearing him down until he agreed. Instead I barreled inside his trailer and demanded his attendance.

Max, his eyes on his computer screen, barely glanced up when I stormed his trailer without knocking. "And good afternoon to you, too, Poet."

I glared at him. "Did you hear what I said?"

"I did. Can you hold on a minute?"

"Absolutely not."

Max tapped on his keyboard. "Thirty seconds then."

"No. I need you now."

"And done." Max closed his laptop, smiled, and looked me up and down. "You look flushed. Are you feeling all right?"

I love Max like a father – which is kind of gross if you think about it too hard because he's my boyfriend's father – but there are times when his sense of humor grates in the worst way imaginable. "I'm really not feeling all that great," I gritted out. "It's been a trying two days."

"Is there something wrong with the trailer?"

"What? No."

"Then what seems to be the problem?"

I wanted to nutshell everything for him, keep my diatribe short. Instead I launched into the tale from the beginning. I was still talking twenty minutes later. "And that's basically it. I have no idea what the lady in the library was doing, but I'm fairly certain it was some kind of mind manipulation."

"That sounds terrible." Max leaned back in his chair and steepled his fingers over his stomach. "Why wasn't I informed any of this was going on?"

Oh, now he really wanted me to melt down. "Because you're rarely around, Max! You come down for dinner, like, once a week and otherwise leave everything to us. We already saw you the night we arrived, so I figured that was your limit for this week."

"While I do enjoy my solitude, that doesn't mean I don't want to be around when my workers – my family, really – need help. You should've called me."

"Well, I'm calling you now." I pulled together my fraying patience. "I need you to be a part of what goes down tonight. It's not just for me. It's for Kade."

Max's sparkplug eyebrows migrated north. "And what's wrong with Kade?"

"I don't know, but I think those things are affecting him, too. He just doesn't seem to realize it."

Max leaned forward, finally alert enough to fully engage in the conversation. "What do you mean?"

"He's acting weird, overprotective and whiny."

"Given what happened to you last night, can you blame him? That must have been terrifying."

"It's more than that. He said he feels as if he's being overcome by fear. That's not like him. He's brave even when he doesn't understand stuff. That signifies that something – or someone, for that matter – outside of the dreamcatcher is trying to influence him. He simply doesn't appear to recognize the signs."

"Well ... ." Max broke off and pursed his lips, his mind clearly busy.

"You're his father, which means he has some mage in him," I pointed out. "If these things – whatever they are – are going for those most sensitive on a psychic level, they might zero in on Kade. Just because he hasn't manifested powers yet doesn't mean he won't now that he's close to regular magic."

"I've been wondering if that would happen. It's not out of the realm of possibility."

"So ... you'll come?"

"Of course I'll come. I wouldn't want to be anywhere else. We'll figure this out. We always do."

I only hoped we could do it sooner rather than later. Kade was fraying quickly – too quickly for me to keep ahead of the meltdowns – and I wasn't sure how much he could take.

13
THIRTEEN

For a change of pace, I was the one sticking close to Kade throughout the rest of the afternoon. He didn't complain, of course, and I honestly believed he thought he was the one hovering over me, but I couldn't shake the feeling that something big (and potentially bad) was about to happen.

Even though interior design didn't exactly blow up my bohemian skirt, I allowed him to take me on another tour of our new office digs. It looked exactly the same – although you would never know it by his enthusiasm – but I made the appropriate noises and congratulated him on a job well done.

We ended up making out on his desk – and mine – before touring the circus grounds to make sure everything was in order. We held hands the entire time, both of us working overtime to project an air of calm, even though we both knew a storm was coming.

The walk around the circus was leisurely. I stopped by my tent long enough to make sure everything was set up – Melissa had obviously been inside to add the finishing touches to the display – and then hit the midway before heading back to help with the dinner preparations.

In typical fashion, Mark Lane, the oily midway head honcho, was waiting for me in the middle of the set-up mayhem.

"Don't worry about us," Mark announced, a cigar hanging from the corner of his mouth. "We got our trucks late, but we'll be finished before darkness falls this evening."

I hated the man on principle – he was a grifter of the highest order – but he was good at his job and I was thankful at times like these (when a paranormal threat was breathing down our necks) that I could trust him to handle his corner of the world.

"That's good." I bobbed my head as I studied the midway. "It looks almost completely put together now."

"Yes, well, my people are motivated." Mark puffed on his cigar, blowing three smoke rings in my face as he grinned. "You don't have anything to worry about."

Kade scowled as he waved the smoke out of my face. "Don't do that."

"Why not?"

"Because secondhand smoke kills."

"Oh, don't worry," I offered, my lips curling. "He'll die long before secondhand smoke becomes an issue for me. I can promise you that."

Mark blinked several times in rapid succession before ultimately shifting so the cigar smoke didn't blow directly in my face. "Better?"

"I'm considering throwing you a party," I said dryly. "I might even make you the piñata for the celebration."

"Has anyone ever told you that your personality needs some work?"

That was rich coming from him. "Believe it or not, you're not the first person to say that to me."

"I didn't think so."

"But you are the most hypocritical person to have the audacity to say it to me," I added, offering him the fakest smile in my repertoire before sobering. "I never thought I'd say this, but we need to have a quick talk."

"Oh, I would like nothing better than to have a quickie with you, baby, but I'm on a timetable." Mark winked at Kade, something that

I'm sure infuriated my boyfriend, and puffed out his chest. "I don't want to miss my deadline."

"The deadline isn't as important as what else we have going on," I argued. "Also, I wouldn't have a quickie with you if you were the last leech on the planet. Don't be gross. You know I don't like it."

"Since when has that stopped me?"

"Okay, let me rephrase that," I said. "You know I'll shrink your unit to the size of a peanut ... without the shell ... if you don't knock it off, right?"

Mark rolled his eyes, but I was amused to see him shift his groin as far away from me as possible. "Well, now that we've discussed circus food, what is it that you want?"

"I want your people inside before dark," I answered without hesitation. "I don't care if you're not finished. You have time to finish tomorrow if it's necessary."

"And why don't you want us out after dark? Wait ... I don't want to know." Mark held up a hand to quiet me. "This is more of your extracurricular nonsense, isn't it?"

"Yes."

"Then I don't want to know."

"That doesn't change the fact that you need to be inside before dark," I shot back. "No matter what you do, don't leave the fairgrounds. It's important."

"Fine." Mark sighed. "I won't leave the fairgrounds. Happy?"

"I'm so happy I'll gladly refrain from making peanut brittle from your naughty bits tonight."

Kade waited until Mark turned on his heel and stalked away. Then, when he was sure no one could overhear us, he burst out laughing. "You have a certain way with words. You make me laugh even when I'm nervous."

I was so happy to hear the laugh I was willing to call Mark back and threaten him some more. We didn't have time, though, so I decided to simply give Kade a kiss. "I'm glad I can serve as a source of entertainment."

Kade graced me with a softer kiss, this one more sensual and full of promise for when things calmed down. "Always."

"ALL RIGHT. I'M HERE."

Max appeared in the communal dining area just as we were cleaning up following our dinner feast. He was dressed in bright track pants and a T-shirt – something I rarely saw him wear – and he seemed ready for business.

"We have pie for dessert," Luke offered, lifting his plate. "Blueberry. It's really good."

"I'll pass for tonight." Max's smile was fond as he surveyed Luke. "I don't want a lot of carbs slowing me down."

"Carbs are good for muscles," Luke argued.

"Yes, well, I don't have need for muscles." Max shifted his gaze to Kade and me. "How is everything so far this evening?"

"It's not dark yet," Kade replied. He looked relaxed, but I could feel the agitation rippling through his skin. "We won't see any action until dark."

"It will be dark soon." Max ran his hand through his snowy hair. "Where did you guys see the ... shades, for lack of a better word, last night?"

"That way." I pointed toward the trees. "I expect that's where we'll see them tonight, too."

"Because you think they're coming from Falk?"

I gave the question serious thought. "I don't know that they're coming from Falk," I hedged. "It's just a suspicion."

"Well, until we know otherwise we'll go with that. Your feelings are usually spot on."

"They are," Luke agreed. "Unless she's not telling me when she has a horrible nightmare that almost kills her and I have to find out from others."

"Oh, let it go," I snapped. "I won't make that mistake again. I promise."

"That's all I ask." Luke polished off his pie before grabbing the paper plate and tossing it in the closest trash receptacle. He looked intense as he stared at the trees. I wasn't used to him being serious – overwrought and theatrical, sure, but not serious – so my anticipation ratcheted up a notch.

"Do you see anything?" I asked.

"The fog is rolling in," Luke replied, inclining his head.

I looked in that direction, my stomach twisting when I realized what looked to be a large cloud billowing in this direction. "That's new," I muttered, hopping to my feet. "Usually the fog is more subtle."

"Yes, well, I don't think it's going to be a subtle sort of night," Max muttered. "Come on. Show me where we should be watching from."

I did as he asked, making sure Raven and Naida weren't far away. Instead of separating this evening, we were all approaching the problem as a group. We were strongest when together and we wanted to show our mystical friends that we were firm in our solidarity.

It took less than five minutes to creep to the other side of the grounds. By the time we arrived at the edge of the dreamcatcher, the fog was so thick we could barely see five feet in front of our faces.

"Don't go any farther," Raven warned, jutting out a hand to still Max when he looked as if he was about to traipse over the dreamcatcher line. "We don't know what will happen if we're on the other side."

Max looked amused that Raven was bossing him around, but he followed her instructions and stopped in his place. "I don't see anything."

"How can you see anything?" Kade queried. "The fog is so thick it's almost impossible to see each other let alone anything else."

"We need some illumination," Max supplied, lifting his hand and sending sparks into the air. They were blue, green, purple and pink, and while they didn't boast a great deal of light they offered enough for me to see the shadows moving on the other side of the dreamcatcher.

"Will you look at that." I gasped as I instinctively moved forward, Kade grabbing my hand to make sure I didn't cross the dreamcatcher perimeter. I knew better than worrying him, but I couldn't stop myself from staring.

There had to be at least fifty – maybe even a hundred – ghostly figures standing on the other side of the dreamcatcher. The fog hid them well until Max utilized his magic to give us an edge. The figures, all transparent, ranged from small children to wizened adults.

While I'd seen ghosts and shades before, this group was more unnerving than usual because they were all dressed in antiquated clothing. We're talking homemade trousers with suspenders to hold them up, ankle-length dresses with thick stockings poking out beneath, and shirts that looked as if they'd been mended so many times they were one good rip away from giving up the ghost.

"Oh, I feel as if I'm in a *Little House on the Prairie* episode," Luke enthused, clapping his hands. "Quick, somebody find the Nellie Oleson ghost. I want to pull her hair."

"I'm more worried about going blind," Dolph said. "Didn't every character on that show go blind?"

"Only a handful," I countered. "You're far more likely to come down with a communicable disease and die than go blind."

"Oh, well, that makes me feel better," Dolph deadpanned.

"You know, now that I think about it, I should've picked a different nickname." Nellie thoughtfully stroked his beard. "I don't like Nellie Oleson."

"Who does?" Luke challenged.

"I'm just saying that it's weird now that I think about it," Nellie said. "In fact ... wait. Wasn't that woman in the woods named Caroline Olsen? Maybe she was a *Little House on the Prairie* fan and conjured up these little ... things ... to mess with us."

As unlikely as I found the suggestion, I couldn't entirely shake off the similarities. "We'll go back and ask her tomorrow."

"Can we please focus on these things?" Kade asked, his voice high-pitched. The man in the hat was back, staring directly at Kade, as if entranced by his beauty.

"Oh, look," Luke teased. "I think Kade has a fan. It's almost as if he wants to start a romance or something with our resident security stud. I think he's making kissing faces."

I stared closer. "No. He's talking. We simply can't hear him."

"What makes you think he's talking?" Raven asked, pushing forward.

"His lips are flapping like he's talking. I've seen the phenomenon before."

"Oh." Raven narrowed her eyes. "I can't read his lips."

"I didn't know you could read lips," Percival said nervously from behind us. "I learn something new about you every day."

"I can't read lips, but I thought I might be able to pick something out."

"Why is he staring at me?" Kade complained, shifting to move away from the man in the hat. "I don't like it. He's creepy."

I had to agree. The dude was definitely creepy. The way his ethereal face moved under the limited light made him look almost skeleton-like. The result was jarring.

"It's okay." I reached out to grab Kade's hand but found he'd retreated farther down the dreamcatcher line. "What are you doing?"

"Trying to see if he's going to follow," Kade answered. "Look at that. He is. It's as if he knows I'm weirded out by him or something."

"He does seem abnormally attached to Kade," Raven noted, her head tilted in such a manner that she looked like a scientist about to run an experiment. "Look at that one." She pointed toward a robust woman standing across the line from Max. "She's following Max like the hat guy follows Kade."

"What do you think that means?" Kade asked.

"I have no idea," Raven replied. "I want to test out a few others. Naida, move down the line and see if anyone follows."

Naida did as Raven asked. None of the ethereal figures followed her. In fact, they paid her zero attention.

"Interesting," Raven muttered. "Poet, you do the same."

I understood what Raven was trying to uncover, so I followed her orders without complaint. One of the figures, another woman, followed me. Even though I couldn't make out her facial features, she looked like the unhappy sort. "She's like my mirror," I said. "The hat guy is Kade's mirror and the other woman is Max's mirror."

"Yeah. It's definitely interesting." Raven licked her lips. "I'm going to try it now." She conducted her own experiment, but none of the figures followed. When she returned, she seemed even more confused than when she'd left. "They're not interested in the pixies or me. That seems to indicate it's not the power they're most attracted to."

"Max is powerful," I argued. "I might not be on the same level as you, but I'm powerful, too."

"Yes, but what about Kade?" Raven's eyes were thoughtful when they landed on my ashen boyfriend. He seemed to be growing more agitated by the second. I wanted to do something to help him, but I had no idea what that might entail.

"Kade is part mage," Luke pointed out. "He might be more powerful than any of us realize. Although ... you sleep with him, Poet. Has he ever blown the lid off your pickle jar while doing ... you know?"

It took me a moment to process the question. "I'll kill you if you're not careful."

"I was just asking." Luke's amusement was obvious. "You can sense things. Have you sensed magic in him?"

I swallowed hard, unsure how to answer. "I don't know," I answered finally. "There are times I think I might've brushed up against something inside him, but it could just as easily be my imagination."

"What does that mean?" Kade asked, his voice cracking. "Am I going to turn into something ... different?"

"I don't think so." I looked to Max for answers. "You're his father. Shouldn't you be able to answer these questions for him?"

"I would if I knew what to say." Max turned grave as he stared at the son he barely knew. "I think it's entirely possible you're more powerful than you realize, son. I don't know why you didn't manifest when you were younger. Perhaps it was simply because you didn't know you could.

"I don't know much about half-mage children," he continued. "In fact, mages aren't supposed to be able to have children at all. That rule has lapsed a bit over the years, but I know there are very few born mages. One in particular – she's become infamous because she absorbed a book to add to her powerbase – has been considered the most powerful mage ever born. I've yet to meet her. I've thought about looking her up."

"Why don't you?" Kade asked.

"My understanding is that she kills first and asks questions later," Max replied ruefully. "I'm strong, but if she's stronger ... well, let's just say I'm not in the mood to die. She has a young daughter. There's debate whether the child will be more powerful than her. I do eventually want to meet them.

"Kade is different, though," he continued. "His mother was human. My understanding is that the female mage of terror is the offspring of two mages, which is definitely frowned upon. Kade is only the offspring of one mage."

"So, you're saying you have no idea if I'll somehow start shooting magic sparkles out of my fingers?" Kade gestured toward the lights Max conjured. "You don't know if these creatures marking me as equal to you and Poet is normal or something bad, do you?"

"I know you're a good man," Max said gently. "If you manifest, you'll be a good mage."

"Like you?"

"You'll be better than me. I've never had a problem with the mage stuff. Being a good man was more difficult. You're already a good man, a better man than I ever dreamed of being. If you're magical too, you'll have a leg up on me."

They were nice words, but I wasn't sure Kade was ready to hear them.

"I don't think I want to be magical," Kade admitted.

"I'm not sure you have a choice, son." Max gestured toward the shade following Kade's every move. "We'll figure it out. You have my word."

"And mine," I added, forcing a smile. "You're not alone."

Kade made an effort to return the smile, but it didn't make it all the way to his eyes. "At least I have that, huh?"

14
FOURTEEN

We spent an hour watching the dreamcatcher ghosts before Raven suggested another test.

"I want to split their focus," she said finally, narrowing her eyes as she stared at the man with the hat. He was so fixated on Kade that it was hard to look anywhere else. "Does anyone else think this guy is all kinds of wacky?"

"Is that your clinical opinion?" I asked dryly.

"No, it's just ... he doesn't look anywhere else." Raven moved to Kade's side and waved her hand. The shadow completely ignored her. "At least the women fixated on you and Max occasionally look at the rest of us. This guy only stares at Kade."

"So, what do you want to try?" Max asked, his gaze on his mirror ghost. "Wait ... I want to try something first." He snapped his fingers, igniting the tips and created a small ball of power.

"What is that?" Kade asked, uncomfortably shifting from one foot to the other.

"It's nothing important," Max answered, flashing a smile for his son's benefit. "It's one of the flashier aspects of magic, if you must know the truth. I simply want to see what it does to our friends here."

I'm not sure what to make of them, but I'm almost positive they're not normal ghosts."

"I definitely agree with you there," Raven said, moving to the dreamcatcher and pressing her toes against the line so she could get directly in the hat man's face. "I don't know that I'd call them shades either. I'm not sure what they are and that totally creeps me out."

"Look at how they're dressed," Kade protested. "They look like extras from a historical reenactment. They must be ghosts. There's no other explanation."

"There are plenty of explanations," Max countered. "Pinning down the correct one is our next task. In fact … ." He stared hard at the woman watching him before letting the small ball of golden flame fly. It smacked directly into the woman, causing the energy crackling around her form to break up. The resulting activity was like a wave coming to shore, and the female form of Max's mirror ghost completely dissipated.

"That was interesting." Raven stepped forward so she could better see the broken parts of the former figure. "Is she completely gone or is it a temporary thing?"

"That is the question, isn't it?" Max was impassive as he stared at the spot where the female ghost had stood moments before. "That wasn't a lot of magic. If they're that easy to get rid of it shouldn't take me long to eradicate of the rest of them."

Kade looked almost relieved by the suggestion. "Do it then. Get rid of them. I'm not going to be able to sleep knowing they're out here."

"Wait a second," Raven ordered, her eyes flashing. "I want to test a few other things first."

"Like what?" Kade challenged. "Why does it matter? If Max can get rid of them he should get rid of them."

"I'm with Raven," Nellie argued. "I kind of want to see what these things can do before we destroy them all. If they're as easy to rip apart as what Max just showed, I don't see the harm."

"Of course you don't," Kade muttered, rubbing the back of his head as he did everything he could to avoid staring at the man in the hat. "You brought an ax to a ghost fight. Your ideas are always awesome."

I shouldn't have laughed – the situation was too surreal and everyone was under too much pressure – but I couldn't stop myself. The sound was low and hollow, but before I knew it almost everyone had joined in with me. Even Kade, however reluctant, flashed a smile.

"I'm sorry," Kade offered, holding up his hands in a placating manner. "I don't know what to make of these things. They make me extremely nervous. I've never seen anything like them."

"I think we can all say that," Max said, moving his attention to the ghost with the hat. He clearly seemed to understand that it was that ghost driving Kade to his emotional extremes. "Raven can run her experiments on them. I'll take out the one bothering you."

"I want the one fixated on Poet gone, too," Kade insisted. "She's the one most at risk."

I opened my mouth to counter the statement, but snapped it shut. Arguing with him in his current state would simply make matters worse.

"Then there's the compromise," Max supplied. "I'll take out the other two mirrors right away and allow Raven to play with the others."

"Great." Raven excitedly rubbed her hands together. "This is going to be fun."

I didn't know if I believed that, but at least she was enthusiastic. "What do you want us to do?"

"First I want Max to oust those two staring ghosts."

"I really don't think they're ghosts," Max noted as his fingers danced with magic a second time. "They're something else. It's intriguing and troubling at the same time."

"Just get rid of them." Raven's patience frayed. "I want to test something."

"I don't think I'm going to like the sound of this," Kade muttered, shoving his hands in his pockets as he watched his father blow the hat-wearing specter to smithereens. The light effect was even cooler this time, as if Kade's friendly ghost had more energy than the previous one. Still, Kade's shoulders sagged in obvious relief when his mirror dissipated. That made me feel better.

"It will be fine," Raven said, grinning. "Let's see what these things can do, shall we?"

RAVEN SEPARATED EVERYONE into teams ... again.

Initially she suggested Kade stay with her while I walk to the other side of the dreamcatcher with Luke, but Kade was having none of that. Even though his courage was clearly bolstered now that he knew Max could so easily get rid of the ghosts, it was obvious he had no intention of letting me wander off on my own ... at least not tonight.

"The ghost problem is in hand," Raven argued. "Your precious Poet isn't in any danger."

"What if the ghosts aren't the danger?" Kade challenged. "What if the ghosts were only sent here to distract us because something else is hanging around?"

That was an interesting suggestion, one I hadn't fully given thought to. "He's not wrong," I said after a beat. "Remy was a human. Er, well, at least she had a corporeal body. She clearly had other attributes and gifts, but she was corporeal."

"So?" Raven asked blankly.

"So Remy isn't a ghost ... or whatever these things are." I gestured toward the remaining figures. They glowed bright under Max's magic, unmoving despite the fact that Max had destroyed three of their brethren. "These things could be simple distractions."

"You're saying that checking the boundaries of the dreamcatcher to make sure it's still intact is the best way to go, aren't you?" Nellie noted.

I nodded. "Basically."

"Okay, we'll break up in teams again," Luke said. "Kade and Poet will take the north. I'll go with Naida to the east, and Nellie and Nixie can go that way." He pointed to the final side of the dreamcatcher. "That means Raven and Max will stay here."

"Everyone has their phones so we can stay in contact, right?" I asked.

Heads bobbed as everyone geared up.

"Be careful and keep your eyes open," Max instructed. "I don't sense immediate danger, but now that I think about it, it's obvious we're dealing with more than what we see. Be diligent and safe."

"That's how I was born," Nellie said, gripping his ax in one hand as he adjusted the bodice on his blue evening gown with the other. "I'm always diligent and safe."

"Yes, those are the two words I always ascribe to you," Max said dryly, his eyes shifting to Kade. "Be careful. I won't be far if anyone runs into trouble."

Kade grabbed my hand and smiled. "I know. I have my bodyguard."

Max's smile was kind. "I was talking to both of you."

KADE AND I SET OUT at a brisk pace. It wasn't cold, the wind didn't hurry us along, but we both felt a sense of urgency that we couldn't quite shake. I wasn't sure how to explain it.

"You seem anxious," I said after a few minutes, desperate to break the silence. "You're okay, aren't you?"

"I'm more worried about you."

The sentiment was sweet but unnecessary. "I'm fine. You're the one unnerved by the ghosts – which I get, by the way, so don't get worked up about it. I find the ghosts more interesting than anything else."

"I thought you said they weren't ghosts."

"I don't believe they are. I don't know what else to call them, so for now they're ghosts."

"I guess." Kade kept his hand wrapped around mine as we walked. "Why do you think that one with the hat was so focused on me?"

I was expecting the question. That didn't mean I had a good answer. "I don't know."

"You must have an idea."

While I often basked in the fact that Kade seemed to think I had all the answers, this one time it hurt because I didn't know what to give him to ease the emotional burden he was clearly toiling under. "I don't know." I gently let my index finger drift down his cheek. "I know that's not what you want to hear, but this is new for all of us."

"Is it wrong that I was happier with the world we were already living in?"

"No." I meant it. "Did you really think you wouldn't inherit something from Max? I mean ... after all you've seen, how could you ignore the fact that you were most likely going to manifest magic in some manner?"

"I haven't manifested, though." Kade was stubborn. I had to give him that. He tugged his hand from me and ran it through his hair before crossing his arms over his chest. "I haven't done anything magical. Not one little thing."

"I think you do a lot of magical things," I teased, going for levity. "You just don't happen to do them when we're fighting monsters."

Kade's expression softened, though only marginally. "Very cute."

"I do my best."

"I know." Kade lowered his forehead to mine and sucked in a steadying breath. "I wondered about it at first. When I found out Max was my father I was terrified I would suddenly be able to shoot lasers out of my eyes or develop claws."

"This isn't a comic book."

Kade was rueful. "I know, but I was more familiar with comic books than real-life horror stories. I thought when nothing immediately happened that I'd managed to somehow avoid the curse."

I furrowed my brow. "Curse? You think magic is a curse?"

"I ... think magic is something I'm perfectly fine without."

"But you think those who wield it are cursed?" I pulled away from him and focused on the dreamcatcher line. This side of the fairgrounds was devoid of ghosts. The fog continued to roll around us, but the creepy factor wasn't nearly as severe as it was on the other side. "I guess, from your point of view that makes sense."

Kade wrinkled his nose. "Wait ... you're upset."

"I'm not." That was a lie. I didn't think adding to the emotional strife already stripping us bare was a good idea, though. "We should walk the dreamcatcher boundary to make sure. I don't think anything has crossed, but it can't hurt to check."

"Wait a second." Kade grabbed my arm before I could wander off. "I want to talk about this."

"There's nothing to talk about." I was trying to appear blasé, but the words came off a bit squeaky. "Everything is fine."

"Everything is clearly not fine," Kade shot back. "You're upset about what I said." He stroked his jaw with his free hand. "I didn't mean to hurt your feelings."

"You didn't hurt my feelings."

"I think I did."

"Well ... they're my feelings so I think I know better."

"Yeah, but I know when I've been an ass and I clearly have been." Kade carefully released my arm and petted his hand over the top of my head. It was meant as an intimate gesture, but it made me feel like a dog and I didn't like it. "It's not that I have a problem with magic," he clarified. "It's that I'm fine not being magical. Do you get the distinction?"

"No. It's hardly important, though."

"It is important," Kade argued. "You think I have attitude because of your magic. You're wrong. I like that you're magical. I'm impressed by what you can do every second of the day. I simply don't think I need to be magical."

"Why?"

"Because my father is magical and I saw what that did to my mother," Kade answered, harsh emotion rolling off him in waves. "I always thought my mother was beaten down because of my father's death. Then I found out the man who I thought was my father was a figment of my mother's imagination. His death isn't what made my mother sad. Max not being part of our family made her said."

"Oh." Realization dawned. "You think the magic made Max a bad father."

"No, I think the magic made it so my mother wanted to keep distance between Max and herself," Kade corrected. "Whether it was right or wrong, she thought she was doing the correct thing ... especially for me. Max was a presence in my life growing up, but I wish he could've been around more.

"Inherently I know that magic won't cause you to kick me out of your bed," he continued. "I like how things are now, and I can't help being afraid because ... because ... ."

I rested my hand on his forearm. "Because it's new and you never thought it was something you would have to deal with," I finished. "I get it." Honestly, I understood better than he realized. "The thing is, magic won't ruin anything for us. I promise.

"I know that it will probably be an adjustment and you'll have to learn how to use your powers – whatever they might be – but it won't ruin anything for us," I continued. "Max is right. You're already a good man. The magic will only enhance that."

"What if I don't manifest?" Kade pressed. "What if I never have powers that I can use to help you guys in the fight against ... well, whatever it is you're fighting against any given week?"

I grinned at his uncertainty. "Then you'll still be the same man you are now. I happen to be fond of that man."

Kade mustered a shaky grin. "You always know the right thing to say."

"Not always," I countered. "In fact ... ." I didn't get a chance to finish. At that moment, the dreamcatcher alerted, blaring so loudly I initially thought it was a tornado warning.

"What the ... ?" Kade jerked his head to stare at the lights flashing over the circus. "What's happening?"

"Something crossed the dreamcatcher," I answered. "I don't know where, though. Usually we get some idea which part has been breached. The alarm is indicating every part has been breached."

"What do we do?"

"I ... ." Something niggled the back of my brain and forced me to snap my eyes toward the field in front of us. I could sense something ... and it was close. "Get back." I moved to shove Kade as far from the dreamcatcher boundary as I could manage. "It's coming."

"What's coming?" Kade tried to wrap his arm around my back, but

I wouldn't let him, instead squaring my shoulders to face what was coming head-on.

"It's here," I said, the wind picking up at the exact moment an ethereal figure popped into view. It barreled toward us, coming fast, and it was wearing a very distinctive hat.

"But ... Max killed it," Kade protested.

"Obviously not." I had no idea what I was going to do to fight the creature, but I was prepared to protect Kade at all costs. Just at the moment the ghost hit the dreamcatcher, it increased in size and began to scream.

I felt power rolling off of it, yet it couldn't cross the line. The dreamcatcher alerted harder as the creature continued to scream. It was stuck on the other side, which was fortunate, because it looked really ticked off.

"What do we do now?" Kade asked after he regained his breath.

That was a really good question. "I have no idea."

15
FIFTEEN

Eventually the ghosts settled down and went back to merely haunting the perimeter, which was creepy but tolerable. We searched the grounds, every inch and every tent, but found nothing out of the ordinary. Max ran a scan and came up empty. There was no indication anything actually breached the dreamcatcher. We were basically more flummoxed than when we'd started.

The circus was due to open the next day so everyone turned in, orders to contemplate other forms of attack issued by Max. Kade seemed solid when we climbed into bed. I could see the figure in the hat – and the woman who seemed to enjoy following me – floating on the other side of the dreamcatcher near our trailer, so I closed the shades tightly and did my best to distract Kade. He finally fell asleep, but I'm not sure how easy his slumber was. Thankfully for me, the charms we laid down earlier in the day kept my dreams free of the torturous figures who wanted so badly to haunt them, so I considered that a win.

The sun was already up when I opened my eyes the next morning. The shades kept the room dark, but my internal body clock recognized when it was time to rise. Kade was still out beside me, so I opted to let him sleep, carefully pulling myself into a sitting position and staring toward the window.

I didn't want to disturb Kade, so I used magic to open the blinds, taking a moment to blink so my eyes could adjust to the light. No ghosts. That was a relief. If they started showing up during the day it would completely throw me off my game. I was used to stuff like this. I was prepared for the unthinkable. I was certain Kade wouldn't be able to handle ghosts haunting us by day. That would be his limit.

"What are you doing?" Kade murmured, shifting so he could run his hand up and down my back. "Is something wrong?"

"Other than it being morning, no." I smiled at his sleepy countenance. "I have to go help with breakfast preparations – and talk about our plans for the day – but you should stay in here and get some more sleep. You might need it if we're up late again."

"No. I'm up." He said the words but didn't put much "oomph" behind them. "I'll help with breakfast."

"You're a man."

"Really? I never noticed."

I snickered. "In case you haven't noticed, the men rarely help with food preparations around here. If you help, people might think your man card has been revoked."

"You're funny." Kade poked my side. "As for the food thing, I have noticed. Why do you women allow it? I'd think you'd be the last person to embrace antiquated gender roles."

"Well, about three years ago there was a revolt and we decided not to cook for everyone else," I explained. "We tried to teach Nellie, Luke and Dolph especially a lesson because we felt they were shirking their duties."

"How did that go?"

"The whining was terrible."

"Luke?"

I bobbed my head. "He was the worst, but Nellie and Dolph weren't any better. They finally bribed us into returning to cooking."

"Really?" Kade was officially awake now … and intrigued. "What did they bribe you with?"

"Have you noticed that the men do most of the heavy lifting when it comes to our personal stuff during moves?"

"Yes."

"We agreed to keep cooking if they took over the packing and unpacking. I think we got the better end of the bargain. I don't mind cooking, but I absolutely hate sweating."

"That's not what you said last night ... and the night before that." Kade was in a playful mood, so I gave in and rolled around with him as he tickled my ribs and kissed my cheek. He seemed much lighter than the night before, which was a relief.

Still, even though we were having fun, I couldn't stop myself from asking the obvious question. "You're better?"

Kade shrugged as he smoothed my hair. My bedhead was always out of control, although he didn't seem to mind. He said he found it cute, which I didn't get, but his fingers were often busy combing through snarls most mornings. "I don't know if I'm better, but a good night's sleep helped things."

"I worried you'd be up all night. I tried to stay up, but I was too tired."

"Well, I don't want you staying up. You need your rest, too."

"But ... you were upset."

"I was," Kade conceded. "Then my brain worked out a few things while I was asleep."

"Like?"

"My mother always said it was a waste of time to worry about things I can't change. Whether I'm magical or not, I can't change it. All I can do is move forward. If I suddenly start having magic spark from my fingertips we'll deal with it. I think I picked the perfect girlfriend if that should happen."

"I think you picked the perfect girlfriend regardless."

"Good point." Kade smacked a kiss against my lips. "I can't change anything, so fixating on it won't do me any good. I am really creeped out about the guy in the hat following me – who wouldn't be, right? – but I can't change that either. All we can do is focus on solutions. That's the plan for the day."

"I'm impressed with your will to succeed," I supplied. "Mind over matter, huh?"

"I have no idea if it will work." Kade turned sheepish. "But I'm going to try. If I focus on external happenings too much I'll miss what's going on right under my nose. The circus opens today. That means we'll have to worry about guest safety. That won't leave me much time to obsess about you."

I feigned outrage. "And here I thought I was the center of your universe."

"Oh, you are." Kade grinned. "I still have a job to do. I intend to do it."

"I think we all do," I said. "Don't worry. I think as long as we stay protected in the dreamcatcher we'll be fine."

"I hope that's true." Kade was the pragmatic sort and I could practically see the gears in his mind working. "Just one question, though. How will we protect the people in the parking lot if we can't cross the dreamcatcher lines and the ghosts come out to play again tonight?"

Huh. That hadn't even occurred to me. "Well, we'll just have to expand the dreamcatcher."

"Can you do that without putting us at risk?"

"It shouldn't be an issue."

"Then I recommend doing it. I'm extremely worried about how things are going to run tonight."

He wasn't the only one worried about the guests. "I'll talk to Raven during breakfast. We should be able to handle the expansion with time to spare before the guests start arriving at noon."

"Let's hope so."

"**EXPANDING THE DREAMCATCHER** is a good idea."

Raven cracked eggs in a skillet while Naida turned hash browns, and Nixie fried bacon and sausage. I handled the toast while the men sat at the table and watched us work.

"It shouldn't take us too long," I said. "Right after breakfast, I figured we'd tackle that before we have to split up for the day."

"What will we do if the ghosts show up?" Luke asked. "How can we explain it?"

That was a good question. "We could close the circus early," I suggested.

"I don't think that's a good idea," Max said, sliding between Kade and Luke at the table and pasting a bright smile on his face. He acted as if it were a normal occurrence for him to join us for breakfast. In truth, I couldn't remember the last time he'd joined us for the first meal of the day. "We have posted hours and we need to stick to them."

"That means it will be dark when we close," I pointed out, arranging the toast on a platter before delivering it to the picnic table. "If the ghosts arrive ... ."

"I don't think they're ghosts," Max stressed. "I'm almost positive they're something else."

"Does it matter?"

"If we're going to fight them in the correct manner it most certainly does matter," Max argued. "We can't approach them like ghosts if they're something else."

He had a point. "Right now, I'm mostly worried about what happens if they show up while the guests are still here," I admitted. "I can't think of a feasible way to explain it."

"I can." Luke's hand shot up as if he was the smartest kid in the classroom. "Why not just pretend that they're something we created for ambiance? You, Raven, Nixie and Naida can put on a fake show if it comes to it and pretend you conjured them. That might actually intrigue the guests."

Hmm. It was an interesting idea. Still, there were a few holes. "What happens if the guests try to cross the dreamcatcher and the ghosts hurt them? The guests are only protected when they stay within the confines of the dreamcatcher. We're expanding it to cover the parking lot, but I'm not comfortable expanding it more than that."

"I agree that's probably not a good idea," Max said. "That will simply create strain on the threads and make it easier for holes to appear."

"So, what do we do?" Nellie asked, grinning when the huge pile of bacon and sausage appeared in front of him. "Sweet Jehoshaphat! That smells like the best thing ever created."

"It smells like grease to harden your arteries," Nixie corrected. "If you're okay with that, eat up."

"I'm fine with that." Nellie shoved a slice of bacon into his mouth and enthusiastically chewed. "Heaven!"

Max smirked at Nellie's reaction. "Ah, I forgot what it was like to eat with you guys regularly. Two meals in a row seems a bit ... much."

"Well, you're stuck now," I argued. "We need to figure out how we're going to explain the ghosts."

"Have you considered that we're the only ones who can see them?" Max queried.

The question threw me for a loop. "I ... no. Why would you assume that?"

"Because everyone in this particular group is magical," Max replied. "We all have abilities. Maybe that's why we can see the ghosts."

"Kade doesn't have abilities," Dolph argued. "He can see the ghosts."

"We don't know that Kade doesn't have abilities," Max clarified. "This is all new to him. We're working on the assumption that he will probably manifest some sort of ability. Everyone out and about last night saw the ghosts ... or spirits ... or shades. Whatever they are, we saw them.

"I didn't see any of the clowns out last night," he continued. "I didn't see any of the midway folks out. We don't know that they can see anything."

I cleared my throat. "That's not exactly true," I said. "I warned Mark to keep his people inside after dark last night. He didn't come right out and say it, but he seemed to understand that something was going on. I think he saw the shadows. Plus, well, Percival was with us and he saw them. To my knowledge, Percival doesn't have any powers."

"He doesn't," Raven confirmed, sliding her eyes to her boyfriend.

"Well, he does have some powers, but not the ones you're talking about."

I'd accidentally seen the powers she was talking about – leather chaps and full clown makeup, and that's all I'm going to say about the subject – so all I could do was press my eyes shut as I fought a shiver of revulsion. "Knock that off," I warned.

"Why do I have to knock it off but the rest of us have to watch you and Kade fall all over each other?" Raven challenged.

"We don't fall all over each other." I turned to Kade for backup. "Tell her."

"I think we're still in that heady space where we've just started a relationship and we might fall all over each other," Kade countered. "It's not the end of the world and I'm not embarrassed in the least."

Well, I was embarrassed. "We do not fall all over each other," I repeated.

"Whatever." Raven waved off my outrage. "As for what Percival saw, we talked about it last night. He saw the hints of movement, but it wasn't as easy for him to make out the figures. Even with Max's magical help he couldn't see them as easily, and said he only knew where to look because we were staring."

That was definitely intriguing. "So maybe we see more because we're magical."

"Or meant to see more," Raven corrected. "If we're the target of a spell and that's why we're seeing them so clearly, that might explain a few things."

"That's a good thought." Of course, that didn't change the fact that we wouldn't be able to test that theory until after darkness fell. "I hope you're right. If not, we're going to have a lot of explaining to do."

"It won't be the first time," Raven said. "We can only do what we can do. Right now, that's run the circus. The show must go on, right?"

I nodded. "Yeah. The show must go on."

MAX WAITED FOR ME TO finish cleaning up after breakfast, drawing me away from the rest of the group so we could still see them but talk in private.

"How is he?"

I didn't have to ask which "he" Max meant. "He slept well, hard even. He needed the rest. He woke up in a fairly decent mood and says he's better."

"Do you believe him?"

I swallowed hard. I wasn't a fan of talking about Kade behind his back, but I understood Max's concern. This was a lot for Kade to take on, and it was our job to watch him until things shook out. We had no way of knowing how things would twist and turn, so it was going to take our entire village to make sure Kade was protected.

"I believe he wants it to be true." I chose my words carefully. "He doesn't want to be magical. I can't decide if it's because he's afraid or he's generally repulsed by the entire idea."

"I'm going with fear."

"I am, too, but only because I have trouble believing we would be together if he were really that turned off by magic," I said. "He let something slip last night. I probably shouldn't tell you, but it involves you so I'm going to. I'm also going to own up to telling you because keeping secrets from him never does me any good."

Max's lips curved. "Fair enough. What is the secret?"

"It's not really a secret. It's simply something he said."

"The suspense is killing me." Max's eyes twinkled. "I think you've been spending too much time with Luke. His storytelling skills are starting to rub off on you."

I scowled. "You're so funny. Anyway, Kade mentioned that his mother was unhappy for most of his life. He had told me before that she was friendly and always wanted to do well by him, but there was a certain sadness about her.

"Last night he said that he always assumed that sadness had something to do with his father passing away so early, but now he knows that story isn't true," I continued. "He thinks the reason his mother wasn't happy is because she couldn't raise him with you and he thinks that she likely blamed the magic for that."

"Ah." Max nodded in understanding. "From his point of view magic has only hurt the people he cares about most. Even you, who he seemingly adores, has been hurt by the very magic you wield."

"I haven't been hurt all that badly."

"Really? My understanding is that you likely would've died if Raven hadn't managed to wake you the other night. That's on top of the injury you sustained in Washington when you were looking for Melissa. I had to heal you then."

"Yes, but ... ." Crap. He had a point. "I guess I can see why he would have an issue with magic," I said after a beat. "I wish he would get over it. I'm afraid if he fights it too hard something is going to explode – and probably literally – because he tends to bottle things up."

"He gets that from his mother." Max smiled fondly at what I assumed was a memory. "We'll watch him. We can't focus on Kade's abilities until we're out of this mess. The most important thing we can do is protect the guests and ourselves. We'll explore his abilities when we're away from this place."

"That sounds like a plan."

16

SIXTEEN

"I want to know who killed JFK."

My first client of the day was Milton Chamberlain. He was eighty and claimed to be along the parade route on the day John F. Kennedy was shot. He also claimed to have seen two shooters disappearing into the crowd and had managed to convince himself that the president's murder was a vast conspiracy involving at least four foreign governments, two rogue governments (I'd yet to fully understand what he meant when saying that) and current high-ranking members of our government.

I could read all that on the surface two seconds after he'd sat down.

I bit back a sigh as I smiled at him. I'd changed into my normal uniform, an ankle-length skirt with bells on the drawstrings and a flamboyant scarf tied over my hair. I wore an over-sized peasant blouse and several chunky bracelets to complete the ensemble.

"You want to know who killed JFK, huh?" I managed to keep calm, but just barely. "May I ask why?"

"Because the government is keeping the truth from us," Milton replied without hesitation. "I know that there's more going on and I want to make sure that the Russians aren't infiltrating the government because of what happened almost sixty years ago."

I knit my eyebrows as I regarded him. "So ... you're worried that Russians have infiltrated our government as part of some conspiracy that originated in the sixties?"

"Of course not," Milton sputtered, annoyance evident. "Are you even listening to me?"

"I'm trying, but I'm having trouble keeping up."

"Of course you are," Milton grumbled, rolling his neck. "You're probably a Russian, too, aren't you? It would make perfect sense. What better place to hide spies than in a traveling circus?"

We were hiding paranormals – and had become quite adept at it – so I couldn't really argue. Still, the man's paranoia set my teeth on edge. His mind was a busy place to live, and not altogether comfortable to visit even briefly. "I can guarantee we have no spies here."

"So you say, but I don't know that I believe you."

"Yes, well, the thing is, I don't know who killed JFK." I chose my words carefully, hoping not to offend him to the point he'd cause a scene. That was the last thing I wanted. "As far as I know, the official story is the truth."

"Oh, come on!" Milton slapped his hand on the table hard enough to cause me to jolt. "Don't play games with me, girlie! I'm serious about this."

I stared hard into his eyes, frustration mounting. "I can tell you're serious."

"So, answer the question."

"I don't have an answer to the question."

"You'd better get an answer."

"Or what?" I was legitimately curious if he would have the stones to physically threaten me. I wasn't worried about an overzealous eighty-year-old taking me out, but I was in no mood for drama.

"Or I'll ... report you to the police for abusing an elder," Milton answered, his face twisting at the words. He gave it some thought and then brightened when he realized what he'd said. "Yeah, that's right. I'll report you for elder abuse. People don't like that."

"Uh-huh." I couldn't muster the energy to be worried about that. "That doesn't change the fact that I don't know who killed JFK."

"You're a psychic," Milton barked. "It says so right on that sign outside your tent. You can tell fortunes and see the future. I'm betting that means you can see the past, too."

He wasn't wrong. That still didn't mean I could see what happened to JFK. In truth, I'd never thought about looking. He was far before my time. It clearly mattered to Milton, though. "Listen, I get that you're upset about this ... ."

"You have no idea how upset I am," Milton exploded. "That man was our president. He was the leader of the free world. He was taken out by a bunch of traitors and commies. How can you not be upset about this?"

"Well ... ."

Before I got a chance to answer, Kade poked his head inside the tent and took a long look around before his gaze finally landed on Milton. He looked more confused than anything. "Is something going on here?"

Hmm. Either he was passing by and overheard or someone else overheard and tipped him off. That was interesting. He always came running when he thought I had trouble. He was reliable that way.

"Who are you?" Milton asked, his eyes flashing. "Are you a spy?"

"A spy?" Kade wrinkled his forehead. "Am I missing something?"

"He wants to know who killed Kennedy," I supplied, rubbing my forehead. I'd barely started my readings for the day and I already had a headache. "He's convinced the Russians did it."

"Oh, well, sure." Kade offered Milton a genuine smile as he shuffled closer to the table. Apparently he found paranoid older Americans adorable. "Why are you so interested in the Kennedy assassination?"

"I was there," Milton replied. "I was on the street. I saw it happen. I also saw people with guns disappear into the crowd and know that there was more than one shooter. One shooter has never made sense. I mean ... one shooter? No way."

"It sounds like you have firm beliefs on the subject," Kade noted.

"The thing is, I'm not sure Poet is capable of telling you who shot Kennedy." He was much calmer than I felt. "She needs to touch something from the deceased person to get a vibe and, unfortunately, we don't have anything belonging to JFK."

That was a lie. Sometimes there was no rhyme or reason to my visions. Sometimes I needed to touch someone, or at least be close enough to pry open his or her head. Still, as far as lies go, it was a convincing one. Er, well, it was a convincing one until Milton opened his mouth again.

"I've got a shoe from one of the secret service agents." Milton dug in the bag he carried. I thought it was a man purse when he first entered – perhaps he needed medication or something – but now I realized he was carrying a fifty-five-year-old shoe in his man purse and the bag somehow seemed sinister. "I figure she can touch this and see what happened."

"Oh, um ... ." Kade's eyes widened to comical proportions as Milton dropped the shoe in the middle of the table. "I bought it off eBay and I have a letter of authenticity and everything."

"Uh-huh." I licked my lips as I stared at the shoe. "Well, I guess I have no choice but to touch it."

"Wait." Kade tried to stop me at the last second but I knew what I was doing. I forced a smile, grabbed the shoe, and concentrated on the energy emanating from it. I wasn't surprised at the images flashing through my mind. They made sense ... in a sick sort of way.

"Well?" Milton was far too eager as he leaned forward. It was as if his entire life relied on this answer. I worried that if I disappointed him it would cause some sort of meltdown or health scare. Instead, I decided to do the kind thing.

"You're mostly right," I said after a beat. "Only one of the men you saw disappearing into the crowd was involved, though. The other was an unknowing patsy and had no idea what happened. The gun you saw was somehow planted on him." I thought giving him a new mystery to puzzle through, something to keep his mind sharp even if he would never figure out the whole story, was the best way to go. "The one man – and I can't see a name, the shoe energy is simply too old – was a partner with Oswald. Perhaps you can conduct some research to find out who he was."

"Oh, I intend to." Milton was so excited it took everything I had to hold back a smile. "What about the commies?"

"They were totally involved."

"The Russians planned it, didn't they?"

"Along with some help from their Cuban friends."

"I knew it!" Milton smacked his hand against the table, his excitement growing. "I can't wait to get home and tell Edith. She's been calling me crazy for ten years."

"Well, you can make her stop doing that now."

"Definitely." Milton clutched the shoe and man purse to his chest as he hurried toward the tent opening. "Thank you. I've been waiting for this day for more than fifty years."

"You're welcome." I heaved out a sigh as I watched him go, amusement rolling through me. "Well, at least he's happy, huh?" When I turned to face Kade, I found him watching me with unveiled interest. "What?"

"Is that true? Did everything he said happen?"

I thought about messing with him, but it seemed somehow unkind given everything we'd been through. "That shoe was stolen off a corpse in a funeral home, and it most certainly wasn't JFK or one of his Secret Service agents. I have no idea what happened that day in Dallas, but I know Seymour Hills of San Diego wouldn't be happy to know that the funeral director stole his fancy shoes."

Kade made a face. "That is so much worse than I expected."

"Hey, I can't control the gift."

"But you lied. Why didn't you tell him the truth?"

"He didn't want to hear the truth, and I was afraid it would kill him," I answered honestly. "I thought it was best to let him keep hope alive. He's elderly. If he has nothing to live for, nothing propelling him, why get up in the morning? I think he needs the mystery, so I gave him a different one to focus on."

"You have a good heart."

"I'm just lazy. I didn't want him melting down in front of people."

145

"Oh, you can't fool me." Kade leaned over and gave me a quick kiss. "You're a great big marshmallow when it comes to some people. I find it endearing and adorable."

"I am not a marshmallow."

"You're Rocky Road ice cream, baby."

I grinned. "Thanks. Can you show my next client in when you leave?"

"Absolutely."

THE REST OF THE AFTERNOON went by in a blur. It was filled with the usual questions.

Will I find true love?

Will I become rich and famous?

Is my spouse or significant other cheating on me?

When will my parents die so I can get my inheritance and quit work?

Is my cat trying to kill me when it sleeps on my face at night?

I was used to those questions and breezed through them, taking a break when the line died down and no one was waiting. I put my "back soon" sign on the tent flap before heading to the food area to grab something quick for lunch before taking on another round of futures.

I opted for shawarma and a soda, isolating myself between the ticket booth and Mark's small office tent near the midway. It was the perfect vantage point to watch visitors.

From all outward appearances, the locals looked normal. That's not as judgmental as it sounds. It wasn't that I expected them to have two heads or wear bad clothing from the eighties or anything. It was more that I thought someone might stick out, that someone might be putting on a show of being normal when, in reality, they were covering for something else … like sending a cadre of ghosts after us.

I was so lost in thought I didn't notice a small boy – he couldn't have been more than eight or so – watching me from next to the dart game. He stood next to an older boy I was sure was his brother, but his eyes were trained on me. When I realized I had an audience, I wiped my hands on a napkin and offered him a smile. He returned it, although there was something wary about his expression.

"Are you having fun?" I asked, hoping he would chill a bit when he realized I wasn't some random kidnapper. I figured that's what frightened him, perhaps that his parents had warned him about strangers and he was being careful that I didn't try to lure him from his brother.

"It's okay." The boy took a tentative step in my direction. His polo shirt boasted an embroidered name: Troy. Either that was his name or someone picked a really odd shirt for him to wear to a fun outing.

"Only okay, Troy?" I gave him a wink when he startled. "Your name is on your shirt."

"Oh." Troy glanced down, his green eyes widening. "I thought maybe you read my mind or something."

"Why would I read your mind?"

"Because you're the fortune teller lady," he replied without hesitation, drifting away from his brother but not entirely closing the distance to me. He was obviously mistrustful, which was probably smart on his part. It was good to be vigilant.

"I am the fortune teller lady," I agreed, tilting my head to the side. "How did you know?"

"My mom said she wanted to visit you before we left. My dad said she was smoking crack to waste money on something like that, but she didn't care."

"Ah, well, that's nice." Really? What do you say to that? "I'll be going back to my tent soon if she wants a reading. I'm just taking a quick lunch break."

Troy made a face I couldn't quite identify, as if he was gearing up to ask a tough question. He finally made up his mind and stepped closer. "Can you really see the future?"

"Sometimes. Why? Do you want to know what's in your future?"

Troy shrugged, noncommittal. "Kind of. I don't know. Maybe."

I smiled. "Well, I wouldn't worry too much. I think you're going to have a bright future ... as long as you focus on your studies and don't misbehave too much, that is."

Troy rolled his eyes. "You sound like my mom."

The way he said it made me think that wasn't a compliment. "I'm sorry if that offends you."

"That's not really what I want to know," Troy said. He kept inching closer, as if the longer we talked the more his fear fled. I wasn't sure that was a good quality in a child in this day and age, but because I had no intention of hurting him I reassured myself that he would be okay.

"What do you want to know?"

"I want to know when I'm going to die."

The question jarred me. He was much too young to be worrying about something like that. "What?"

"I want to know when I'm going to die," Troy repeated. "I think it's soon."

My heart rolled at the words and I swallowed hard as I debated how to proceed. "What makes you think you're going to die soon? Are you sick? Have you been sick?" There was nothing I could do to fix a human ailment like cancer or leukemia … and that was the first notion that popped into my head. He looked relatively healthy, though, so I forced the assumption out of my head and focused on his clear eyes. There had to be a reason for the boy's melancholy.

Troy shook his head, causing the invisible fist wrapped around my heart to ease its grip. "I'm not sick. Well, I puked after the movies the other night, but that's because I ate three packages of candy all by myself."

"I bet you won't do that again."

"Not until Halloween."

"Okay, well, why are you so worried about dying if you're not sick?" I was genuinely curious. Troy was far too young to let heavy thoughts like that ruin his day. "You should have fun instead of worrying about stuff like that. It's the circus, after all. The circus is supposed to be fun."

"Yeah, but this circus is surrounded by ghosts and I'm the only one who can see them," Troy replied, causing my heart to stutter. "They're everywhere. And if I'm the only one who can see them, that must mean they're here for me, right?"

I glanced around to make sure no one was listening before kneeling so I was at eye level with Troy. "Ghosts? You see ghosts?"

The boy nodded, his green eyes full of worry. "I pointed them out to my brother, but he couldn't see them."

"Where?"

Troy pointed toward the now-familiar tree line. "They're over there. One of them is even wearing a hat. He's been waving at me."

I had no idea what to say. "They're not here for you," I blurted out quickly, hoping I sounded more reassuring than I felt. "I promise. They're here for … the circus."

"They haunt the circus?" Troy didn't look convinced.

"They're here for us," I answered. "They're … part of the show."

"Oh." Apparently my answer made sense, because he brightened considerably. "Are they really here to be part of the show?"

"They really are," I confirmed. "But they get unruly sometimes, so don't go over to talk with them. They don't like it."

"Oh, I don't want to talk to them. They're weird."

"They're definitely weird." I straightened as I looked over the crowd for a familiar face. Unfortunately, anyone I could talk to about this was either busy or elsewhere. "You be good and stick close to your brother and parents, okay? I promise those ghosts aren't here for you."

"I'm just glad I'm not going to die." Troy was earnest. "That would've really blown monkey chunks."

"The biggest monkey chunks in the world," I agreed. "You're okay. I'll make sure of it."

17
SEVENTEEN

I raced straight for the dreamcatcher line, narrowing my eyes as I scanned the strip of land separating the circus grounds and the trees. There was nothing there, no ghosts or shadow movement. It looked like a perfectly nice, sunny day.

Except Troy said he saw ghosts. Sometimes children can more easily see certain things because their minds aren't closed off to possibilities, but I was dumbfounded that Troy could see the ghosts when I couldn't. It didn't seem possible.

Yet I believed him.

"What's going on?" Nellie appeared behind the beer tent – this wasn't a dry event, which I think we all preferred because the ghosts were going to drive us to drink – and he looked concerned.

"I'm not sure." I flicked my eyes to him, grimacing at his new dress. "Is that ... velvet?"

"Pink velvet." Nellie smoothed the front of the dress and grinned. "I ordered it online. It's fabulous."

I blinked several times. I never quite "got" Nellie. He liked to cross-dress, which I was fine with, but sometimes I thought he did it only to irritate others and sometimes I recognized he did it because he was a slave to fashion. He was an odd guy ... who I loved despite his eccentricities.

"It's definitely fabulous," I said finally, taking a moment to finger the heavy straps. "It also looks as if you'll be able to wear it into battle without risking a wardrobe malfunction."

Nellie's smile was sly. "Nothing wrong with a good wardrobe malfunction!"

"I'll have to take your word for it." I turned my attention back to the dreamcatcher line. It remained quiet, untouched and unbothered.

"What's wrong?" Nellie prodded. "I saw you by the midway. You went almost completely white when talking to that boy. I know something's bothering you."

"He said he thinks he's going to die."

Nellie remained calm. "Okay, but ... he's a boy. He probably watched some horribly violent movie and got it stuck in his head. Half the fun of being a kid is overreacting about stuff and getting scared by horror movies we shouldn't have watched in the first place."

"That's what I thought at first, or that he was sick and I didn't realize it. That's not why he thinks he's going to die, though."

"I'll bite. Why does he think he's going to die?"

"Because of the ghosts only he can see," I answered without hesitation. "He says they're all around the circus and some are waving at him. His brother can't see them. He believes they're here for him."

"You've got to be kidding me." Nellie swore under his breath as he gazed at the trees. "I thought those things were only coming out at night."

"I did, too."

"So ... why can't we see them?"

"Maybe they don't want us to see them." I worked various scenarios through my head. "Maybe they want us to see them at night, but they're only here to observe during the day and don't want to tip us off."

"That would suggest someone is issuing them orders."

"Or they're coming up with plans themselves."

"Except they don't exactly seem like great thinkers," Nellie countered. "I definitely think someone is controlling them."

That was my initial thought, too. Now I wasn't so sure. "Keep your eyes open," I said finally. "Make sure everyone is on top of their game. Don't let the guests wander over the dreamcatcher."

"Do you think the ghosts will hurt them?"

"I have no idea. Better safe than sorry, though, right?"

"I think that depends on whether or not you look good in pink velvet." Nellie offered me a lopsided grin. "It's best to be fearless when it comes to fashion."

I couldn't stop myself from returning the smile. "Good to know."

I WAS HYPER-VIGILANT for the rest of the day, going through the motions during readings and returning to the dreamcatcher boundary on every break to make sure nothing had changed.

Time crept by.

When darkness fell and the inevitable fog followed, my circus workers were clearly edgy. The locals, however, didn't seem at all twisted by the eerie ambiance. They ignored the shifting fog and winds, oblivious of our anxiety.

I found Troy as he was leaving, his brother standing close to him, toward the front of the circus as their parents used the restrooms before hitting the parking lot.

"What do you see?" I lowered myself to a knee so I was closer to Troy's height and scanned the area on the other side of the dreamcatcher.

"They're brighter now," Troy replied, his features more ashen than earlier. "They're everywhere."

"Yeah." I could see the ghosts, too, although they hadn't fully formed yet. Now they were back to being the shadow hunters Caroline first warned us about, faceless blobs. Just bits of movement that were hard to make out. It wouldn't be long until they were completely back. Thankfully they didn't glow without magical aid because I had no inclination of how to explain what we were dealing with to fearful guests. "They're not here for you."

Troy's expression remained grim. "You don't know that."

"Trust me. I'll get you to your car and you'll be fine."

Troy's brother, Marcus, who looked to be about thirteen, fixed me with a suspicious look when he saw me talking to his sibling. "He's not interested in being kidnapped," the older boy said, indignant. "If you try to take him I'll scream because my parents will ground me if he goes missing."

I rolled my eyes. "Troy and I are old friends. I'm not trying to kidnap him. We're simply talking about ... other stuff."

The brother looked me up and down, his gaze lingering on the vee in my shirt as his interest coalesced. "What kind of stuff?"

Oh, geez. Teenagers should come with a manual to wade through the inappropriate sexual years. All those hormones made them slaves to stupidity. This kid was a walking idiot of some insanely high level. "Serious stuff," I replied without hesitation. "You probably wouldn't understand."

The look Troy shot me was full of profound gratitude as a little color returned to his cheeks. He was bolder when his parents returned. "This is my mom and dad."

"Poet Parker." I extended my hand toward the mother because she was the one who looked most worried about my intentions. This wasn't my first time soothing a worried parent, and I knew exactly how to approach her. "I met Troy earlier on the midway. I'm second in command here at Mystic Caravan. It's my job to make sure everyone is having a good time."

"Oh, well, of course." The woman looked visibly relieved as she straightened her shoulders. "I'm Vivian Brooks, Troy's mother. Do you spend a lot of time wandering around getting to know guests?"

I nodded. "I'm the resident fortune teller, but I take breaks throughout the afternoon and it's part of my job to tour the grounds."

"Oh, well, that's nice." Whatever reluctance she held onto faded as she gripped Troy's hand and smiled at me. "We had a fabulous time, if you're looking for feedback."

"I'm glad." I meant it. "Are you leaving now?"

"We are."

"I'll walk with you to the parking lot. I was heading in that direction anyway."

"You were?" Vivian furrowed her brow but ultimately shrugged before falling into step with me. "May I ask how often you travel? I'm fascinated by the little community you seem to have built here. I mean ... look at that." She pointed at trailer row. "Do you all eat together every meal?"

I understood her curiosity. Everyone wondered on some level how we lived our lives. "I wouldn't say we eat together every meal." I kept my voice amiable as I carefully watched the shadows. If one of the shadow hunters made a run at Troy I'd have to fight. I had no idea what that would entail, but there was no way I would let the boy get hurt. I made a promise, after all.

"We have big dinners together almost every night," I continued, doing my best to pretend the subject didn't bore me. "We are mostly on our own for breakfast unless we need to coordinate something, and then we usually talk business over our meal. We rarely eat lunch together because we've usually got so much going on."

"Oh, well, that's interesting." The woman focused on our trailers as we passed. "Do you have children running around?"

"You mean traveling with us?" I wanted to laugh out loud at the suggestion but I thought that would make her uncomfortable. "There are no children who travel with us. This isn't really a life for children."

"Who is it a life for?" Troy asked, his young face full of interest and intrigue.

"Those who want to see the world," I replied as I smiled at him. "It's not an easy life and most people in this business don't have families, so the travel isn't a hardship."

Understanding passed over Vivian's face, but Troy obviously didn't grasp what I was saying.

"You don't have a family?" he pursed his lips. "I thought everyone had a family."

"Not really." I didn't want to get into a philosophical discussion with an eight-year-old, but it appeared that was on my evening agenda. "You see, the thing is, I had a mother and father when I was younger, but they died when I was a teenager."

"Oh, that's too bad." Vivian clucked her tongue as she shook her head. "How did you end up with the circus?"

I saw no reason to lie. "I was on the streets in Detroit when I ran into the owner of Mystic Caravan. We got to talking, he asked about my skills set while buying me a meal I desperately needed, and then he offered me a job.

"He told me it was never going to be easy and required a lot of hard work," I continued. "He told me that he watched his workers closely and thought I might fit in. He also told me there are different kinds of family."

Troy flicked his eyes to his mother. "But ... I already have my family."

I chuckled at his expression. "I can tell you're a worrier."

"He definitely is," Vivian agreed. "He's a sensitive soul. I don't know where he gets it from. His father and I aren't like that."

Sensitive soul. Hmm. That's how most of my teachers described me before it became apparent that I could read minds. I couldn't help but wonder if Troy was suffering from the same affliction. I almost immediately discarded the notion. If he could read or infiltrate minds he would've tipped his hand earlier. I had no doubt he was sensitive. That didn't mean he was psychic, though.

"I'm sure he'll grow out of it," I offered. "Besides, there's nothing wrong with being sensitive. Some of my best friends are sensitive. As for family, while I don't have any left – or at least I have no idea where the people I do have left are – I have a new family of sorts."

Troy tilted his head to the side. "You do?"

I nodded. "Sometimes you're born into a family and sometimes you make one yourself."

"Do you like your new family?"

I pictured Nellie's velvet pink dress and thought about Luke's constant meltdowns. "Most of the time," I said finally. "Every family argues, just like you and your brother. It's the nature of the world. But every family loves, too."

Vivian beamed at me as Troy scowled.

"I don't think my brother loves anything but his PlayStation," he grumbled, causing me to laugh.

"I think you'll find out differently as you get older."

I MADE SURE TROY and his parents were safely loaded into their vehicle, offering a wide smile and enthusiastic wave as they pulled out of the parking lot. I remained rooted to my spot until Raven joined me, her expression bemused.

"I never pictured you as the motherly sort," she drawled. "You were doting on that kid. What gives?"

"He's either psychic or overly sensitive," I replied. "He can see the ghosts."

"I think a lot of people can see the ghosts now that it's dark," Raven countered. "I've seen a few people glance in their direction. Most of them convince themselves they're imagining things. If they look like they're going to say anything, I crawl into their heads and give them a nudge in the opposite direction. He's a kid. He's more apt to believe."

"It's not that. He saw them bright as day ... and during the day."

Raven stilled, her expression thoughtful. "He saw them during the day? How can you be sure he really did see something and didn't make it up?"

"He mentioned the one in the hat waving to him."

"Son of a ... !" Raven viciously swore under her breath. "Well, that just figures. Here we thought they were only coming out at night, but it turns out they're here all day. I wonder why we can't see them."

"Yeah. I've been thinking about that." I rolled my neck until it cracked and turned to walk back to the fairgrounds. Security was emptying out the place, which was good for what needed to be done, but it would be at least an hour before we were free to take on our shadowy friends. "I think either they don't want us to see them and they're purposely shielding their existence or the sun is keeping them hidden between planes."

"You think they're on a different plane?" Raven was understandably intrigued as she stopped next to my trailer and stared at my mirror shadow. The woman followed me from the circus to the parking lot and back, the way she carried herself somehow suggesting she was grim ... and possibly angry.

"I think they *might* be on a different plane," I cautioned. "That plane could be really close, though, like one hop over. That's why we have an easier time seeing them at night."

"Because the veil between the worlds is thinner at night," Raven mused, tapping her chin as she watched the apparition. Without Max's magical help and thanks to the increasing fog, the ethereal figure wasn't easy to make out. "I'm glad they don't glow. We would never be able to explain them if they glowed."

I chuckled. "I was thinking that same thing when I walked Troy and his family to their car."

"Did you think they would be attacked?"

"No, but if the ghost with the hat waved at Troy, that means he wasn't watching Kade," I replied.

"Oh." Realization dawned on Raven. "You think the ghost was torn about whether he should watch Kade or the kid. That probably does mean there's something special about the kid."

"Probably," I conceded. "He's on his way home, though, and the ghost is still here." I pointed toward the corner of trailer row, to the spot where the ghost in question watched something only he could see. I had a feeling Kade was there performing some task or wrapping up with the security personnel, but I wasn't ready to head in that direction quite yet. "Have you considered that maybe they're not here to hunt us as much as scare us into staying put?"

Raven jerked her head in my direction, surprise flitting through her heavy-lidded eyes. "You think they're trying to keep us here?"

"I think it's definitely a possibility. I mean ... if we're here and focused on them, we're not looking elsewhere."

"Like ... where?"

I shrugged. I didn't have an easy answer. "Like Caroline's house. Like Falk. Like ... the woods. I don't know. Think about it. The first night we were here you thought you heard a wendigo. We haven't heard the noise since. That seems odd."

Raven pressed the heel of her hand to her forehead, her mind clearly working overtime. "You're right. I almost forgot about the wendigo because we were so focused on the ghosts."

"Maybe that's what someone wants us to focus on."

"Maybe." Raven glared at the ghost as the obviously female spirit watched us, her body language signifying overt disdain. If I didn't know better, given the way she planted her hands on her hips, I'd think she was mocking us. "I want to run a few more experiments tonight."

"I figured you would."

"I'm sick of these things."

"That makes two of us."

18

EIGHTEEN

Once we were sure the grounds were empty (and the clowns and midway folk locked away for the night) we returned to what was quickly becoming our regular spot to study the specters. I wasn't surprised to find Max in attendance, his expression serious as he watched the figure with the hat do a little a dance for his benefit.

"I'm really starting to hate that guy," Kade muttered, shaking his head.

"You're not the only one." I moved to his side and linked my fingers with his. "You're not the only one he's been following."

Kade's eyebrows flew up toward his hairline. "What do you mean?"

I related my afternoon adventures with Troy. When I was done, everyone started speaking at once.

"What is he?" Dolph asked.

"Do you think the ghosts are really watching everything we do, even during the day?" Nixie asked.

"I want to smash all their faces in with my ax, but that won't do any damage, so we need to figure out what else to do," Nellie exploded. "The more violent the better."

It wasn't funny, but I couldn't help but smile at the reactions. "I think Troy is okay. I'm guessing he was only a curiosity because he was here. The hat ghost is clearly still hanging close and fixated on Kade."

"Yeah, and it's not creepy at all," Kade groused, making me laugh out loud when he shot the ghost the finger. "I hate this guy."

"I think he knows that," Max mused. "That's his entire purpose. He wants to irritate you, unnerve you. Stop being such an easy mark."

Kade's mouth dropped open. "Well, excuse me for living."

Max sighed but didn't back down. "I'm not trying to offend you. In fact, it's the opposite. I'm trying to get you to realize that you're playing right into these creatures' hands.

"I think Poet is right," he continued. "The ghosts aren't here to glean information from us. They're here to distract us. Someone wants us to stick close to the fairgrounds and not venture anywhere else. I think that's a directed effort."

"But what are they trying to keep us from?" Luke asked, appearing out of the gloom behind me and moving close. He had full makeup on from his work in the main tent, which usually put him in a good mood, but he was all business. "What do they want?"

"I don't know." Max looked as frustrated as I felt. "I've tried scanning them for information. I've come up empty."

"I've tried the same," Raven supplied. "There's nothing there. That's why I don't believe they're really ghosts."

"I think we all agree with that," I said. "They're not ghosts by any stretch of the imagination."

"Shadow hunters," Nellie said. "They live in the shadows and hunt us. Your friend Caroline gave them the name, and she's right. That's what they're doing."

Hmm. That was interesting. "Maybe they're doing the same thing to her," I suggested after a beat. "Maybe they're keeping her locked in her house at night and that's why she still lives there."

"I don't know," Luke hedged. "We didn't spend much time with her, but she didn't seem unhappy with her surroundings. I think she likes the isolation."

"Or she's getting something from it," Naida suggested, frowning at my mirror woman and making a growling sound in the back of her throat. "This one is different." She pointed for emphasis, so there could be no confusion about who she was talking about. "The guy with the hat is more animated, but I think she's in charge."

"What makes you say that?"

"There's something there."

"You can read her mind?" Raven asked. "I've tried with several of them and found blank slates. It's as if we're in a classroom and the teacher is yet to write anything on the board."

"I can't see thoughts," Naida replied. "There's still something about this one. She seems more ... intense. She watches Poet's every move. And I swear she's actually thinking before acting."

I stared at the figure in question, sticking out my tongue and blowing a raspberry to see if she would react. Sure enough, she bobbed her head back and forth, like a really angry chicken that wanted to go nuts on me if given the chance. She didn't move to cross the line, though. She stayed exactly where she was.

"I don't know that we can prove that," I said after a beat. "She does seem different, although I can't be sure I really believe that or it's simply because you pointed out her actions."

"So, what should we do?" Luke asked. "We haven't made a lick of progress since these things first appeared. If we're going to test the theory that they're here to stop us from leaving, isn't the obvious next step to allow someone to cross the dreamcatcher?"

Kade immediately balked. "No way. I don't like that idea one bit."

"He's not necessarily wrong," Max said, feigning patience. "We can't do nothing. If we expect results, someone needs to cross the line. I can do it."

He was already moving when I extended a hand and grabbed his arm. "Wait. I don't think that's a good idea."

"And why is that?" Amusement licked Max's features. "You said yourself that I'm the strongest one here. I should conduct the test for that very reason."

"That's exactly why you shouldn't," I countered, firm. "You're the only one who can heal, yourself and others, if something happens. If they attack and manage to do actual damage – which I'm not sure is a possibility, but we are operating in the dark – then we need you to handle the healing. I believe you have to be conscious for that, right?"

Max shook his head. "I hate to admit it – mostly because I can already see what you're going to suggest next – but I get what you're saying."

"Poet is definitely right about Max not crossing the boundary," Raven said. "Because she's going to suggest she be the one to do it, I think we should simply cut to the chase and agree that she makes the most sense."

"Oh, thank you so much for volunteering me," I drawled.

"You were going to do it yourself, and you know it." Raven was unruffled. "You make the most sense because you have a mirror ghost. Max can't do it, and we're not sure Kade can protect himself. That leaves you."

"Wait." Kade's face flushed, and even though the illumination was limited I could see the worry glittering in his eyes. "This is an absolutely terrible idea. She's already been attacked once."

"Which simply means we know they're interested in her," Raven said pragmatically. "She's the best person for the job."

Kade wasn't ready to acquiesce. "What about Nixie or Naida? They're magical."

"But the shadow hunters show no interest in them," Luke pointed out. "The best test is the one that helps us get to the heart of the matter quickly."

Kade was stymied. "You're willing to risk Poet's life for a test?"

"I'm willing to be right here and yank her back across the line if necessary," Luke corrected. "We're stuck in unchartered territory. We don't have a choice."

Kade gazed from face to face. Finally, his eyes landed on me, and I felt anger and worry colliding as he fought to maintain his temper. "You're going to do it no matter what, aren't you?"

I held my hands palms out and shrugged. "I think I have to. We need answers."

"But ... ."

"It'll be okay." I reached over and wrapped my fingers around his wrist. "Look at all the backup I have. This won't be like what happened the other night when I was sleeping. Raven and Max are here to yank my butt out of the fire if it gets too hot."

"I don't like it." Kade kept his voice low. "Something could happen."

"And something even worse could happen if we don't figure out what these creatures are capable of," Max pointed out. "I think it's necessary."

"That's easy for you to say," Kade grumbled. "She's not your girlfriend."

"That doesn't mean she's not dear to me." Max patted his shoulder. "I understand this is difficult for you, but we really need to make it happen."

"Fine." Kade forced out a sigh, resigned. "If something happens to her, I'll kill all of you."

"Duly noted." Max winked at me as Kade gave me a quick kiss. "Don't go too far out, Poet. We need to be able to grab you quickly if something happens."

"I understand." I tugged on my skirt to straighten it, my eyes landing on my mirror as I sucked in a breath. "Here I go."

I took one brave step over the line, my eyes flicking between the shadows as I waited. At first, the creatures showed zero interest. It was as if I hadn't done anything of note. Then my mirror moved closer.

I stared into her sightless eyes – they were more empty sockets – and frowned when I realized she was mimicking my stance. She posed exactly like me, her head tilted to the side, and it was very clear she was mocking me.

"Under normal circumstances I might like your attitude," I offered. "These are not normal circumstances."

The specter moved a bit closer and I swore she was smiling, even though she didn't have a mouth.

"It's clear she's trying to intimidate me," I volunteered. "It won't work but I think that's what she's trying to do."

"Definitely," Max agreed. "I ... Poet, look out!"

The quick change in his demeanor caused me to jolt. It was too late. The ethereal woman moved fast and already had her ghostly fingers wrapped around either side of my head before I could react.

Watch.

She didn't say the word out loud, but I heard the command in my head. I fought the panic washing over me, but the darkness invading my mind didn't make it easy. I tumbled into the abyss despite my best efforts, and then I fell for what felt like forever.

I FELL SO LONG I thought I would never hit bottom. I didn't thump when hitting the ground as much as slide into existence. I recognized right away I was in another time, though. The place seemed somehow familiar. This was hardly the first instance when my subconscious was taken on a wild ride so I recognized the signs of my new reality.

"What am I doing here?" I glanced around, my eyes narrowing when I recognized what looked to be a tall building rising down a cute pathway that cut through various buildings and tents. "That's the Falk Mill."

"Very good."

I practically jumped out of my skin at the second voice, swiveling quickly to find a woman standing behind me. She was dressed in a skirt made of natural fibers. It ran almost to her feet. Her hair was pulled back in a tight bun and her cool blue eyes were accusatory as she looked me over.

"You're the mirror ghost," I blurted out for lack of anything cooler to say. "I recognize you."

"I'm not sure what you mean by that." The woman crossed her arms over her chest. "You're ... interesting."

That was rich coming from a ghost who I didn't think could possibly be a ghost. The fact that she managed to yank my mind through time was simply too much to comprehend. "Who are you?"

"It doesn't matter."

"It matters to me," I persisted. "I need to know who you are."

"What good will knowing my name do you?"

"I'm not sure."

"Then why should I give it to you?"

"It's simply polite," I gritted out. "When grabbing someone by the head and forcing them to time travel you should offer your name first."

I couldn't be sure, but I was almost positive that the woman's lips curved as she fought a smile. "Fair enough," she said finally. "I am Gillian Dodd. This is my home."

Gillian Dodd. Gilly. "This is your home?"

Gillian nodded as she turned her attention to the bustling activity around us. I could tell right away that this was Gillian's memory because the other people – the ones walking to and from the store and fields – paid us no attention. "I lived here for five years. That was the longest I lived anywhere. This is definitely my home."

I swallowed hard. There was something about the way she watched the others that told me she wasn't a big proponent of home being where the heart is. "What happened to you here?" I remembered the other dream, the one in which I was tied to a stake and seemingly burned from the inside. "What was going on here?"

"Come with me." Gillian's tone told me she wasn't in the mood to be trifled with. "We don't have much time."

"Why is that?"

"Your friends will have you back with them very quickly – they're not happy, by the way – and you only have a short time to see what you need to see."

"And what's that?"

"The ruination of a town."

She was so ominous I could do nothing but make a face at the back of her head. "That was a bit dramatic."

"So is what's about to come." Gillian stopped at the top of a hill and pointed. "Do you see that?"

I followed her finger with my gaze, my heart constricting when I saw what looked to be a stake in the center of the town. "I see it."

"There will be a reckoning tonight, although my tonight is long in the past."

"They think you're a witch, don't they?" It was the only thing that made sense. The stories I'd heard and the dream I lived through were both pointing to the same conclusion. "They decided you're a witch and responsible for warping the saw blade."

Gillian nodded. "I was single after the death of my husband and stayed to help. That turned out to be a mistake. Nobody trusts a single woman."

"It's too bad you weren't born in a later time. That's no longer true today."

"Yes, well, we can't change things like that." Gillian licked her lips as she watched a man affix ropes to the stake. "You can't save me. You can't stop what happens."

I had no idea why she was telling me that. "Okay, but ... you have to be showing me this for a reason."

"I need you to know."

"But ... why?"

"Because some things shouldn't be forgotten, or buried."

She was talking in riddles. "Why are you guys hanging around the circus? I mean ... what do you hope to accomplish by doing that? Did someone send you?"

"Everything will make sense in time." Gillian's eyes were sober when she locked gazes with me. "Your friends are about to take you. Remember what you saw in the dream. Remember what you saw here. You'll figure it out."

"How can you be sure?"

This time Gillian's smile was completely genuine. "Because I have faith. It's the only thing that sustains me. Now, go. Think hard. The answers are there if you put everything together. I promise."

"POET!"

I bolted to a sitting position on the ground. Somehow, while I was out, Kade and Luke had managed to drag me back over the dreamcatcher so Max and Raven could heal me. I wasn't nearly as jarred by this visit to the past as the previous one.

"Are you okay?" Kade threw his arms around me and tugged me close. "You scared the crap out of me."

"I'm fine." I patted his back and met Raven's gaze over his shoulder. "I know who Gilly is."

"I figured that woman wanted to show you something," Raven said. "What happened?"

"Gillian Dodd. She moved to Falk with her husband, but he died. She stayed behind and was accused of being a witch."

"That explains what you saw in your dream," Max said. "They were burning her at the stake."

I immediately started shaking my head. "No, they didn't burn her."

"What did they do?"

"That's what we need to find out. I'm not sure what they did, but I guarantee it wasn't good. If we find out what happened to Gillian I think we'll be able to piece together everything that happened in this town."

"And what if we can't find records on Gillian?" Raven asked. "It was a long time ago."

"Then we'd better start looking first thing in the morning. I think we're stuck if we don't find that specific answer."

Raven exhaled heavily and nodded. "Okay. At least we have somewhere to look."

I was excited by that prospect. We were finally getting somewhere.

19

NINETEEN

I thought Kade would be a hovering mess the next day. I slept long and hard, no disturbing dreams. That allowed him to drift off without having to worry about me, and he was more pragmatic when he woke in the morning.

"What's the plan today?"

He sat next to me at the picnic table, breakfast finished but the cleanup remaining. He seemed almost chipper, which was fairly impressive given how shaken I knew he really was.

"It's a normal day at the circus." I wiped the corners of my mouth with my napkin. "We all have jobs to do, including you."

"You know what I mean." Kade sipped his coffee. "You're not going on another adventure across the dreamcatcher today, are you?"

It was as close as he was willing to come to admitting he was terrified. I took pity on him. "I have no intention of leaving the fairgrounds. I promise. We're going to need another planning session before we decide how to proceed."

"We're also going to need to get some research in," Raven added. "I'm taking my computer to the House of Mirrors. I can spend time trying to ascertain exactly who Gillian Dodd was and what happened to her in Falk."

"Even if you find that out, what good will it do?" Kade was plaintive. "Maybe we should pack up and take off today. We'll claim we have an emergency or something and leave." Multiple heads snapped in his direction, causing him to widen his eyes. "What did I say?"

"This is the circus," I reminded him. "We don't pack up and take off for no good reason. That's not how we roll."

"But ... you're in danger."

"I wasn't in danger last night," I countered. "She wanted to show me something, not kill me."

"You're only here because Max and Raven acted quickly."

"She had no intention of keeping me." I was positive that was true. "In fact, I think she was trying to show me what happened to her the night of the nightmare. I don't think she realized what she was doing. She's not trying to hurt me."

"You don't know that."

"But I feel it." I patted his hand. "I need you to chill. I understand this is new to you and it's a struggle because of the interest the guy in the hat is showing you, but we have to take this one step at a time.

"I'm not finished," I continued, holding up a hand to still him when his mouth moved to start what I was sure would be a righteous argument. "This is what we do. Hunting monsters is as much our purpose as entertaining the masses. I know it's hard for you to grasp, but I really wasn't in any danger last night. She was simply trying to communicate."

"What if she's only pretending to want that?" Kade wasn't ready to let it go. "What if she's trying to placate you so she can lure you away and ... I don't know ... eat you?"

It took everything I had not to burst out laughing. I knew it would only compound his frustration if I did. "She says I'll understand when I put everything together. I believe that. I wish you had faith in me to believe the same thing."

Kade scowled. "Oh, that was low."

"I know."

"Fine." Kade was resigned as he shook his head. "I can't stop you. I don't want to stop you because you know what you're doing. I just ... please be careful."

"I'm always careful."

Kade's scowl was back. "I'm going to pretend you didn't say that because I've watched you almost die several times since we've met."

I kept my smile in place despite his annoyance. "I think that's probably best."

"Yeah, yeah."

MELISSA STUCK CLOSE TO my tent after the circus opened. At first I thought it was because she was ready to get back to work – and she absolutely loved reading fortunes and interacting with the public – but eventually I realized she was hanging so close because someone had put her up to it.

During one of our coffee breaks, I nursed my mocha and fixed her with a serious look as she busily scanned the crowd and practically ignored my presence. "Was it Luke or Kade?"

The question clearly stymied her because she flicked her eyes to me, confusion evident. "I don't know what you're talking about."

"Someone told you to watch me," I pressed. "I'm guessing it was either Luke or Kade. If I were a betting woman I'd lean toward Kade."

Melissa made a huffing sound as she looked away from me. She was clearly uncomfortable being called out directly. "Maybe I just want to get some work in. Have you considered that?"

"I did ... for the first hour," I conceded. "Then I saw the way you were watching me and realized something else was going on. It's okay. I'm not going to melt down. Kade sent you, didn't he?"

Melissa was sheepish. "He might have stopped by my trailer and suggested it was time to re-enter the work force," she said. "I've been working behind the scenes but staying away from the customers. He told me to suck it up and take care of you because I'm alive thanks to what you did."

The sentiment was both sweet and grating. "Well, I don't think that's exactly fair to you. What you went through was traumatic. I'm perfectly fine. If you feel more comfortable returning to your trailer, I'm okay with that."

"Kade won't be okay with that."

"I can handle Kade."

Melissa's lips twitched at my cocksure attitude. "Yeah, well, I think I'll stay. He wasn't wrong about me needing to rejoin the real world."

"I think you rejoining the real world is great," I admitted, hoping I didn't sound like an exuberant mother as I drained the rest of my coffee and tossed the empty cup in the nearby trash receptacle. "I also think you should do it on your own timetable. Don't force yourself to live on someone else's schedule."

"You did save me."

"I wasn't working alone."

"No, but you did the heavy lifting." Melissa shifted from one foot to the other, clearly uncomfortable. "I'm here because of you. I understand that."

"That doesn't mean you have to force yourself to mingle before you're ready."

"I'm okay." Melissa looked as surprised with the declaration as I felt. "I don't feel great or anything, but I'm okay. I think anticipating having to rejoin society was actually worse than doing it. Now that it's over, I feel ... better."

"But not good, right?"

"Definitely not good. I think that's still to come."

"Well, it's a start. Who doesn't love a good start?"

"I just want to put one foot in front of the other and keep marching." Melissa squared her shoulders. "Before long, I won't have to remind myself that it's necessary."

"That's a very healthy attitude."

"I certainly hope so. If I fall apart again, I think it will take forever to pick up the pieces."

Sadly, I couldn't help but agree.

THE AFTERNOON SHIFT seemed to take forever. I had annoying client after annoying client asking me to make sure they would achieve success or snag a rich man. One even demanded I make sure he married a Victoria's Secret model. It took everything I had not to explode a few times.

Perhaps sensing my irritation, Melissa volunteered to take the last hour of readings. I thought it might be too much for her, but then realized it was better to let her try and fail than to not try at all.

I didn't go far, planting myself outside the tent so I could pre-screen the people waiting in line. Most of them were the usual dregs who wanted something for nothing – as if Melissa could wave a wand and give them everything they desired without them ever lifting a finger – but there was one couple I couldn't quite wrap my head around.

I watched them a long time, my curiosity propelling me closer. The man didn't have a care in this world. His mind was a blank slate. He stared forward without speaking. The woman next to him kept up a steady stream of inane chatter. She said a lot, but nothing of substance. I figured out quickly that she was talking to cover for his lack of verbal skills.

Just because he didn't have anything on his mind didn't necessarily mean something was wrong. Through all my years of mind reading and psychic invasion, the one thing I learned was that the female mind was often much busier than the male counterpart. That's not sexist. I once scanned a man for an entire football game and the only time he registered thoughts were when his team scored, made an error, the cheerleaders came on or a beer commercial hit the screen. That's not to say men don't think. For some reason, though, it's easier for them to zone out.

What I was seeing now was nothing like that.

"What's going on?" Nellie appeared at my side. I sensed him a second before he showed up, so I wasn't surprised.

"What makes you think anything is going on?" I asked, not bothering to look at him. I couldn't drag my eyes from the man. He looked to be in his late forties, nicely dressed, his hair combed and kept. He stared into nothing, and didn't register the movements of anyone around him. If I didn't know better I'd think he was in some sort of walking coma.

"I've been watching you for twenty minutes," Nellie replied, matter of fact. "You haven't moved a muscle. All you've done is watch the people in line. I've known you long enough to recognize that means something is going on."

"Something is definitely going on," I agreed, puckering my lips as I debated the possibilities. "That guy isn't there."

Whatever he was expecting, that wasn't it. Nellie slid me a sidelong look and tilted his head. "Who isn't there?"

"That guy with the blond hair." I inclined my chin, making sure not to point and draw attention. "His head is completely empty."

"Oh, is that all?" Nellie chuckled, genuinely amused. "I hate to speak ill of my gender, but that's a man thing. Look at the woman with him. She's chattering away nonstop. The blanking out is probably just a defense mechanism so he doesn't have to comprehend whatever she's saying. I've seen it before."

"You're not psychic."

"No, but I am a man."

"Yeah, well ... ." I narrowed my eyes as I studied the woman. She was perfectly coiffed, her manicure pristine, and she seemed to be having a good time. The only problem was, she kept talking about things that had little to no substance. "I need to figure out what's going on with her."

I pushed away from the tent and inched closer to the couple, careful to make myself as unobtrusive as possible. The woman didn't even glance in my direction and yet somehow I recognized the moment she picked up on my presence. She didn't stiffen. She didn't jerk her head to meet my steely gaze. She simply continued talking.

"I think we should definitely switch to decaf, Stanley," she blathered. "We're getting older and all that caffeine isn't good for us."

I stood still, delicately unraveling my powers so I could slip inside her head. It wasn't difficult – I'd done it numerous times before – but I wanted to make sure she didn't notice the invasion and cause a scene. That wouldn't end well for anybody.

"I'm so sick of television today," she prattled on. "All the violence and sex. It's unseemly."

I thought I would stumble across a name at first entry, but I couldn't find anything remotely resembling a moniker. That's one of the first things I learn about most people. That was a piece of information very few individuals cared about hiding. This woman was different.

"I wish they had wholesome shows on, like when I was younger," the woman continued, her eyes trained forward as the line moved. "Things like *The Brady Bunch* and *Bewitched*. Who doesn't love *Bewitched*?"

That was a very good question. I pressed harder into her psyche, my stomach quivering when I realized I was about to smack into a wall. I tried another avenue of attack but came up with the same outcome. "Son of a ... !"

Nellie remained at my side. He was always looking for a fight and I was his best option considering the doldrums of the day. "What is it?"

"She's closed off her mind."

"What does that mean?"

"I can't get in."

"I know that, but ... I thought you could invade anyone's mind."

"Usually that's the case," I offered. "There are a few people who can fight the process – Max, Raven, Naida – but this is different. This woman is ... strong."

Nellie glanced back at the woman, this time looking at her with fresh eyes. "Look at her hand. She's leading the man forward and talking, but he doesn't engage with her at all."

"That's because there's nothing in his head." My alarm ratcheted up a notch as I glanced around, fervently hoping Kade would make one of his hourly stops to make sure I was okay. He tried to play the visits off, as though they were part of his job, but I knew better. "We need to talk to her."

Nellie didn't bother hiding his surprise. "How are you going to do that? You can't just walk up to her and say, 'Are you a crazy hell beast who is hollowing out your husband's brain? If so, I think we should have some coffee.' She'll make a scene."

I rolled my eyes so hard I thought they might twist into the back of my head. "I'm not going to ask her that."

"Then what are you going to ask her?"

I had no idea. I simply knew I needed to get her away from the crowd. "I don't know. You need to come with me, though. I might need backup."

"I don't have my ax."

"You can't chop off heads in front of people anyway."

"That's why I think most people are stupid," Nellie sniffed. "Who doesn't like a good head chopping?"

"Just … come on." I didn't mean to be short with him, but my psychic senses were on overload. Something was very wrong here. I approached the woman from the rear, hoping to catch her off guard. She was staring at the exact spot I landed in before I could open my mouth. "Hello, ma'am." It was a struggle to say anything that made sense. "I'm with Mystic Caravan. I'm making my rounds to ensure everyone is having a good time."

"I'm having a terrific time," the woman offered. "Thank you for your hospitality."

"Oh, I'm here for more than that," I enthused. "I'm here to tell you that you and your husband have been randomly selected for free midway tickets. All you have to do is come with me to the administration trailer and we'll make sure they're in your possession in just a few minutes."

The woman didn't blink. She simply stared. "I'm not much of a midway fan."

"I am," the man in front of her in the line offered, grinning. "I'll take the tickets."

"Yes," the woman said. "Give them to him."

"Unfortunately they're non-transferrable."

"Well, that is a shame." The woman's tone was clipped as she urged her husband forward. "We're just here for a reading and then we're leaving."

Instinctively I grabbed her husband's arm and poured everything I had into his head. He didn't so much as shift his eyes in my direction. He was completely vacant. If thoughts could echo, mine would do that within his cavernous head. "Sir, you don't look so well. Would you like to go to the emergency tent and sit down, maybe have some juice?"

He didn't speak. He didn't look at me. He just ... stared. It was eerie.

"He's fine." The woman narrowed her eyes to slits. "He's not much of a talker. He always says I make up for it and talk for both of us."

I could see that. The woman's mind was empty, too. No matter how I pushed and prodded, I couldn't make headway past the barrier she created. She recognized what I was doing, and her smile was sly as it spread across her face.

"You don't need to stick so close." She raised her voice so everyone in the line could hear her. "We're happy as we are. I'm sure you have other guests to attend to."

"Listen ... ."

She didn't give me a chance to finish. "We don't need anyone hovering. We're perfectly fine."

She'd put me in a difficult position. We both knew it. If I remained it would look as if I was harassing her. Even worse, if I tried to force the situation and drag her away it would cause a scene that no one wanted. I couldn't allow either of those things.

So, instead of pushing forward, I drew back. "Enjoy your day at Mystic Caravan Circus."

The woman beamed, although her eyes were alive with mayhem rather than mirth. "I intend to."

20
TWENTY

I had no idea what to do about the woman. She remained in line with her husband, who was essentially nothing more than a functioning zombie that didn't crave brains for dinner. He stared at nothing. She chattered away. I watched them with keen eyes and a heavy heart while internally freaking out about exactly what was happening.

Nellie lost interest in my obsession not long after we started watching and disappeared. I figured he had better things to do but I realized that was not the case when Kade rounded the corner and headed in my direction.

"What's going on?" Kade kept his voice low as he moved in close, giving the appearance that we were having a romantic interlude despite the fact that he was clearly disturbed by whatever Nellie had told him.

"Nellie whipped you into a frenzy, didn't he?" I was now agitated by more than one thing. "He shouldn't have done that."

"Nellie wisely tracked me down to spread the word that you're ready to go to battle with a woman," Kade clarified. "He thought I might want to be part of that."

"You just want to see two women fight in case clothes start flying."

Kade arched an eyebrow. "I want to make sure you don't do anything to expose us. Even more important than that, I want to make sure you're safe. That's the most important thing to me."

I heaved out a sigh, frustrated. "I'm sorry. I just ... there's something wrong with that woman."

"What woman?"

I pointed out the woman in question, biting back a coarse laugh when he slipped his arm around my waist and pulled me in for a hug while he stared. He was a smooth operator when it came to things like this and his actions today actually managed to calm me.

"So this is about equal parts spying and copping a feel, right?"

Kade's lips curved against my forehead. "Something like that. What's up with that woman?"

"She can shutter."

"Meaning?"

"Meaning she's either psychic or a witch. I guess she could be some other variation, but she's definitely paranormal. What's worse is that she knows I was trying to get into her mind and failed."

"Did she say anything?"

"No, and I couldn't call her on it with so many people hanging around. She's made a big show about staying in line and refusing to leave. I couldn't very well grab her by the hair and drag her away."

"No, you couldn't do that," Kade agreed, his gaze intense as he eyed the woman. She was closer to the front of the line now, so we were staring at the back of her head. "Nellie said something about the husband, too."

"Oh, his mind is blank."

"Like he's thinking about being someplace else?"

"He's not thinking at all. There's nothing in there. He's a hollowed-out shell."

Kade worked his jaw as he gazed into my eyes. "I don't know what that means," he said finally. "How does something like that happen?"

"I have no idea." That was the truth. "But it's not normal."

"Is it temporary? I mean ... is it something you can correct?"

"I don't know. I don't know what was done to him."

"Well, we'll focus on her for the time being. I ... ." Kade broke off as an incoming text dinged on his phone. "Son of a ... !" He viciously swore under his breath.

I was instantly alert. "What's wrong?"

"Some guy is throwing punches on the midway. I have to head over there." Kade looked torn as he glanced between the woman and me. "Try not to do anything with her until I get back." He gave me a quick kiss and bolted in the direction of the games and rides.

I watched him go, flummoxed, and then followed. If the woman fled while I was helping Kade I would probably be furious with myself. I was in charge of the entire circus, though, and if a fight was breaking out I had to be there to stop it ... or at least survey the damage when it was over.

Kade was quicker, his legs longer, and he disappeared into the crowd as I struggled to keep up. He was already in the thick of things, hands between bodies, by the time I arrived. I took a moment to survey the situation. Mark stood close to the ticket booth, fury evident on his pinched face as he planted his hands on his hips and yelled at the two men to stop fighting.

Madcap Marlene, one of the midway workers, screamed like a horror movie victim as she gestured wildly. Kade had one hand wrapped in one guy's shirt and another on the second fighter's collar and he was struggling to maintain control of the situation.

I decided to help and strode directly up to him, resting my fingertips on the arm of the guy who seemed to be foaming at the mouth as he lobbed obscenities at anyone who would listen. "Calm down." It was an order, not a request.

Kade widened his eyes when the man ceased struggling and fell limp. "What did you do?"

I ignored the question and focused on the man. "What seems to be the problem?" I kept my voice calm.

"He shoved into me," the man replied, vaguely gesturing to the other man Kade had in his grip. "He forced me to spill soda all over my wife."

"That hardly seems worth a fight, does it?" I knew I sounded like a scolding teacher but I enjoyed being in charge so I didn't mince words. "Did he apologize?"

"No." The man's eyes flashed. "He didn't say a word. I would've been fine if he'd apologized."

I arched a challenging eyebrow, dubious.

"Fine. I wouldn't have been fine, but I would've gotten over it a lot quicker," the man conceded, throwing up his hands. "He didn't apologize. He just stood there like a robot and pretended he couldn't hear me."

An alarm sounded at the back of my brain. "What?"

"He stared right through me, as if it were a game," the man replied. "He pretended I wasn't saying a word, that I wasn't talking to him. The more he did it the more it drove me insane."

I flicked my eyes to the second man, taking in the lax way Kade held his shirt because he didn't put up a fight, and his glazed eyes. "Oh, crap," I muttered under my breath as I stepped closer.

Kade must have recognized my worry because he took control of the situation. He released the man I spelled to calm down and gave him a serious look. "No more fighting. If you get caught throwing punches again, you'll be removed from the premises. Do you understand me?"

The man nodded, sheepish. "I didn't mean to cause a scene."

"Well, don't do it again." Kade forced a smile as he watched the man go. "Show's over, folks. Go back to your regularly scheduled fun." He sounded jovial, but I recognized the edge in his voice.

But I couldn't focus on Kade. I had other things to deal with. I slammed my consciousness into the quiet man's mind, not caring in the least who was watching. There was no way a random person in the crowd could identify what I was doing. It wasn't difficult to slide through the man's barriers – mostly because they didn't exist – and once I had a chance to look around I understood why.

"There's nothing here."

Kade stared at my face for a long beat. "I don't understand what that means. I know you tried to explain it to me, but … it still doesn't make sense."

I sucked in a breath as I tried to explain what I saw. "He's like a droid that hasn't gotten his marching orders yet." My voice was barely a whisper. "He has an operating system, which means he can perform basic functions, but he can't think or reason for himself."

Kade frowned as he released the man. Sure enough, the blank individual didn't do anything but stare straight ahead. "Okay, this is creepy. If there's nothing in there, how did he defend himself? I saw him throw at least two punches when I was heading this way."

"Maybe he has a suggestion implanted somewhere." I got as close as I could to him and stared into his eyes. "Maybe someone is controlling him."

"But ... why?"

"I don't know. I ... ." I broke off, something occurring to me. "Oh, crap!" I started moving back through the crowd, heading for my tent.

"Where are you going?" Kade ignored the empty man and followed me. "Don't you think we should deal with this?"

"What were we doing right before you got called away to handle a fight?" I challenged. "Who were we watching? Melissa is in that tent. That woman knew I was watching her and had no intention of leaving unless something bigger happened to draw my attention."

Kade increased his pace. "This day just keeps getting weirder."

I couldn't argue with that.

THE LINE OUTSIDE my tent was gone. If I was worried before, I was downright panicking now. I barreled through the flap, absorbing the scene in an instant.

The first blank man stood to one side, not moving. His wife stood in front of the table, an evil look on her face. Melissa was also on her feet, the table serving as a buffer, and her features were ashen as she clenched her hands into fists at her side. That was a good sign; she was ready to fight.

Unfortunately for the woman who should've had the sense to run, I was in the mood to fight, too.

"And what's going on in here?"

Melissa looked to me, relief flooding her features. "There's something wrong with her ... and him."

"Yeah, I figured that out." I glared hard at the woman, throwing out a blanket of powerful magic and watching with grim fascination as it settled over her. It was a net of sorts, just like the dreamcatcher, but on a much smaller scale.

As if in slow motion, the woman slowly turned to face me. She looked slightly different, somehow older, and my stomach clenched as she sneered. "Do you think you can control me?"

"I think that you're under the mistaken assumption that you can control everyone else," I countered. "That's not going to happen on my turf."

Kade appeared behind me, his breath heavy. He didn't insert himself into the middle of things, instead opting to move to my right so he could take up position between Melissa and me. It was clear he was ready to throw himself into action should the need arise. Once comfortable with his stance, he asked the obvious question. "Why didn't she run?"

"Obviously she doesn't think we're a threat," I replied. "I find that ... interesting."

"I would use the word disturbing," Kade argued.

"What is she?" Melissa asked, her anxiety high enough that I felt it in my bones. "I can't see in her head ... and he has nothing in his head."

I briefly glanced at the unmoving man. He appeared to be lost and docile. I didn't know what to make of the phenomenon. "I don't know what she is."

"I'm a woman visiting the circus." The woman made a big show of smoothing the front of her blouse. It was an attractive ensemble, but there was something dated about it. "Why would you think I'm doing anything else?"

"We're not stupid." I saw no reason to play games. "Were you controlling the man on the midway, too? Did you force him to cause a scene to distract us?"

"I have no idea what you're referring to. I'm simply here with my husband. Who doesn't love the circus?"

I took a menacing step in her direction. The small net I threw over her remained intact, but I could feel tears appearing in the fabric. As she talked, she simultaneously broke through the magic. She was powerful.

"What are you?" I tilted my head as I watched the net continue to erode. "Are you a witch?"

"I'm not a fan of labels." The woman – or creature – made a big show of studying her fingernails. "I like to think of myself as a progressive. Although I'm also a Libra on weekends."

I was guessing she didn't mean "progressive" in a political sense. "And why did you want Melissa?"

"Who says I wanted the girl?" The woman's lips curled into a sneer. "She's not a regular in this tent, or hasn't been since you opened. Why would I possibly want her?"

She was tipping her hand, but only enough to give me a few clues that didn't make sense. "So, you've been watching us?"

"I think she's saying that she's been watching you," Kade corrected, his expression unreadable. "This is your tent."

The woman barked out a laugh. "I think you're reading the situation wrong."

"And how is that?" Kade challenged. "You were outside Poet's tent. You created a distraction to get inside and take up residence. It seems to me you're focused on Poet."

"It seems to me that you're the one focused on your little friend here." She wiggled her fingers in my direction, as if I were nothing more than a pesky child annoying the adults. "Not everything is about her. In this particular instance, for example, nothing is about her."

Something about the way she said the words set my teeth on edge. "Seriously, what are you?"

"Beyond your control."

"If that's true, why not tell me what you are? I mean ... you're not afraid of me, are you?" I was calling her chicken. That rarely works, but I had no idea what else to do. I was too leery to get close to her and I couldn't rule out the fact that she could engage her human robot in the corner and send him in our direction. He probably wouldn't put up much of a fight, but he was a distraction all the same.

"I'm not anything," she replied calmly. "I'm nothing ... and yet everything."

"I hate it when bad things talk in riddles," I groused, shaking my head. "That makes them all the more irritating."

"What do you think we should do with her?" Kade asked. "I mean ... should we take her into custody? We can lock her in one of the animal cages until we figure out what to do with her."

The woman's eyes lit with mirth. "Do you think I'll allow you to take me, boy?"

Kade shrugged. "I don't think you have much of a choice. You're our prisoner. Poet has control of you."

Ugh. I wished he hadn't said that. At the exact moment the words escaped his lips the net I had thrown shredded and the woman – whatever she was – took control of the situation and lashed out with a bolt of magic that threw me across the tent.

I landed on the ground in front of her husband, my knees aching at the jolt. He was moving before I registered what was happening, his hand wrapping around my throat and causing my eyes to bug out of my head as my oxygen supply was cut off.

"Poet!" Kade turned in my direction, which was exactly what the woman wanted. She intercepted him, planting her hands on either side of his head and causing his eyes to widen.

"Kade." His name came out as more of a gurgle than a gasp, but I fought the husband with everything I had, silently apologizing to him even though I knew he couldn't understand before forcing a burst of scorching magic into his wrists.

He didn't react to the pain. Not a blink, not a lessening of his grip, nothing. Crap!

The next bolt of magic I sent out was ten times stronger than the first. It was full of electricity and I watched with a sick feeling in the pit of my stomach as the man's eyes fluttered back in his head and he released his hold on my throat. He fell backward, hitting the ground with a loud thud. I couldn't waste time checking on him; I had other things to deal with.

With the first breath, I blinked back the fog threatening to overcome me. With the second, I swiveled toward the woman and Kade. They were locked in some sort of mental struggle, the woman's eyes bulging as she tried to do … something.

"Let me in," she growled, spittle forming at the corners of her mouth as she fought for supremacy of Kade's mind. "I want to get in there and see."

Kade didn't respond, instead remaining still. I forced myself to my feet despite the pain shooting through my body and took two long strides toward them. As I approached them, Melissa slammed a chair into the back of the woman's head. The blow didn't dissuade her, but it was enough to cause her to turn and growl.

"I'm going to eat you, little girl," she hissed. "I'll eat all of you."

I had a limited opportunity, so I embraced it. I slapped my hands on either side of her head, mimicking the position she took with Kade, and poured everything I had into her.

Her eyes widened further, which seemed impossible, and then they rolled back into her head. She was dead before she hit the ground. I wasn't far behind her, my strength flagging as I slid to the ground.

Thankfully I didn't lose consciousness. I saw stars floating through my eyes and my breath came in ragged gasps. I was alive, though, and all three of us were standing.

"Well, that was fun," Melissa said blandly. "And here I thought the circus would be boring."

21
TWENTY-ONE

We had a dead body and what appeared to be an empty-headed man to contend with. Those were the only two things going through my mind when I swiveled to shift my legs out from underneath me and sank to the ground.

"Close the flap, Melissa," I croaked as I rubbed my hands over my face and forced myself to focus. I'd expended a fair amount of energy killing the woman. It wasn't so much that it would throw me for a loop for an extended amount of time but it was enough that I was a bit shaky.

Melissa did as I asked without comment or complaint, allowing me to focus on our really big problem. Unfortunately for me, all Kade could focus on was what almost happened.

"Why did she do that?" He looked a little dazed.

"Because she was evil and crazy and thought it seemed like a good idea at the time," I replied dully, patting his arm. "We can't focus on that right now. We have to make sure no one realizes she's dead, which means we have to be proactive."

Kade stirred, flicking his eyes to the woman on the ground. "She's dead? But ... how?" He seemed surprised by the news.

"I exploded her head."

"You exploded her head?" Kade remained unmoving but incredulous. "May I ask how you did that?"

I blinked several times in rapid succession, biting back a curse so hot it would've singed his hair. He didn't understand what had happened. It wasn't his fault. Even though he seemed to fit into our group seamlessly, I often forgot that he wasn't always a part of it and still had a lot of learning to do. This was one of those instances, but I was on a timetable and I didn't know if I could spare the time to teach him.

"That woman was trying to get inside your head," Melissa supplied as she returned to us after closing the tent flap. "My guess is she was trying to either absorb whatever magic she thinks you have or trying to turn you into a mindless zombie like her husband."

Speaking of her husband .... I flicked my eyes to the corner and found the man in exactly the same spot he'd stood during the fight. He didn't so much as stir when his wife died. In fact, he showed absolutely zero emotion.

Kade was incredulous. "Is that what she was trying to do?"

"I think she was trying to absorb your magic." I was calm but firm as I replied, grabbing the woman's purse so I could root around inside. "She seemed to recognize you were special. She went for you rather than me, which means she thought she could get more out of you."

"But I can't do anything." Kade's eyes flashed with impatience. "Right now I'm nothing but a man."

"You're more than that, but we don't have time to deal with your emotional breakdown right now – and I am sorry about that – but we have to focus on the fact that we have a dead body and need to get her out of here." I tugged the driver's license from the woman's wallet. "Erica Claire. She lives in Eureka."

I left the woman's license on my table before moving to the man and pawing through his pocket for a wallet. I read out loud when I found his license. "Stanley Claire. I guess that answers the question about whether or not he was her husband."

"So, what do we do?" Melissa asked. She was surprisingly put together given what just happened. She was probably running on adrenalin. Since she was more useful than Kade at this point, though, I would take it.

"I need Nellie and Dolph," I answered without hesitation. "Go get them and explain what happened. Make sure you pull them away from guests before you say anything. They'll know what to do."

Melissa bobbed her head. "Okay. I'll be right back."

Kade waited until it was just the two of us to speak again. "They'll know what to do?" He was incredulous. "Has this happened before?"

"Has this exact scenario happened before? No. Have we had an instance where an attack left us with a dead body when the circus was full of people? Yes."

"And what's the plan?" Kade sounded stronger as he fixed me with a curious look. "How are you going to handle this?"

"It's pretty simple." I was grim but determined to get it out. "We have to get the woman to her house so it can appear she died in her bed – the medical examiner will find nothing suspicious about her death as long as it happens at home – and then we need to get her husband into the right hands so he can get some help."

"What kind of help?" Kade shifted his attention to the vacant man. "He's not in there."

"No, but we don't know if that's a permanent condition," I explained. "We don't know that when we end this – whatever this is – that he won't go back to what he was before. I have no idea what this woman was, or what kind of magic she used. I can't fix him until I have more information. Even if I get that information, I might not be able to fix him.

"We can't watch him in the meantime, though," I continued. "We need him to get the proper care he deserves. We also need to make sure we're not on the hook for this woman's death."

"Even though she totally had it coming," Kade muttered under his breath.

"Despite that," I agreed. "Our other problem is that we need to move the body when it's still daylight because the second it gets dark the ghost things are going to be back to lock us in here."

"So you think Dolph and Nellie are going to be able to move a body out when this place is crawling with people?"

I nodded without hesitation. "Don't worry about it. We've got it under control."

Kade threw up his hands and scowled. "Oh, well, if you've got it under control. Clearly I have nothing to worry about."

"You really don't."

"I wish I could have as much faith as you."

"It will be fine." I was seventy-five percent sure that was true. Mentioning the other twenty-five percent seemed like a poor idea given the circumstances. "We'll work together and everything will turn out completely fine."

"I hope you know what you're doing."

He wasn't the only one. "I know exactly what I'm doing."

Kade heaved out a resigned sigh before pulling me in for a quick hug. "Good." He briefly buried his face in the hollow of my neck. "Thank you for doing whatever it is you did to save me."

"You're welcome." I ran my hand up and down his back. I didn't say that I thought he was capable of saving himself from that situation because it felt like adding fuel to an already raging inferno. He had no idea what he was dealing with and I couldn't take time out to hold his hand until we were clear of this potential catastrophe. "It's going to be okay. I promise. As soon as Nellie is here, things will be better."

"I've never heard anyone say that about Nellie, but I guess I'll take your word for it."

I chuckled despite myself. "He's good in a crisis."

As if on cue, Nellie picked that moment to stroll into the tent. He didn't seem surprised by the scene. Rather, he seemed amused and gung-ho to be involved in a body transfer. "It's been a while since I've had to move a body during the day." He didn't sound particularly worried.

"At least six months," I agreed. "I have her address. And we need to make sure the police find her husband because he can't be on his own. Oh, there's also another blank guy wandering around the midway – at least there was ten minutes ago. You need to track him down and get him into the hands of the authorities, too."

"Got it." Nellie's smiled as he leaned down to stare at the woman's lifeless eyes. "I'll need one of those ice cream refrigerators, a leash for the dude and a slight distraction to get her loaded into one of the trucks."

"I can handle all that."

Nellie brightened considerably. "Have I ever mentioned that I love this job? It's never boring."

Kade rolled his eyes. "You have the weirdest sense of humor."

"You say that like it's a bad thing. Now ... let's get this witch in a freezer, people. She's not getting any fresher."

BY THE TIME the ghosts returned to line the dreamcatcher we had the fairgrounds empty of visitors and were back in our usual spots so we could study them. Max illuminated the entire area – mostly in an effort to pierce the fog because it was especially thick tonight – and it wasn't hard to ascertain that we were being inundated with twice as many ghosts as usual.

"Will you look at that?" Percival was agog as he took up position next to Raven. He still had a purple clown wig on and oversized shoes that irritated every inch of me. I tripped over them twice before glaring so hard he wisely moved to the other side of his girlfriend.

"Everything is handled," Nellie announced as he joined us, his face flushed with excitement. "We got the woman inside and put her on the couch. Made it look like she had an aneurysm or something.

"We searched the house, but only had a few minutes to spare," he continued. "We didn't see anything out of the ordinary. Of course, we couldn't look as thoroughly as we wanted."

"What about the husband?" Kade asked.

"We let him outside to wander the neighborhood. We dropped the other guy you told us about in the police station garage."

Kade's mouth dropped open. "You did what?"

Nellie snorted, genuinely amused. "Don't worry. We parked

around the block and kept an eye on guy number one to make sure he didn't wander into oncoming traffic. Then Dolph mentioned to one of the neighbors that he thought it was weird the guy was just standing in the yard. The neighbor called for help and we left when the police were a block away. We listened on the scanner to make sure they took him into custody. They did, by the way, and he's being transported to the nearest hospital.

"As for the second guy, we blanked the cameras in the garage – there was only one working anyway – and dropped the guy as close to the underground door as possible," he continued. "We watched him until two officers came in from patrol. They took him inside after trying to talk to him for a few minutes, so he's being taken care of, too."

"That's good." I fixed him with a sidelong look. "How was it getting back here?"

"The ghost things are around the parking lot but they seemed fine letting us in."

"I wonder how they would be letting you out."

Nellie pursed his lips. "That's exactly what I was wondering. I mean ... look around. Those things are two deep and I don't think there are any gaps in the ghost line. They clearly want to keep us inside."

Something occurred to me. "That must mean something is going on outside the line." I turned to search the small crowd for Max's face. As if sensing I was looking for him, he broke from the conversation he was holding with Kade and slowly turned in my direction. "I have an idea."

Nellie snorted. "I have a feeling this is an idea that lover boy isn't going to like."

I had a feeling he was right. "Stick close. You might have to help persuade him if things go the way I think they're going to go."

"Like he's going to listen to me."

"He probably won't listen to any of us," I conceded. "That doesn't mean he'll ultimately have a choice. Come with me."

"YOU CAN'T BE SERIOUS."

Kade was even more worked up than I'd expected when I laid my plan out for Max.

"I don't see where I have a lot of choice." I forced myself to remain calm despite his heaving chest and furious eyes. "They want us locked up tight in here tonight. There has to be a reason for it."

"And you think the reason is in Falk?" Max was hard to read at the best of times, but his expression was absolutely blank now. "How can you be sure?"

"I can't be sure." That was true. "It does make the most sense."

"It does?" Kade's eyebrows hopped as he turned shrill. "Nothing about this makes any sense. Those ... things ... are haunting us every night. They're crawling into your head. They're trying to hurt you. What's your response? To run out there and give them another shot."

He was overwrought. I couldn't blame him – this was out of his comfort zone – but I also couldn't indulge his meltdown.

"Kade, I need you to calm down." I looked down as I searched for the right words to soothe his frazzled nerves. "I get that you're freaking out about multiple things here, but we're in a bad spot. I mean ... a really bad spot.

"That woman was sent to us today on a mission," I continued. "She was supposed to mess with us, distract us, and maybe even hurt us. Either she didn't understand how strong we really were or she was woefully unprepared for her job.

"She's not the only one out there," I said. "We know there's at least one more because of the woman I saw at the library. I'll wager that we have a lot more enemies than we initially envisioned."

"So what does that mean?" Kade's voice was plaintive. "How does running into the woods in the middle of the night when we're under siege by ghosts make any sense given what you just said?"

His heart hurt. I could plainly see that ... and even feel it because we were so closely linked emotionally. I wanted to soothe him, but I couldn't. In fact, all I could do was make things worse.

"Someone hosted a bonfire at Falk the other night," I reminded him. "I think it was the people we're looking for. They conjured these

... things. I still don't know what they are, but they're not our primary concern. Whatever is happening in Falk is what we need to focus on. These ghosts have been placed here to distract us."

"You don't know that," Kade muttered.

"She's right," Max countered calmly. "We need to see what's happening in Falk. It's very obvious that the person pulling the strings wants us distracted and on our heels. We need to go on the offensive."

"And how is she supposed to get through those ghosts and get to Falk?" Kade looked smug, as if he'd somehow won the argument with a single question.

"She'll use magic and have a little help from me to blow an opening in the perimeter," Max replied. "She'll make it through."

Kade stared at his father for a long moment, something dark passing between them. When he finally found his voice, he was resigned. "Fine, but I'm going with her."

This was the part that was going to bother him most, essentially rip his heart in two. I didn't see where dragging out my inevitable response was a benefit for anyone. "You can't."

Kade balked. "You're not going alone."

"I'm not," I agreed, resolved to get through this no matter how angry he was. "Raven is going with me."

"She is?"

"Yeah, I am?" Raven made a face. "Why am I going with you?"

"Because it makes the most sense," I replied. "Naida, Nixie and Max will stay here to hold down the fort, maybe conduct a few more experiments. They'll blow a hole through the ghosts, and that will give us an opening. We should be fine after that.

"If we get in trouble out there, Naida will know," I continued. "She'll also know if it's trouble they can help with or if it's better to leave us to fend for ourselves."

"Don't say things like that," Kade hissed.

I gave myself a second before responding. "I know this is going to be hard on you. A lot has happened in a short amount of time and you're all twisted up inside. You're going to fight and insist on going with us because you're head of security."

"Ha!" Kade extended a finger in my direction. "That's right. I'm head of security. You didn't think about that, did you?"

"Um, dude, she's the one who brought it up," Nellie pointed out.

Kade's face remained immobile. "I'm going with you. I won't allow you to wander out there without backup."

"You don't have a choice, Skippy," Raven said. "You might very well have power in those masculine hands of yours – and it might be a lot of power – but you're afraid to use it. That's fine. We can walk you through it later. For now, though, we need power."

Raven wasn't the type to back down, so she barreled forward despite the unhappiness emanating from Kade. "We can't take you because you'll become a liability," she continued. "If we're protecting you we won't be able to protect ourselves. We could all die if that happens. You have to stay behind."

Kade looked to me for support. "You need me."

"I need you for a lot of things," I conceded. "But you can't come for this. We need to move fast and be able to hide if necessary. You're not ready to do that. You have to stay behind."

"But ... ."

"No." I offered up a firm headshake. "I know this is going to eat at you, but we don't have time to mess around. We need to see what they're doing in Falk. You can't come with us. That's final."

22
TWENTY-TWO

Kade remained bitter as I changed from flowing skirt to black trousers and tennis shoes. I tied my long hair into a ponytail so it wouldn't get in the way, and shrugged into a hoodie to cover my T-shirt. Raven did the same several feet away, Percival at her side, their heads bent together as they whispered between themselves. I changed by myself because Kade refused to help. I felt isolated before I was even separated from my group.

He was being petulant – I think he knew that – but that didn't change his attitude. He was furious, angry beyond words, and he struggled to let the fury go long enough to say goodbye.

That grated more than I wanted to admit.

"Don't look behind you," Max instructed, moving in front of me. "That will be your instinct, to look over your shoulder to see if anything is giving chase. What happens if you do that?"

Max had started training me on certain escape techniques when I was a teenager and he found me trying to pick his pocket in Detroit. Instead of busting me, turning me over to the police, he saw something he liked and offered me a job. The first few weeks after that were difficult, mostly because I wasn't used to following rules, but eventually I came to see Max as my savior rather than jailer. I'd had a better life ever since.

"I'll trip because I'm not watching where I'm going," I answered perfunctorily. I'd seen enough horror movies to know that was true, so he didn't need to drill it into my head. "I know not to look behind me." I zipped my hoodie as high as it would go, close to my chin. "We'll be okay. We know what we're doing."

"I know that." Max squeezed my shoulders and glanced to his left, to where my eyes naturally gravitated. Kade stood staring at the taunting ghosts and gripping his hands into fists at his sides. He didn't so much as glance at me, which caused my heart to flutter. "I'll take care of him." Max lowered his voice to barely a whisper. "You take care of you. If something happens to you out there, he really will never get over it. You need to make sure that doesn't happen."

I nodded and forced a smile. "I never thought I'd be one of those women who has to temper her actions for a man."

Max chuckled, low and throaty. "That's not what you're doing. He's upset. He doesn't understand. If he could go with you it would be a way of keeping some control. That's not possible – and he truly understands that, whether he'll admit it or not – so he feels as if he can't offer you anything. That's not easy for a man like him."

"And what kind of man is he?"

"An alpha-hole," Luke answered automatically as he moved to my side, his eyes lighting with mirth as I scowled. "What? He's totally an alpha-hole."

"He is not," I shot back, taking a moment to make sure the laces on my sneakers were tied tightly.

Max furrowed his brow. "What's an alpha-hole?"

"It's nothing," I automatically answered.

"It's a book and movie thing," Luke countered. "It's an alpha male – think Arnold Schwarzenegger or Sylvester Stallone in all their movies – who thinks he needs to tell a woman what to do to protect herself.

"In this case, Poet is the one with the knowledge and Kade is the one pouting because he can't go with her," he continued. "That makes him an alpha-hole."

"He's not an alpha-hole," I countered. "He's just ... struggling. He doesn't want me to be off on my own."

"I don't want it either," Luke admitted. "I'm worried. Maybe I should go with you."

"You might slow us down, too," I argued. "You can't shield yourself with magic and you can't physically fight these ghosts. You'll probably be a distraction."

Luke made a face. "That's my payback for calling your boyfriend an alpha-hole, isn't it?"

"It's just the beginning of my payback." I looked to Raven and found her watching me with an expectant gaze. "Are you ready?"

She nodded. "We should go now."

"We're ready to blow a hole in the ghosts," Naida volunteered. "As soon as you're ready, we'll scatter them. That should give you an opening. Use it to run as fast and as far as you can. I don't know if they'll follow you when they regroup, but if they do you'll be on your own."

"We know." Raven's expression twisted with impatience. "Let's get it over with. The sooner we leave, the sooner we come back."

"Yeah." I nodded. "Let's do this. I ... ." I didn't get a chance to finish what I was saying because Kade slid in front of me, grabbed the front of my hoodie and pressed a sloppy kiss to my mouth.

"Oh, I knew he couldn't let her go without making up," Luke teased. "He's kind of cute when he gets handsy, isn't he?"

"That's the exact opposite of what I was thinking," Max said dryly. "I was wondering if anyone had a blindfold handy."

Kade ignored the conversation and pulled back far enough to stare into my eyes. "Please be careful."

I wrapped my fingers around his wrist, giving it a squeeze as I nodded. "It's going to be okay. We know what we're doing. We've been taking care of ourselves for years. This is no different."

"It's different to me." He smoothed the back of my hair and pressed another kiss to my forehead. "We're going to fight about this when you get back because ... well, I'm probably going to need to fight about something. Don't take it personally."

I smirked. "Sounds like a plan."

"Don't let him kid you," Luke interjected, leaning closer to me and winking. "He's going to fawn all over you when you get back. He'll forget all about fighting. Luke knows all and sees all."

"I hate to admit it, but he's probably right." Kade gave me one last kiss, this one brief. "Go. Be careful. I'll be really angry if you don't come back."

I saluted. "Duly noted."

Raven and I prepared ourselves to run while Max and Naida moved into position on either side of us. Naida looked excited for whatever she was about to do. Max looked grim and determined. Together they made quite the picture, and I was glad they would be the ones protecting those I loved most while I was gone.

"When I tell you to run, just do it," Max instructed, raising his hands. "Don't wait. Just run."

"I know." I rubbed my sweaty palms over my thighs. My heart pounded crazily. "We're ready."

"Okay." Max threw his hands in the air and whispered something I couldn't quite make out. I felt the magic gathering on the wind – a wind Naida created – and then he threw the power he was collecting at the ghosts. "Now!"

I didn't have to be told twice. I bolted over the dreamcatcher, slipping through the opening Max created without a backward glance. I felt Raven next to me even though I didn't look to her for confirmation that she followed. I focused forward, as I was supposed to.

Out of the corner of my eye I saw the ghostly features twisting in agony as whatever spell Max flung at them took control and froze them in place. It was a curious sight to behold, but one I couldn't fixate on.

Instead I focused on running. I was into the trees and heading straight for the trail when I finally allowed the tight grip of panic to relax around my heart. The woods were dark and desolate, devoid of ghosts … or specters … or whatever they were. We were free and on our way to Falk.

Now the truly hard part would begin.

RAVEN WENT WITH the group that returned to Falk after our first visit – the time when I took a detour to the library, which turned out to be horrific in its own way – so she knew exactly where she was going. She was a natural runner. I struggled to keep up with her.

We ran full tilt until we hit the outskirts of Falk. By tacit agreement, we didn't light the path in front of us, instead relying on instinct to make sure we didn't trip. In some ways it was better because we honed our innate skills and relied on inner determination rather than outer influences. In others it was more nerve-wracking because one wrong step could put us both at risk.

Still, despite the heightened anxiety, we arrived at Falk unscathed.

"No one followed us." Raven stopped at the edge of town to catch her breath. The only reason I recognized our location was because I'd seen it during our tour. I knew exactly where I was – close to that foundation that intrigued Luke enough to point it out – and I glanced over my shoulder to make sure we were alone.

"The ghosts either didn't notice we left or chose to stay behind to watch over everyone else," I noted, running the back of my hand across my forehead. "I didn't sense them in the woods."

"I've yet to sense them, which is how I know they're not real," Raven supplied. "They're not ghosts. I don't even think they're shades."

"So ... what are they?"

"That's the question of the evening." Raven flicked her gaze to the pathway that led to the heart of Falk and pointed toward a glimmering light to the west. "You see that? That's the other question of the evening. Why are people having a bonfire in a ghost town in the middle of the night?"

I narrowed my eyes as I stared. She was right. There was clearly a bonfire roaring. While I couldn't see any movement around the fire that would suggest someone was tending it, I recognized right away that we were probably not alone. "That can't be a coincidence."

"No," Raven agreed. "Someone is out here. Odds are, whoever it is, they're intent on keeping us at the circus. That's what the poltergeist and pony show is with the ghosts. They're not real."

"Any idea how they're creating them?"

"No, but I plan to find out. If it's something I can master it could be a useful trick for the House of Mirrors. Even more than that, it could serve as a distraction for us during a battle."

I stilled. "Wait ... you want to steal the ability, not stop it?"

"Oh, I want to stop them from using it on us," Raven replied without hesitation. "That doesn't mean I don't want to test it on someone else."

"You're a rare and fascinating creature."

"I tell myself that every single day."

Raven and I fell into step together as we picked our way along the path. We didn't speak of it – it wasn't necessary, after all – but we wove a camouflage web around us as we walked. It would hide our movements from whoever had started the fire, and it would also mask our scents. There was nothing we could do to quiet our feet, though, so we purposely picked a slow pace to make as little noise as possible.

The closer we got to the fire, the more apparent it became that we weren't alone. Voices filtered through the wind as we closed the distance, although making out words was exceedingly difficult.

On a whim, I grabbed Raven's arm and dragged her off the trail. We were far more likely to be noticed out in the open. It took longer than it should have to make it to a spot where we could crouch low and hide while observing what was going on. However, it was worth the effort because we had a clear view ... and what a sight it was to behold.

"Wow!" Raven kept her voice low as she stared at the women dancing around the fire. They almost looked like ghosts themselves thanks to their filmy dresses and the way their shadows danced against the night sky. "It's like a scene from *Outlander*."

It took me a moment to get what she was referring to. Now that she mentioned it, though, it did look a lot like the pagan ritual at the beginning of *Outlander*, the one that drew Claire back to the stones that she would eventually pass through. "What do you think they're doing?" It was a struggle to keep my voice low, but thanks to the singing and dancing around the fire, the odds of anyone hearing us unless they were directly on top of us weren't great.

"They're clearly casting a spell." Raven tilted her head to the side and stared at the women. "I think most of them are human."

"How can you be sure?"

Raven shrugged. "I can't. It's just ... I usually get a feeling when another paranormal being is around. Even if I can't identify what they are or the type of magic they wield, I can recognize them. I don't sense that here. I ... it's weird."

I tugged on my bottom lip as I considered her words. "I don't sense anything either, but I'm not as strong as you are in that department."

"Sometimes you're stronger depending on the situation. This situation is ... otherwordly."

That was an interesting word choice. "Do you think they're from another plane of existence?"

"I ... um ... no." Raven finally shook her head. "They're normal women. Sure, some of them might have a few magical abilities – maybe all of them do, for all I know – but they're simply women. I have no doubt about that."

My eyes fell on a familiar face on the far side of the circle and I extended a finger. "Remy Langstrom."

Raven knit her eyebrows. "The woman from the library?"

"Yeah."

"Hmm." Whatever Raven was thinking she kept to herself as she watched the young woman (who I knew had an old face and soul) cavort with the others around the fire. "Well, I think we knew she was involved. You can't be overly surprised that she's here."

"No, but ... she's creepy. She obviously has magic. I told you what she did with her appearance."

"That could be a simple glamour," Raven countered. "You use them all the time. In fact, if I remember correctly, you made yourself look like a clown once. The image still haunts Kade from time to time."

Of course she had to bring that up. "He's mostly over it."

"I don't know why he hates clowns so much. I think they're kind of fun."

She was dating one that boasted a fake British accent, so that didn't surprise me. "You know why he hates them. It's the same reason we all hate the clowns, including you. There's something unnatural about a grown man who wants to dress like that."

"I don't think Percival is unnatural."

I decided to split the difference because now wasn't the time to get into a fight. "I think Percival is the lone exception."

Raven looked understandably dubious, but she kept her opinion to herself as she focused on the dancers. "Do you notice there are no men present?"

Subconsciously I'd noticed, but I hadn't given it any thought. "That sort of makes sense," I said. "Pagan priestesses wielded most of the magic. Historically, I mean."

"Yeah, but ... it's the middle of the night." Raven rocked back on her haunches as she concentrated on the dancing. "Don't these women have husbands ... or boyfriends ... or even fathers? That one over there looks about sixteen. How can nobody be missing her?"

"Maybe her mother is here."

"I guess that's possible." Raven didn't look convinced. "Why are no men involved, though? Even the pagan practices of old involved men."

I pictured Stanley and the glazed expression on his face. "Maybe they're doing something to the men."

"Like what?"

"Like sucking out their brains to use for ... I have no idea what. Maybe they're using the essence of the men in some sort of ritual."

"I guess I could buy that, but how has no one noticed these zombified men walking around?"

"Perhaps you have to be looking for them to see them." My eyes drifted to Remy, who seemed to be enjoying her younger form as she hopped from one foot to the other. Her dress was ethereal, seemingly from a costume shop, but it flowed around the fire, creating a beautiful tableau that made the eye dance. "It's interesting."

"I don't know what to make of it," Raven admitted after a beat. "I don't know what they're trying to accomplish with the dance, and I have no idea what sort of ritual this is. I also think there are too many of them to risk asking questions and drawing attention to ourselves."

I wanted to argue the point, but I knew she was right. "Well ... I guess we'll have to do more research."

"I guess. This isn't the answer I was hoping for."

We couldn't risk staying longer. They would discover us if we didn't make our retreat. I opened my mouth to tell Raven just that when an unearthly howl filled the air.

The dancers didn't respond other than to throw their heads back and sing louder. It was a language I didn't recognize, a melody that didn't trigger a memory. The creature we couldn't see howled again, as if urging them forward.

I slowly turned my eyes to Raven. "Are you thinking what I'm thinking?"

She nodded without hesitation. "It's a wendigo."

"It's a wendigo that has some tie to these women," I corrected.

"Yeah, like a pet or something." Raven wrinkled her nose. "We have to get out of here. We can't risk them seeing us."

"We need to be careful of the wendigo. Obviously it's active."

"They're not afraid of it."

"No, but we're not them."

Raven nodded in understanding. "Yeah. Let's get out of here. I'm not sure how much more we can learn tonight."

TWENTY-THREE

I sensed a presence behind us as we headed back to the circus. It wasn't that I saw someone so much as I felt a mind brushing against mine as we hit the trail heading back. I did the one thing I wasn't supposed to do and looked over my shoulder, widening my eyes when I caught sight of a young woman – she had to be in her mid-twenties at the most – following us. Thanks to the large moon's illumination (and her cream-colored dress), I had no problem picking her out of the gloom.

Raven grabbed my arm when I stumbled, keeping me on my feet. "Look ahead," she barked, obviously annoyed. "Don't look back."

"We're being followed," I gritted out, cursing myself for making such a rookie mistake. Thankfully I didn't tumble head over heels and incur a head injury, because that would've left us in a world of trouble. "It's one of the dancing women."

"I know." Raven remained facing forward. "I can sense her. She's ... curious. I guess that's the best word. I don't sense danger from her, but I don't think it's wise to stop."

"What if she has information to share?"

"And what if she's a distraction to stop us from getting back to the circus?" Raven challenged. "Do you want to take that risk?"

Part of me did. "If we can get answers …."

"And what if we get attacked instead?" Raven wasn't in the mood to capitulate. "What if we get overwhelmed and our friends have to come out here to fight for us? Do you think Kade will stay behind in that scenario? Do you want him in danger?"

I shrank back in the face of her fury. "No. It's just … she's freaking following us. There has to be a reason."

"And we'll figure out that reason when we get back to a position of power." Raven was firm. "Now, come on. Pick up your feet and stop looking over your shoulder. If you trip again, I'm leaving you."

Sadly, I was fairly certain she was telling the truth, so I focused on the path and forced thoughts of the trailing woman out of my head.

It didn't take long to get where we were going. I saw the ghosts illuminated on the other side of the dreamcatcher when we closed the distance. They seemed to have recovered from whatever magic Naida and Max dosed them with, and they completely covered the boundary.

"Crap!" Raven made a face as she pulled up short and rested her hands on her knees. "We're going to need help getting back in there."

I took the opportunity to glance over my shoulder and found the young woman still following, although she slowed her pace when we stopped to watch us with wary eyes. I opened my mouth to call out to her, perhaps invite her to join us, but Raven slapped her hand over my mouth before I could say something stupid.

"Don't even think about it." Her irritation was off the charts. I could feel it sparking in her fingertips. "If you yell to her the ghosts will hear."

I slapped her hand away and worked my jaw, tamping down my own frustration as I fought to maintain my cool. "We need to contact Max and tell him we're ready to return."

"I'm on it." Raven briefly pressed her eyes shut. I had no idea what message she sent, but she was quiet for only a few seconds before she focused on me again. "He says we'll know when it's time to run."

That was interesting. "I wonder what he has up his sleeve."

"I don't know, but it better be good." Raven turned back to look at the woman. She was barely moving now, standing in the tall grass and openly staring. "Do you have something you want to say?" She kept her voice low, but it carried a bit through the eerie fog. "Is there a reason you're following us?"

The woman looked around, her eyes briefly falling on the ghosts before turning back to us. "You watched the ritual." Her voice was deep, throaty. She didn't sound as young as she looked. "How did you get out?"

"That doesn't matter," Raven replied, looking to the sky when a magical barrage of sparks arced over us. "I think that's our sign."

"Yeah." I cast one more look at the woman before turning and facing the melee in front of us. "Ready?"

"Go now." Raven gave me a shove and we both started running. The ghosts remained where they were until right before we reached them, and then something – probably Max – shoved them to the side and created a path.

The ghosts screamed their disapproval as they flopped away from us, but we were already on the other side of the dreamcatcher before they regrouped enough to close the opening.

Kade was on me before I caught my breath, pulling me in for a tight hug. "Are you okay?"

It was hard to regain my breath but I nodded. "I'm fine."

"What happened?" Nellie asked, appearing at my elbow. "Did you see anything good?"

"We saw ... something."

Kade smoothed my hair, some of which had come out of the rubber band, and stared into my eyes. "That was the longest hour of my life. You're sure you're okay?"

I nodded to appease him. "We didn't get close to anything dangerous. In fact ... ." I remembered the woman and jerked my eyes to the dreamcatcher line. She was still there, her hair blowing in the breeze as she stood behind several ghosts and stared.

"Who is that?" Luke asked, instantly alert.

"I don't know, but she's hot." Seth, our resident tiger shifter, had apparently joined the group during my excursion with Raven and was clearly enamored with our new visitor. "Quick, someone invite her over the line. I want to see her up close and personal."

"We're not doing that," Kade fired back. "You don't know anything about her. In fact, she could be evil and deadly for all you know."

"She's hot." Seth refused to back down. "It's easy for you to draw a line in the sand and say we're not going to invite her over, but you already have a woman. You don't understand what true loneliness feels like."

Seth looked earnest, but I knew him well enough to roll my eyes. "Stop being a pain, Seth," I ordered, causing his lips to twist into a grin. "Kade is right. We don't know anything about her ... other than the fact that she followed us from Falk."

"Was she the only one there?" Max asked, moving closer to me so he could give me a long once-over. "No injuries to heal?"

I shook my head. "I almost tripped when I realized she was following us, but held it together."

"You held it together?" Raven arched a challenging eyebrow. "Where was I when this happened? Wait, was this when you looked over your shoulder and almost fell on your face, but I saved you from a fate worse than death?"

I scowled. "Fine. Raven caught me." I glared at her. "You didn't have to bring it up. I felt stupid enough without you ratting me out."

"That's why I'm here," Raven sneered before flicking her eyes back to the woman. "I don't understand why she followed us. More than that, I don't understand why she didn't raise the alarm when she realized we were watching their ritual."

I didn't understand that either. "I guess we could ask her." I moved closer to the dreamcatcher boundary and focused on the woman. "Who are you?"

She shrugged. "Does it matter?"

"It might," I replied. "Do you need help? I mean ... are you trying to get away from them? If you do need help, we might be able to offer some."

"As long as you're not eating people or offering human sacrifices," Luke called out.

"You can't help me." The woman was matter of fact. "I've been here since the beginning of time. It's far too late to help me."

I squinted as she moved a bit closer, the illumination Max tossed over the area so we could see the ghosts allowing me a better look at her face. When I did, things clicked into place and I gasped.

"What is it?" Kade wrapped his arm around my waist. "Do you feel sick? Do you need to lie down? I'll take you back to the trailer."

"Now is not the time for sex," Luke chided. "We have a crisis on our hands."

I thought Kade might lunge for him, actually try to wrap his hands around my best friend's neck, but he was too worried about keeping me on my feet. That was unnecessary.

"I'm not going to fall down," I said, finding my voice. "I'm fine."

"Then what happened?" Kade pressed. "Why did you make that noise?"

"Because ... Luke, what was the name on that driver's license we found in the woods? The one next to the blood?"

"Oh, that?" Luke furrowed his brow as he concentrated. "Amanda Stevens. Twenty-four. Blonde. Blue eyes. License says she weighs a hundred and ten pounds, so she's probably actually ten to fifteen pounds heavier than that."

I stared pointedly at the woman. "Really."

Luke followed my gaze, realization dawning. "Oh, geez. That's her!"

"That's who?" Raven asked, pulling away from Percival long enough to infiltrate our conversation. "What are you talking about?"

"The license we found in the woods next to the blood," I answered. "It belonged to Amanda Stevens. I'm pretty sure this is Amanda Stevens."

"What?" Raven couldn't hide her surprise. "She just said she's been here a long time. That blood was fresh days ago."

"We don't know the blood belonged to her," Max reminded us. "We only know that her license was there, and blood was on the ground." He tilted his head as he moved closer to the dreamcatcher, waving his hand imperiously to make several of the ghosts move to the side so he could have a better view. "What are you doing here, young lady?" He adopted his stern voice, so I knew he meant business. But Amanda didn't so much as lower her shoulders as she regarded him.

"This is my home," Amanda said breezily. "You're the outsiders here."

"We're visitors," Max corrected carefully. "We're not trying to infiltrate your group or destroy your home. We're merely trying to understand what's going on here."

"Perhaps you're limited in what you can understand."

"And perhaps you're not as dedicated to the cause as you would like us to think," Max shot back. "There's a reason you fled whatever was going on in Falk this evening. What was that again?"

"A pagan dancing ritual," Raven replied without hesitation. "They had a fire going. There had to be at least thirty of them of all ages – it wasn't just young women – dancing in dresses. They sang."

"And then a wendigo howled again," I added. "They reacted to the wendigo howling, as if they were doing something in tandem."

"Really?" Max was intrigued. "What are your ties to the wendigo, Amanda? Do you serve it?"

I'd never heard of anyone serving a wendigo, but Max was smarter than me, so I thought there was a decent chance he might know better.

"We serve the night." Amanda was almost blasé as she regarded our fearless leader. "We serve the night and the night will swallow you whole."

"Is that what happened to you?" I asked. "Did the night swallow you?"

"I've always been part of the night."

Hmm. That was interesting. I filed her response away to ponder later and focused on our more immediate issues. "Why are you working with a wendigo? I don't know what's going on with you guys, but it's clear you're connected to the monster that's roaming around out there."

"I think they're also connected to the zombie men who keep popping up," Raven added. "It's all women out there dancing. I get that pagan rituals were often performed by women, but it doesn't make much sense for there to be absolutely no men."

"That's a good point." Max nodded, something unsaid passing through his eyes before he obviously decided to change course. "What do you guys hope to accomplish with this little game that you're playing? I mean ... do you think you can just lock us away and carry on as if nothing is happening?"

"You don't understand." Amanda was clearly losing interest in the conversation because she kept turning to look back in the direction of Falk, as if something was calling her away from us. "You are not of the night. You can't understand this."

"Do you want us to help you?" I called out as she turned. "Is there something we can do to help you?"

"There is no helping me." The woman's voice grew faint as she disappeared into the fog. "Stay out of the night. The full moon is tomorrow. That's when we will be at our strongest."

I was gobsmacked by the warning, but not enough to give chase for more information. Instinctively I knew she was already gone.

"Oh, that's too bad," Seth lamented, his expression hangdog. "I thought she might stay so we could have a party."

"You heard her," Luke challenged. "She's of the night. You can't handle something that cliché-ridden and annoying. It's out of your wheelhouse."

Seth snorted. "Good point. Still, she was hot."

"She was also lost," I added, causing Seth to turn sheepish. "We need to find out what happened to her. There's always a chance we can reverse it."

Max nodded as he stroked his chin. "Yes. I want to make a few calls. I might have an idea or two about this, but I want to be sure before I set everyone off."

I wanted to press him but knew it would be wasted effort. "We should all go to bed. We'll regroup in the morning and compare notes."

"Sounds like a plan."

KADE WAS LARGELY SILENT for the walk back to our trailer. Once we were inside, safely locked away, he remained quiet as he brushed his teeth and stripped down to his boxer shorts. I was surprised when he climbed into bed next to me and didn't immediately snuggle close.

Apparently he was still angry.

I cleared my throat, anxious to get the argument behind us so I could sleep. There was no imminent rest for me if he refused to make nice. "I know you're upset," I started. "I'm sorry about what happened – mostly because I know it wasn't easy for you – but that was the only way we could get things done."

Kade stared at the ceiling as he laced his fingers and rested them on his flat abdomen. "And what are you sorry about?"

"Upsetting you."

"Not risking your life?"

Oh, geez. He really was turning this into a thing. "I didn't see where we had a choice."

"I know you didn't."

"So, you're angry?" I was beyond frustrated ... and exhausted.

"I told you from the start that I was going to be angry when you got back."

"I know, but ... I thought you'd get over it."

"Because you're so cute?"

"Because fear of what might happen is worse than recognizing that there was real danger we managed to avoid."

"Ah."

Crudsticks. I hated the detached tone of his voice. "I'm sorry. Can't you just let it go?" I rolled and rested my chin on his shoulder. "I didn't want to leave you behind, but I wasn't sure what to expect out there. It's not a crime to want to keep the person you care about safe."

"It's not," Kade agreed. "That's what I wanted to do for you."

"Oh, well ... ."

"But you wouldn't allow me to do it."

"I couldn't," I clarified. "There's a difference. We had to opt for the best plan of attack we had available at the time. And, look, everything worked out. I'm perfectly safe. Heck, I'm safe and we're in bed together. I think you should forgive me on principle."

Kade's eyes glinted under the limited light allotted by the nearly-full moon through the unshaded window. He didn't look at the ghosts dancing outside, even though I was certain one was the guy in the hat who so tormented him. "I should forgive you, huh? No payback or sexual favors, just forgiveness and nothing more."

It took a moment, but I realized relatively quickly that he was messing with me. "Oh, you suck." I poked his side. "I thought you were really upset."

Kade slid his arm under my waist and pulled me against him before I could escape. "I was upset while you were gone," he said. "I kept thinking about all the terrible things that could've happened to you, things I couldn't stop or fight. I didn't like the feeling."

I felt helpless. "That's what we do. We fight monsters."

"I know. You're unbelievably brave. That doesn't mean I can simply turn off the fear."

I'd lost track of the conversation. "Does that mean you're going to stay angry all night? I really need to get some sleep and I can't if you're pretending to be angry at me."

"Who said I was pretending?"

"Kade."

"Poet." Kade mimicked my voice and kissed my forehead. "We're not arguing. I simply need to wind down. That probably won't happen until halfway through the night, so you'll have to make do with half a makeup."

"Fine."

"We'll make up the right way in the morning," he added, causing me to smile.

"Fine." I kissed his cheek as I got comfortable. "This is starting to come together. Whatever big thing they're planning, it's going to happen tomorrow. That's why Amanda warned me about the full moon."

"Then we'll make sure we have everything together to fight it tomorrow." Kade tightened his arm around my back. "We'll work it all out. I have faith."

That made one of us. I had no idea how to untangle the mess we found ourselves mired in. It was too convoluted, and we were running out of time.

24
TWENTY-FOUR

Kade definitely wanted to officially make up in the morning, so we were late to breakfast. Preparations were well underway when we arrived, and I didn't miss the look of derision on Raven's face when she caught sight of me.

"How did it go with lover boy last night?" she asked when I grabbed a bowl and container of eggs so I could begin scrambling them.

"He's fine." He was. After a good night's sleep he was much better and seemingly more settled. I knew he wouldn't be completely back to his normal self until we left this place in the rearview mirror. It was more than the prospect of him manifesting magic – although that clearly bothered him – it was also the worry of the unknown.

Everything we'd faced before had been something that we either already knew how to fight or could research. This was entirely new.

"He's fine?" Raven arched a dubious eyebrow. "He seemed upset last night."

"He was upset because he couldn't go with us." Something occurred to me. "Speaking of that, how do you handle things with Percival when stuff like this pops up? Does he get worked up because you run off without him?"

"Percival is a coward."

I waited for her to expound. When she didn't, I was even more confused. "But ... are you saying that he would let you die to save himself?"

"I'm saying that he cares about appearances more than bravery. You saw him the first night we got here, right?"

I nodded.

"Percival volunteered to hang around the fire with Nellie, Dolph and Luke in case something appeared out of the fog," Raven said. "He didn't do that to be brave. He knew those guys didn't want him hanging around, but he thought people would assume he's brave simply for offering."

"But what would he have done if they said yes?"

"He would've stayed with them, although he wouldn't have been happy."

"What would he have done if something attacked?"

"Probably screamed like a woman and pissed himself."

I bit the inside of my cheek to keep from laughing at her matter-of-fact response. "Okay, I can actually see that. I guess my next question is, doesn't it bother you that he's not brave? I mean, especially here. Cowards don't last long in this company."

"I don't know that I believe that," Raven hedged. "As for bravery, I'm not sure it's necessary. I've been around a long time – centuries – and I've seen all kinds of men. I don't necessarily need a brave one. I think I'm beyond that."

"You went after Kade when he first arrived," I pointed out. "It was clear he was brave from the start. You only backed off because we got together."

"I didn't back off because you got together," Raven countered. "I backed off because it became clear that he only had eyes for you. If I thought there was a chance to drive a wedge between you, I would still be in it."

She was a walking riddle sometimes. Whenever I thought I understood what she was, how she responded to life, I always got knocked back a step or two because Raven defied categorization. "But I thought you really liked Percival," I said. "You told me that yourself a few weeks ago."

"I do like him."

"But ... ." I was confused.

"You need to put things in order to be able to live with them," Raven supplied. "Each life item has a special box. You have a box for Kade ... and one for Luke ... and another for Max. Sometimes those boxes seep into each other, but you're happiest when you can deal with one box at a time.

"I don't look at life the same way," she continued. "I don't need separate boxes. Everything is an experience that can be enjoyed on its own or with others. I don't even need good experiences. I simply enjoy the adventure."

It was an interesting point of view. It made me uneasy just thinking about it, however. "I think I'll stick to my boxes. Chaos lies your way. I'm never comfortable with chaos."

Raven chuckled. "I think you're best sticking with your way, too. The thing is, Kade and Percival aren't the same types of men, so my approach to Percival is different from your approach to Kade.

"You and Kade are suited for each other, even though things sometimes get uncomfortable," she continued. "You're both worriers. You're both brave. Percival and I are something else. We don't operate on the same wavelength as the two of you."

Part of me thought that was an insult but I couldn't quite figure out how. "Well, as long as it's working for you."

"It is."

"Well, good."

"The question is, will this work out over the long haul for you?" Raven queried. "When Kade manifests – and mark my words, it'll happen – he'll hop from one box to another. You must be ready for that."

I was already prepared for that occurrence. "He'll be okay when that happens. He's strong."

"I agree."

"It's harder waiting for it," I added. "Once it becomes a reality he can look forward instead of in every direction to see where the attack will come from. He's waiting to trip. He won't."

"That's a healthy attitude. But it still won't be all roses and kisses when it does happen," Raven pointed out. "There will be an adjustment period."

"I'm fine with that. I'm pretty attached to him."

"Oh, really? I never noticed," she drawled. "I can't believe you've hidden it so well."

"Is that a dig?"

"Yes."

"Well, okay then."

MAX APPEARED BEFORE THE breakfast dishes were cleared. He carried a notebook and folder. He looked as though he hadn't slept much. I didn't know what to make of that – he was almost always calm and together, after all – but he didn't give me a chance to ask him how he was. He was all business as he grabbed a mug of coffee and settled at the end of the table.

"I think I know at least some of what is going on."

No one reacted with shock. There were no audible gasps or applause. Instead, several sets of eyes settled on Max and waited for him to explain.

"First, we're going to be attacked tonight." There was no easing us into the bad news. He preferred ripping off the bandage and diving right in. "It's a full moon. In addition to that, it's a blood moon. In addition to that, it's a full thunder moon."

"We only have one moon," Kade argued. "How can one moon be so many things?"

"It's simply something that happens." Max rubbed the back of his neck and sipped more coffee before continuing. "A full thunder moon is generally one of the lesser moons. We don't spend a lot of time worrying about it because it garnered its name due to the time of the year. It's summer. It storms more in summer, hence the name.

"This year the full thunder moon happens to coincide with a blood moon," he continued. "It's also a super moon, if you can believe that."

"I'm completely lost," Kade admitted.

"A blood moon happens when there are four lunar eclipses in a row," I explained. "Each month there's a different name for the full moon. We're entering the full thunder moon. That's generally nothing to worry about."

"A blood moon is generally nothing to worry about either," Raven offered. "It's simply an odd occurrence."

"The problem is that all of these moons are happening simultaneously," Max explained. "What do you get when a blood moon, super moon and full thunder moon coincide?"

"Herpes?" Nellie asked innocently, earning multiple groans from around the table.

Max was not even mildly amused at the lame joke. "I haven't slept yet, Nelson. I would tread lightly if I were you."

Nellie was appropriately abashed. "Sorry. It's not herpes. Please continue."

"It's a lunar event," Max volunteered. "That means a variety of things, including the fact that our shifters will be stronger – and wilder – while our magic is harder to control."

"That should mean their magic is harder to control, too, right?" Kade asked.

Kade was always one to look on the bright side. I couldn't help but smile at him. "In theory, yes." I patted his knee under the table. "The thing is, Amanda Stevens warned us last night. She warned us about the full moon."

"You're assuming she was warning us," Nixie argued. "What if she was actually trying to intimidate us?"

"Why would she do that?" I was honestly curious. "She seemed more intrigued than threatening. I think she wanted us to know something was coming, perhaps to save us from whatever fate befell her."

"We still have no idea what her deal is," Luke pointed out. "I don't spend a lot of time with neurotic chicks, but that one seemed freakier than usual."

"She was hot, though," Seth interjected.

"So was the chick in *Basic Instinct,* and we all know how that ended," Dolph pointed out. "You said you thought you knew what was going on, Max. The moon can't be the whole story."

"The moon has very little effect on what is happening," Max said. "I only pointed out the moon because it's going to make things extremely hard for us this evening. That means we need to come up with an appropriate story to close the circus before dark."

I was stunned. I couldn't remember Max ever closing the circus early, no matter the danger. "Are you serious? We're closing at dusk?"

"We have no choice." Max was firm. "They're coming for us tonight. They won't be alone."

"Okay, back the truck up." Kade held up his hand to garner attention. "I think you should tell us what we're up against here. And then, as a group, we'll decide the best way to plan around the attack."

"Fine. I called a friend in Europe." Max shuffled through his portfolio. "I asked if he'd ever heard of a wendigo working with humans. It turns out that's not nearly as rare as I thought. It was common in the old world, an occurrence that most believed didn't hop the pond to become part of paranormal mystique here. It still happens overseas all the time."

"But what do they hope to accomplish?" Naida asked. She was clearly intrigued, but wanted to get the whole story before reacting. "How do they even train a wendigo?"

"They didn't train it." Max tapped the top sheet in the file. "This is some information my friend had tucked away. It's a history of Falk."

"What?" I craned my neck to read the sheet, ultimately reaching in front of Kade to snag it. "Why would they need a history of Falk in Europe?"

"Because something terrible happened here," Max replied without hesitation. "You were right about what you saw, Poet. That woman – I think you said her name was Gillian Dodd, right? Well, she's in this file."

"Something tells me you're about to tell a terrible story," Nixie said.

"I am." Max sucked in a calming breath. "I'm going to keep it short because we don't have much time and there's a mountain of planning to do. Falk did well for a number of years. I don't want to say that it thrived because survival was always hard in those times. But it did pretty well for itself and the people living there. The residents thought the entire town was somehow blessed.

"Then came a bad year," he continued. "The gardens struggled. The groves didn't yield as much fruit. The road between Falk and Eureka became muddy and risky to traverse. That was all before the mill blade warped."

"Are you saying the blade warped overnight?" I asked.

"That's the story, but who knows how much of that is fact," Max replied. "The thing is, it could've been warping for years and the workers noticed only when they could no longer use it. The residents freaked out when it happened, thinking they'd fallen under an evil omen."

"And that's where Gillian Dodd comes into play," I mused. "They thought she was a witch."

"They did," Max confirmed. "They thought she was a witch, but rather than burn her at the stake they decided to cleanse her. I think it's fair to say that the means they chose are why we find ourselves in this predicament today."

I was practically salivating. "What?"

"They whipped her. They starved her. They sexually assaulted her. This was all to cleanse her of the demon, mind you."

My stomach tilted. "What else did they do?"

"When she was close to death, to prolong her life, they fed her human flesh. They told her it was one of her victims, a small child who'd starved because of the failing crops."

Things slipped into place. "Gillian Dodd is the wendigo."

"Ding, ding, ding. We have a winner." Max shot me a fond smile. "You always were quick on the uptake."

"Wait a second, I don't understand," Luke pressed. "Are you saying this wendigo has been running around for, like, ninety years?"

"Pretty much," Max confirmed. "The Falk townspeople assumed Gillian was going to die and tossed her into the woods to suffer until her end. But she didn't die. Thanks to the human flesh and her anger, she transformed into a wendigo. And when she went back to Falk, it was with a purpose."

"She killed all of them, didn't she?" Nixie asked, her voice small.

"No." Max shook his head. "She killed some to sustain herself, but her anger was the driving force. She was forced to eat human flesh while suffering the torments of the damned. She didn't willingly consume it. Apparently that allowed her to maintain a remnant of her soul."

"She's a wendigo with a partial soul?" I thought about what I'd seen in the dream. "She was trying to warn me away from Falk in my dream. She has more powers than a normal wendigo ... by a long shot."

"Yes, I'm pretty sure she's responsible for the ghosts, too," Max offered. "They're not ghosts, by the way. They're nothing. I think they're replicas of the people of Falk – maybe even partial shades, although I think that is a stretch. She's been trying to keep us out of the woods by utilizing the ghosts."

"She doesn't want to eat us," Raven surmised. "She has a conscience but knows there are times she can't stop herself. She really has been trying to do right by us."

"Yes, but the women you saw doing the dance are another story," Max said. "They're part of a coven."

I balked. "Not the one I read about. Everything I saw said they were disorganized and had no idea what they were doing."

"I don't know if it's the one you read about, but the women you saw out there are definitely a coven," Max argued. "There were three of them originally. Gillian enslaved those who stayed in Falk, forced them to do her bidding and provide her with food – livestock – as long as they stayed. The women didn't like it, fought back, and tried to enslave her. They succeeded, but the town was too far gone by that point.

"Those women stayed in the area through the years, passing on power and insight to other witches," he continued. "Their numbers started to grow in the seventies. It wasn't squatters taking over Falk – er, well, I guess squatters could've been there, too, but they weren't the main problem. It was the witches. They were trying to make Gillian their slave, make her kill for them."

"They were providing the greed," I deduced. "Greed is often a motivating factor for a wendigo. Gillian was turned into a wendigo against her will, and then these women provided the energy to keep her going."

"Yes, but the women became stronger along the way," Max said. "They became full of themselves and absorbed power whenever they could. Gillian is the one making the ghosts appear to keep us out of the woods. The women you saw dancing are enslaving her and pose a threat to us."

"So ... how are we going to fight this?" Kade asked. "Are you going to kill all those women? They're human, aren't they?"

"We don't discriminate here," I reminded him. "The human women are worse than the wendigo in this case. They have to be stopped. I mean ... they took Amanda Stevens and somehow co-opted her mind to get her to join. They must be trying to grow the coven for a reason."

"I don't care about the reason." Max slowly rose to his feet. "I care about stopping them. I'm leaving this information with you and taking a nap. I expect everyone to have suggestions for the upcoming fight by lunchtime. As for closing early, we have no choice. We'll have a hard enough time protecting ourselves. We can't add patrons to the fray."

25
TWENTY-FIVE

We had a better idea of what was stalking us – and even what we had to do – but that didn't mean we could ignore our circus duties. Max always stressed that the circus must come first and our monster-fighting efforts second. We had to stick to that.

I changed into my normal clothing for a performance day – an ankle-length skirt, peasant blouse and scarf – and found Kade watching me from in front of the closet when I glanced up. "What?"

"Nothing." He shook his head and offered a smile. "I was just thinking about what Max told us. Is the moon really a big deal when it comes to a fight like this?"

"The moon is powerful. I know that probably doesn't make sense to you, but it does influence mood and happiness in humans. We have abilities, so we're often affected on a grander scale."

"Are you worried about this thunder moon thing tonight?"

I chuckled at his derisive tone. It felt good to laugh, even if it was only fleeting. "I'm more worried about it being a super moon. That will probably make the witches stronger and more unpredictable. The same can be said for our crew. We have training to fall back on, but … well, it's going to be a long night."

"I figured that out myself." Kade shuffled to a stop in front of me and leaned over to kiss my forehead. "We have time to figure this out. Max said we would talk at lunch."

I had no idea where he was going with this. "I heard what Max said."

"I know. It's just ... you're not going to go running around the woods or something, are you?"

"That's, like, the fifth time you've asked me that since we stopped here. I don't often go running around the woods for no apparent reason."

"You did last night."

"I had a reason last night."

"Yes, well, it wasn't a reason I could stomach very well," Kade hedged. "I want to make sure I don't have to worry about you."

"You don't have to worry about me." I softened my voice and met his gaze. "I've got a job to do, and it doesn't involve moving away from the dreamcatcher. I promise."

"Good. It's not that I don't trust you, but I am extremely fond of you. I would be crushed if something happened to you."

I didn't want to encourage him – the mother hen routine was getting a bit old – but I couldn't help taking pity on him. He was dealing with a lot and was essentially admitting he couldn't take another blow. "I'll stick close to the circus grounds. You have my word."

"Thank you." Kade gave me a soft kiss, lingering a moment before pulling away. "I'll be making the rounds all day. I'll stop to see you a few times just to make sure things are okay."

"That sounds lovely." I winked as he moved to leave the bedroom. "By the way, I'm really fond of you, too."

Kade's grin was so quick and sly it warmed my heart. "Keep it that way. We still have to christen the other rooms in our new trailer."

"I'll keep that in mind."

"And the office trailer."

Oh, now he was just being a perverted pain. "Don't push it."

"I have to be true to myself."

"So ... basically you're saying you're a sex fiend."

Kade nodded without hesitation. "Basically."

MY FIRST CLIENT OF the day was a thirty-something housewife. Upon initial entry, I thought she was going to be an easy read and quick twenty-five bucks. I couldn't have been more wrong.

"I want to know who my husband is sleeping with – I'm sure it's that girl who answers phones at his office twice a week – and I want to know which hitman I can hire to bump them both off."

I wasn't often surprised, but this was a new one. My mouth dropped open as I stared her down. "Excuse me?"

"You heard me." Nicole Haskell, all platinum blond hair from a bottle and overdone makeup from Wet N Wild, rested her hands on the table. She wore a well-pressed pink suit and a grimace that made my stomach clench. "I want to know who my husband is having an affair with and who I can hire to kill him and get away with it."

I shuffled the tarot cards and searched for the right way to approach the request. My first inclination was to hop in her head and see how serious she was about the murder aspect. I was barely inside when I realized she was very serious and took a mental step back.

"What makes you think your husband is cheating on you?" I asked, briefly wondering if I could talk her out of the belief. "I mean ... you need a solid reason to want him dead."

"I have a solid reason. He's cheating on me."

"But ... how do you know that?"

"You're the psychic. Shouldn't you already know the answer to that question?"

I pasted a pleasant smile on my face even though the last thing I wanted was to be nice to the woman. "I haven't dealt the cards yet. I can't see anything without the cards to guide me."

"Oh." Nicole was properly abashed. "I guess that makes sense."

"It helps to have a foundation in place when you cut the cards and I start dealing."

"And why is that?"

The question caught me off guard. Most true believers – and that's what Nicole apparently was – fell over themselves to agree with whatever I said because they believed I could change certain outcomes. "I don't make the rules. I merely have to follow them. The spirits make the rules."

"And what are these spirits telling you now?"

"That I should find out why you believe what you believe," I replied without hesitation. "So, again, why do you think your husband is cheating on you?"

Nicole heaved out a sigh that was more petulant teenager than grown wife and mother, but she tapped her fingers on the table and was resigned when she answered. "At first it was just little things. He got a call after dinner one night – we never get calls that late – and he took the phone in another room to talk. Obviously he was talking to his girlfriend."

I forced myself to remain calm. "Perhaps he was planning a surprise for your anniversary."

"Our anniversary isn't for six months."

"Maybe he was talking to a work colleague."

"He owns his own business – he's a real estate agent – and there are only a few other people in the office. The work colleague I'm concerned about is Kelly Biscuit. No, that's her real last name. She's eighteen and perky." Nicole made a face as she imitated the young girl, forcing me to bite the inside of my cheek to keep from laughing. "She's been at the office for six months and she's always hitting on all the men. I know she's the reason that Daryl has been acting odd."

"You must have more evidence of an affair than what you've shared so far?" I certainly hoped so, because I was under the impression that Nicole was completely off her rocker.

"Of course I have more evidence," Nicole scoffed. "The call was just the start of it. He's also taken to having late dinners twice a week. He never had late dinners before. He says he's trying to woo clients in a different way, but I know that's not what he's doing.

"He also started going to the gym to get in shape," she continued. "He says he wants to share a long life with me, but he spends all his time looking at what he thinks are muscles – he's started shaving his chest and everything – and posing in front of the mirror.

"He's on a diet, has a computer I can't get on so he can surf the web, and he had a strange charge show up on his credit card last month that he doesn't think I know about," she said. "I looked at the bill when he was in the shower, and I know he bought something at Victoria's Secret. He didn't buy that for me. That means he bought it for someone else."

Huh. I hated to admit it, but she had quite the case of circumstantial evidence. That couldn't be good. "Okay. Cut the cards." I handed over the deck and waited for Nicole to hand it back. "Are you sure you want to go the hitman route?"

"Oh, I'm sure." Nicole made a face that would've been hilarious under different circumstances. "I want him to pay for what he's done, for ruining our family, and for making me crazy."

Despite the husband's actions, I had trouble believing Nicole wasn't crazy before Daryl married her. He might have lit the fuse to help her blow up Wacky Town in her brain, but she was well on her way to planting the dynamite before that.

"Well, let's see what we have here." I doled out the cards and stared at them while giving myself a chance to shift into Nicole's head a second time. It was an uncomfortable place to visit – she was wound really tight – but I picked up on another few clues before I focused on the reading.

When I flipped up the last card, the tower card, I knew exactly what I was dealing with ... and it was all I could do not to laugh.

"Well, huh."

"What do you see?" Nicole leaned closer. "Is he sleeping with that little tramp at the office?"

"No." That was the truth. I wasn't simply lying so she wouldn't commit a murder. "He is not sleeping with the tramp at the office. She is, however, sleeping with another man in the office who is married. I believe his name starts with a G."

"Gary Parry? You've got to be kidding."

"There's a guy named Gary Parry? No wonder all I could see was laughing in my head when I tried to focus on his name. And, yes, he's the one sleeping with the office tramp."

"Oh." Nicole was mollified, but only slightly. "But what about all the other stuff Daryl is doing? What about the underwear? There's no explaining the underwear."

There was one way to explain it. "Your husband isn't buying the underwear for anyone else."

"He certainly didn't buy it for me!"

"He didn't," I agreed. "He didn't buy it for anyone else either." I willed her to see what I was trying to say. I didn't want to spell it out.

"Oh." Nicole's face went dark as realization dawned. "Are you saying that Daryl is ... gay?"

"No." I immediately started shaking my head. "I don't see anything that indicates he's gay. He simply likes pretty underwear, and boxers won't do. He's afraid to tell you because he thinks you won't understand."

"I don't understand."

I didn't blame her. I was a "to each his own" kind of woman, but I couldn't imagine Kade and I sharing underwear. It was one of those things that simply refused to compute. "Well, if you love him, you need to find a way to understand," I prompted. "He needs love and support. He's still the same guy. He simply likes thongs and hipsters. Oh, and apparently he's considering some Spanx."

"Oh, really?"

"He likes to look good in the underwear. He goes to cheap hotels on the nights you think he's having dinner with others just so he can walk around in the underwear of his choosing. It's harmless."

"Geez." Nicole kicked back in the chair and crossed her ankles as she regarded me. "It almost would've been easier if he was having an affair."

I was happy to see the urge to purge her husband from the face of the planet had vacated when I risked another brief jaunt into her mind. Now she was simply confused. "You can make this work."

"How? I mean ... should I stop by Victoria's Secret, buy him a gift and give it to him when I tell him I know?"

"That sounds like a promising idea."

"Yeah, well, it sounds weird to me." Nicole made a clicking sound with her tongue. "Do you know what his favorite color is for this stuff?"

I grinned. She wasn't such a bad person after all. "Try rascal red."

"That sounds ... frightening."

"Not as frightening as what you were imagining."

"I guess you have a point."

I MADE IT THROUGH most of the morning session with relative ease, opting for a break right before lunch and leaving Melissa in charge of my tent.

Kade was true to his word, stopping by to see me twice during his rounds, offering a flirty smile and saucy salute when he thought no one was looking. I knew he was waiting for me in the communal dining area now – that's where we all agreed to meet to strategize – so that's where I headed.

I kept a smile in place as I walked, my mind brushing against a few others as I cut a path toward trailer row. I read the surface thoughts of the guests' minds and some of them made me laugh, like the man who was trying to figure out a spot where he could disappear for a nap and the woman who was convinced the calories of the food wouldn't count if she made her kids order it.

It was only when my mind brushed against a barbed wire fence that I stopped in my tracks, my eyes slowly moving from left to right as I searched for the source. This mind wasn't blank. Whoever I was dealing with wasn't emptied out like the two men I'd come into contact with the previous day. No, this mind was shuttered ... just like the woman I'd killed.

I found who I was looking for right away. She looked to be in her fifties, although she was well preserved. She clearly hadn't gotten much sun or smoked because her appearance reflected youth.

She stood next to the ticket booth closest to the food trucks, a purse clutched in her hand. Her brown hair was pulled back in a smooth bun, and she wore twill pants and pink sandals as she watched everyone flutter to and fro.

She wasn't alone. She had a man with her, who looked to be about sixty and had a glazed look on his face. I figured out right away that he'd been hollowed out like the other two. I still didn't understand the phenomenon, but it was easy to recognize.

I risked a glance toward trailer row, computing how long it would take me to get there and return with someone to help my spying. I immediately discarded the notion because I knew it was a waste of time. I didn't want to lose this one. In fact, I wanted much more from her ... including a chance to interrogate her to my heart's content.

That wouldn't be easy. I had to get her away from the crowd and find a place to lock her up. I knew right away where that was and an idea formed.

I remained rooted to my spot and stared at the woman until she finally shifted her eyes in my direction. I felt the exact moment when she realized she was being watched, then did my best to feign nervousness and turned on my heel to disappear into the crowd.

I was trying to make the woman think I was afraid of her, so I looked over my shoulder twice. It took everything I had not to cry out in triumph when I realized she was following. This was going to work. I simply had to get the other pieces in place before I directed the woman where I wanted her to go. I sent out a magical message to Raven. I explained what was happening and then sent the final part, which was a simple order: *Be ready.*

I was certainly ready to get ahead in the game. I was tired of working from a position of weakness.

26
TWENTY-SIX

It was a game.

That's what I told myself as I strode through the circus grounds. I wasn't afraid of what harm the woman could cause me. I'd already proved I could handle myself when faced with someone like her. I was more worried about what she would do to others in an effort to control me, perhaps change my course of action.

I gave her one more look before disappearing into the House of Mirrors, shifting my eyes to the second floor, where Raven stood next to the railing, waiting. She nodded as we snagged gazes, watching as I pressed my hands to my face and called to the magic coursing through me.

It was a simple glamour. I'd cast the spell on myself a hundred times. In this instance, though, a lot of thought went into the appearance I opted to take.

The reflection staring back at me from the myriad of mirrors was generic. I turned my hair blond, left my eyes blue, and shifted my clothing so it matched the dresses I saw swirling around the fire the night before.

I was ready.

I strode through the first room and pointed myself toward the second, stopping underneath Raven long enough to confirm the trap was set. "We're ready, right?"

Raven nodded. "Dolph and Nellie are outside to handle the husband. I'll wait until they enter and then trail behind, bringing up the rear so to speak. This should work."

"Let's hope so. We need a little help on this one."

"So, let's make sure we get it." Raven winked before making small shooing motions with her hands. "You need to get moving. I'm pretty sure she's just outside."

"What if she doesn't come in?"

"I don't think she'll be able to stop herself. You're too enticing of a target to ignore. I know that from personal experience."

I didn't bother to hide my scowl. "You're a real pain sometimes."

Raven was unfazed. "It keeps me young."

I bolted into the second room when I heard footsteps by the front door, making sure I was out of sight before the woman entered. I positioned myself so my new reflection showed in every mirror in the second room. It was a trick of the design, something Raven showed me a long time ago during another takedown. I hoped it would work as well this time.

The woman didn't talk as she moved through the first room. I couldn't read her mind, but her presence was a fixed point and it wasn't hard to keep track of her. I felt rather than saw her startled reaction when she moved into the room where I hid.

She stepped into the middle of the space and did a slow turn, her gaze landing on every mirror as she tried to ascertain the source of the image. I knew that Raven had managed to clear out the building thanks to my mental warning, probably stationing someone at the entrance as soon as our quarry entered.

The woman slowly rotated until she faced me, her eyes gleaming when we finally came face to face. "Very cute."

I remained where I was, my glamour intact, and merely smiled. "I thought so."

"You wanted me to follow you."

I bobbed my head. "I did."

"Why?" The woman glanced around, clearly suspicious. The man merely stood in the center of the room staring at nothing. He was an eerie accessory, a walking handbag of sorts, and the way he reacted, devoid of anything, set my teeth on edge.

"Because I wanted to talk to you."

"How do I even know you're the same woman I saw on the circus grounds?" she challenged. "This could all be some elaborate hoax."

"It could," I acknowledged. "Does it matter? You guys have been running an elaborate hoax on us all week."

"I have no idea what you're talking about."

"Oh, don't start lying at the start of our relationship," I chided, wagging a finger for emphasis. "That won't bode well for what's to come."

"And what's to come?" The woman turned haughty. Obviously she wasn't worried that I posed a threat. "I'm not afraid of you. In fact, you should be afraid of me. The fact that you're not – or at least pretending you're not – shows exactly how stupid you really are."

I pursed my lips to keep from laughing. Her ploy was unimaginative and weak. "You followed me in here because you thought you could take control of me, didn't you? I'm betting you have questions of your own."

"I don't have any questions." The woman's eyes moved fast as they bounced between mirrors. "We should take this outside. This place is too much of a distraction for a proper conversation."

Now it was my turn to go on the offensive. "And what makes you think I want a proper conversation?"

"I ... ." She didn't have a chance to finish. It was already too late. She felt Raven move in behind her at the moment the silver-haired lamia pressed her hands to both sides of the woman's head.

"Sleep," Raven commanded, smirking when the woman listed to her side and began to topple.

I opened my mouth to warn Raven that she was going to fall, but Raven clearly understood that because she took a step back and allowed it to happen. She looked grimly satisfied by the loud thud the woman's body made as it bounced. "That was easy, huh?"

That wasn't exactly how I'd term it but we'd managed to accomplish our goal so now wasn't the time to pick a petty argument. "It's done. We need to move her into your office. We can't risk anyone seeing her."

Raven rolled her eyes. "Why do you think I called for Dolph? I'm not new."

"Let's just do it." I was nervous as I darted my eyes toward the front door. "We have no idea how these chicks communicate. Reinforcements could be coming."

Raven sobered. "Good point. Let's start threatening her for information. Ooh, can I be bad cop?"

"I think that we should probably both be bad cop."

"You're right. That is best."

MARIE DALTON LIVED IN Eureka. Her husband, Chet, for all intents and purposes, was a walking vegetable. He didn't say a word ... or make eye contact ... or even show concern for his wife. He was a void.

We placed Chet in the corner, admonished him not to leave, and then focused on Marie once we had her magically tethered to a chair. It didn't take her long to regain consciousness. When she saw that Raven and I were watching over her, she immediately screamed for help. She looked smug when she finally finished.

"You're going to get arrested for this," Marie spat, her eyes flashing. "Your guests will call the police and you're going to find yourself in a world of hurt."

"Did you hear that, Poet?" Raven was obviously amused as she folded her arms across her chest. "We're going to be arrested. I can't remember the last time I was arrested."

I could. It was in Detroit and the cops were considering making an example out of me because it was the third time I'd gotten caught picking pockets on Woodward. I promised it would never happen again – that was my normal refrain – and a judge took pity on me. Two days later I tried to pick Max's pocket and he taught me a very valuable lesson, before ultimately offering me a job.

"We're not all that worried about being arrested," I supplied after a beat. "This room is soundproofed."

"Magically soundproofed," Raven added, her grin malevolent. "That means you can scream all you want and we're the only ones who can hear you."

Marie shifted on her chair, perhaps testing the ropes that held her. Her expression was dark as she glanced around Raven's office. "How great for everybody concerned. I love a good kidnapping."

"So do we." I was purposely blasé as I shined my fingernails on the front of my shirt. "We have some questions for you. You have a few options, of course, but we hope you choose to answer the questions quickly and honestly. That would be best for all of us."

"Best?" Marie looked as if she was about to turn into a rabid dog she was so worked up. "I think I'll pass."

"That's certainly your prerogative. Things won't end well for you if that's really your decision, though, because we're going to get answers either way."

"And how do you propose to do that?" Marie's tone was mocking. "Are you little girls going to pull my hair until I cry?"

"Something like that." I looked to the door when there was a quick knock, not surprised in the least when Kade let himself into the room. He quickly took stock of what was happening and turned to business.

"This is her?"

Raven nodded. "Marie Dalton. She's local. Her husband is a zombie. She followed Poet. Now she's under our control."

"Nellie gave me the high points." Kade's eyes briefly landed on me. "Who is your friend?"

It took me a moment to figure out why he would ask such a ludicrous question. The answer came when I got a gander of myself in the mirror over Raven's desk. I was still wearing my glamour. I hadn't bothered to switch back.

I pressed my hands to my face and shook my head until my hair turned dark and I was back in my regular clothing. Kade took an immediate step back when he realized what was happening, his confusion turning to amusement when I gave him a pointed look.

"Sometimes I forget you can do that," he teased. "I don't suppose you want to dress up like a *Baywatch* lifeguard for me one night, do you?"

"I don't suppose so."

Marie cackled, amused by the conversation. "Did you hear that, girlie? He wants you to pretend to be someone else. He's not happy with the current model. I bet that happens to you all the time."

"Hey!" Kade glared at the woman, his temper coming out to play. "I said nothing of the sort."

"Ignore her," I instructed, running a hand over my hair to make sure it wasn't standing on end before continuing. "We're probably going to have to torture her for information. She doesn't seem forthcoming. I'm not sure you want to be around for that."

"I'm fine with torture." Kade leaned his hip against Raven's desk and studied Marie. "Has she said anything yet?"

"Just the usual nonsense that occurs when we kidnap someone for interrogation." I offered Marie a serene smile. "We haven't really started yet."

"Oh, is that supposed to frighten me?" Marie rolled her eyes. "I'm not afraid of you. There's nothing you can do to make me talk."

I exchanged a quick look with Raven. I knew that wasn't true.

"We're going to start by asking you questions," I said. "If you don't answer, then we will entice you until you do what we ask. You won't have a choice in the matter. Do you understand?"

"I understand you're both little girls playing in the wrong puddle," Marie snapped. "You have no idea what you're messing with."

"Let's see if that's true." I smiled brightly. "How do you control Gillian? We know she's a wendigo, but you guys are controlling her ... at least to a point. How are you doing it?" I decided to go for broke with the first question because I didn't want Marie thinking we were operating in the dark.

Marie did her best to hide her shock, but she was a poor actress. I could see the worry shooting through her eyes before she managed to shutter the panic. "What's a wendigo?"

"A cannibalistic creature," I replied without hesitation. "A former human who is turned into a monster through greed and gluttony. The thing is, most wendigos turn by choice. Gillian Dodd was turned against her will. She's not a true wendigo. She's some sort of weird hybrid."

"I ... you ... she ... how can you possibly know that?" Marie gave up all pretense of continuing her act. "That's a secret. No one is supposed to know that."

"We're not normal people," Raven drawled, tracing the blade of a silver letter opener with her fingertips as she stared. "We're something a little more than what you're used to dealing with."

"You probably want to believe that, but it's not true." Marie was back to being defiant. "You're common, everyday gutter trash. There's nothing special about you."

Instead of reacting out of anger, which I was worried about, Raven only snorted. "You're terrified. I don't blame you. Things are about to change for you and all of your ... sisters."

"They are," I agreed, exerting control over the conversation. "Now, we need to know how it is that you control Gillian. There has to be something you're doing to keep her from killing you."

"I have no idea who Gillian is."

"Don't lie!" Raven was clearly at her limit. She took two long steps, stopped in front of Marie and slapped her hand against the woman's forehead. "Reveal."

"What are you doing?" Marie struggled against her bonds, panicked. "Stop whatever it is you're doing."

"Reveal," Raven repeated, keeping her hand in place.

Marie made a growling sound as the magic coursed through her. "You have no idea what you're dealing with. We will end you."

"Reveal," Raven commanded. "Reveal. Reveal. Reveal."

Marie stopped struggling. Her body went slack and she stared at her feet as the shimmering lamia magic washed from the top of her head to the bottom of her feet. She was completely under our control now. It was about time.

"How are you controlling Gillian?" I asked. "There must be a trick to it."

"I don't know how they control her." Marie sounded defeated, her shoulders slumped. "They don't tell us stuff like that. Only the originals get that information."

"Who are the originals?"

"The ones who were there from the start."

I looked to Raven, confused. "Are you telling me that the women who first cursed Gillian are still alive?"

"No, but the lines are."

"Oh." Realization dawned. "The ancestors of the originals are the ones with the power." I ran my tongue over my teeth, considering. "Who are the originals? Who has the power?"

"I only know about Caroline."

Something stirred inside of me. "Caroline Olsen is one of you?" That didn't jibe with the woman I'd met the second day we were here. That woman was a loner, clearly not part of a coven. "How can that be?"

"She's an original. She has the power to control everyone if she wishes."

"But ... is she the one behind all of this?"

"I only do what I'm told." Marie's voice turned whiny. "I didn't plan this. I didn't want this. I can't turn back now. It's too late."

"What's too late?" Kade asked. "Why can't you turn back?"

"My soul will shatter if I do. You can't come back if your soul is shattered. I'll become ... her ... if I turn back. I'm part of this. I have to fight or I'll be truly lost."

She wasn't making sense, blathering and whining, but I managed to partially follow her train of thought. "You were recruited, promised something of value, and then threatened when you wanted to back out. There are a lot of recruits, aren't there?"

"More all the time."

"And Caroline is leading you?"

"Caroline is an original."

That wasn't really the answer I was looking for, but it seemed to be the only thing Marie could offer. "And the men you're with," I prodded. "What's wrong with them? Can they be fixed?"

"They're the price."

"The price for what?"

"To live forever." Marie let loose a shaky breath, causing me to realize she was softly sobbing. "They're the price and the prize is to live forever. It's not worth the price. It's so not worth the price."

I shook my head. "Criminy. This is such a mess. That old lady built her own army and now she's wielding it against us, while the woman who is supposed to be the monster is actually the victim. How do we fix any of this?"

Raven shrugged. "I have no idea, but I'm looking forward to trying."

That made one of us.

TWENTY-SEVEN

"We have to go back to Caroline's house," I announced to everyone at lunch. "We don't have a choice."

"Are you sure?" Max was calm as he ate his pasta salad and sipped his iced tea.

"I'm sure." I related my adventure with Marie, leaving nothing out. "She's locked in a cage in the animal tent right now until we can decide what to do with her. We soundproofed it and charmed the doors so no one can enter. We can't keep her in there forever."

"Definitely not." Max used his napkin to wipe the corners of his mouth. "Do you think Caroline will willingly give you information? If she is behind this she's probably more powerful than you realized."

"I didn't sense any magic that first day," I pointed out. "Maybe she's not powerful. Maybe she keeps control of Gillian with a cursed object or something."

"I guess that's a possibility." Max rubbed the back of his neck, uncertain. "I don't think you should go alone."

Kade, who had been largely silent while I told the story, stirred. "She's not going alone. I'm going with her."

Max gave his son a sidelong look. "That's a start. I think we need to send another person."

"I can go," Luke volunteered, his hand shooting in the air. "I wouldn't mind seeing that old bat a second time. I thought she was harmless, too. Obviously I missed something."

"I think you should stay here," Max countered. "I think Poet needs magical backup."

Raven groaned. "You're talking about me, aren't you?"

Max nodded. "I am."

"I already did a lot of work today," Raven whined. "I also hiked into the woods last night. I don't want to go again today. I'm tired."

Max ignored the whining. "I want two of you with magic there to back each other up. I will hold down the fort with Naida while you're gone. Kade can serve as something of a lookout for both of you.

"It's daytime, so I don't expect to run into trouble with the apparitions," he continued. "It should be a quick walk and easy interrogation. You said she was old. She shouldn't be a match for you if that's truly the case."

"What if she's more than we realized?" I asked. "I didn't sense anything about her the first time. Maybe that's because she's stronger than I am."

"I don't believe that." Max forced a smile. "While we're getting closer to answering all of the questions lingering over this one, I don't think we're there yet. Caroline seems too easy of an answer."

"I dosed Marie with magic myself," Raven argued. "She couldn't lie to us. She didn't have the power to fight what I did to her."

"I didn't say she was lying. I think she's a foot soldier and doesn't know the whole truth."

"And what do you think the whole truth is?" Kade queried.

"More than we've been led to believe." Max focused on me rather than Kade. "I suggest you make your trip to Caroline's house now. I want everyone back on these grounds an hour before dusk. We will be under siege tonight."

"Not if Caroline has the answers," I pointed out. "This might all be over in an hour."

Max patted my head and grinned. "I like that you still have a naïve streak every now and then. It shows that you're not completely jaded."

I scowled. "You don't know. We might be able to solve everything with this visit to Caroline."

"I don't think so, but I'm hopeful you will." Max shifted his eyes to the table. "No dessert?"

And just like that we were on our own. Ah, well, sometimes I preferred it when the big dog didn't want to jump in and save us.

IT DIDN'T TAKE US LONG to find our way back to Caroline's house. The hardest part was picking the right path. Ultimately I remembered what Luke said and scanned the trees. It was the roof that gave it away.

"There." I pointed. "Hopefully she won't give us too much grief about stopping in unannounced."

"Yes, that would be the true travesty of the day," Raven drawled.

I ignored the sarcasm and headed straight for the house, allowing my senses to unfurl in an attempt to pin down Caroline's location. The house was empty. I picked up on that right away. The small storage shed to the left of the house was another story. "She's in there."

"Then let's get her," Raven said, adopting an expression that had me believing she was gearing up for war rather than a pleasant conversation.

I laid my hand on her arm to still her. "We need to talk to her first. Max is right. We don't yet know what's happening."

"We know most of it," Raven challenged. "We also know this old lady is in the thick of things. I'm not going to give her a pass because you're suddenly feeling sentimental. You know as well as I do that we need answers and she's the only one who can give them."

"I'm not saying that we should give her a pass. I'm simply saying that we should ask questions first and attack second."

"And what if I don't want to do that?"

"Then we'll take a vote." I expectantly shifted my eyes to Kade. "Who votes we talk to her before smiting her?"

Kade met my gaze without blinking. "I think we should kill her."

I openly gaped. "She hasn't done anything to us."

"According to Marie, that's not true," Kade countered. "Marie said she was one of the originals. That means she's in charge."

"Yes, but Marie was hardly one of the great thinkers of our time," I pointed out. "She didn't understand what we were asking. She has no knowledge of the important stuff."

"I still think we should kill her." Kade was firm. "She can't hurt us if she's dead."

I was flabbergasted. It was rare I could use that word and mean it. "I can't believe you guys." I rubbed my forehead as I tamped down my churning emotions. "She could be innocent."

"Really?" Raven looked smug when I risked a glance in her direction. "You think the old lady who lives in the middle of the woods is harmless? We're talking wendigo-infested woods here. She has ties to the original family that enslaved a woman because they thought she was a witch, then force fed her human flesh ... but only after torturing and sexually assaulting her. You think she might be innocent?"

I refused to back down despite Raven's rather obvious feelings on the subject. "We don't know what she's guilty of. I'm not going to allow anything to happen to her until we find out."

"Then you're an idiot," Raven fired back.

"And you're a bloodthirsty pain in the butt." My temper got the better of me and I planted my hands on my hips. "I'm in charge. What I say goes. No killing until I say it's okay. Understood?"

Raven looked as if she wanted to argue, but ultimately she held her hands palms out and shrugged. "You're the boss."

"That's right." My anger was still firing on all cylinders when I turned back to the house and found Caroline leaning against a nearby tree. Her goat was not around this time, but she had an amused look on her face. "Well, hello."

Raven jolted at the woman's sudden appearance. "Where did you come from?"

"I was about to ask you the same," Caroline said dryly. "I recognize this one." She pointed at me. "You other two are newbies. I thought I told you I wasn't the sort who enjoyed visitors, girlie?"

I gave her a considering look. "You also told me about shadow hunters, mentioned fractured souls and indicated you had nothing to do with outsiders. I'm sure you understand that I have a few questions about all that after recent events."

"What recent events would those be?"

"The ones where the witches in the woods are conducting rituals and enslaving a wendigo to their cause," I answered without hesitation. "The ones where the wendigo is sending dreams to try to protect us. She's also sending ghosts to cut us off, make us afraid, and keep us away from danger. Those are the types of things I want to talk about."

Caroline heaved out a sigh, resigned. "I knew the second I heard they were planting you folks in the field out yonder that it wouldn't end well. I told Gillian things would get bloody."

I thought about Amanda Stevens' license and the puddle of blood. "I think things turned bloody before we got here."

Caroline scuffed her foot against the ground as she shook her head. She looked to be debating a big decision. "How much do you know? I mean ... you figured out the wendigo stuff. You're the first to do that without coming face to face with her. How much do you know about the rest?"

"Treat us like newbies."

Caroline squinted at Kade, taking an extended moment to look him up and down. "I think the blond guy was more handsome. You should go back to dating him."

Kade shook his head. "Hey!"

"I don't date the blond guy," I said hurriedly. The last thing we needed was to go off on a tangent. "Tonight is a super moon. We know something bad is going to happen as soon as the sun sets. What we don't know is what part you play in all of this."

"Don't you know? I'm the bad guy." Caroline's eyes twinkled when I stared. She sobered quickly. "My great-grandmother was the bad guy, though I'm still part of it to a certain extent." Caroline didn't invite us into her house to get comfortable for the story, so I remained in front of her, arms crossed, and tapped my foot as I waited for her to continue.

"Those were different times. You have to understand. I don't think the women of Falk started out wanting to be evil. In fact, it wasn't all the women who got involved and set this thing in motion. It was three of them."

"Three townspeople?" Raven asked.

Caroline nodded. "They thought the run of bad luck was the fault of one person. I don't know why they focused on Gillian, although I have my suspicions. She was recently widowed and a workhorse, from what I can tell. She was also young and the men liked to look at her.

"The group was made up of three people," she continued. "Harriet Spencer, Laura Bishop and Grace Olsen. Grace was my great-grandmother. They got everyone worked up and insisted that Gillian needed to be cleansed to save Falk."

"I saw all of that," I offered. "Gillian showed me. I didn't realize what I was seeing at the time. Why did they make her eat human flesh?"

"I have no idea. They never said. It's not in any of the journals I've read."

"Did they realize what they were creating when they did that?" Raven asked.

"No." Caroline almost looked sad. "I think they wanted to torture her before killing her. It was important they make it look like a ritual that was supposed to save her, even though they offered her up to their husbands for sex first. She was tossed out like garbage after that. And when she rose she was out for blood."

"She killed people," I noted, "but she still maintained part of her soul. How?"

"Her soul was cracked, like your friend you brought out here the other day," Caroline answered. "But it wasn't broken. She managed to hold onto a sense of self. She ruled the roost around these parts, but not for long. The same women who insisted she be cleansed managed to enslave her."

"How?" I pressed. "We need to know how if we want to free her."

"They took a mirror that belonged to Gillian – something passed to her by her mother – and cursed it. It was an old ritual. A blood ritual. As long as someone has the mirror and Gillian can't find it, she'll always be under that person's control."

"Do you have the mirror?" Kade asked.

Caroline shook her head. "I'm sure this is hard for you to believe, but I've been trying to free Gillian for years. I was born into this position. My mother raised me to know I had to keep control of the wendigo, that it was evil. I believed that, right up until I got lost in a storm.

"Gillian found me," she continued. "I was terrified and thought she was going to eat me, but she saw me home. I was deeply grateful, but my mother tortured her for the good deed. That's when I realized my mother was the monster.

"The problem is, it's Harriet who kept possession of the mirror," she said. "It's her ancestor who has the power over Gillian. I stayed with the group a long time trying to get my hands on the mirror. It never worked out."

"Did you ever see it?" I asked hopefully.

"No. I left the group twenty years ago. This has been my family homestead since long before I was born. I hear those women when they come out to dance and cavort. I know what they're doing. I've been trying to figure a way to save Gillian before it's my time to pass over, but the clock is winding down for me. Once I'm gone, Gillian will be on her own again."

"Do you communicate with Gillian?" I asked. "Can you talk to her?"

"She communicates with pictures in her mind," Caroline explained. "Very rarely she can muster words, but it's not easy for her. I think that's how she tried to talk to you, right? The images in your head. She saw you in the woods that day, realized you were different. She's so tired and ready for rest that she was hopeful you'd be able to help her."

I chose my words carefully. "Even if I could find the mirror, I don't know that we could help her. She has to survive somehow."

"The rest of them feed her scraps, not enough to thrive but enough to survive," Caroline supplied. "Gillian doesn't kill people. She hasn't since she first woke as a wendigo and went on that initial killing spree. She's been good ever since."

"She's still a wendigo," Raven pointed out. "How do you expect her to survive out here once we free her?"

"She doesn't want to survive. She wants to go. I'm dying, you see. I'm her only friend. I've got maybe six months before this cancer kicks my ass and then she'll be truly alone."

I knit my eyebrows. "I thought you said you didn't go to doctors."

"Yes, well, I lie sometimes." Caroline shrugged. "Sue me. What's important is that I'm not lying about this. Gillian doesn't want to kill. She's never wanted to kill. The evil resides in those other women."

I had no doubt about that.

"What about the women they're recruiting?" I asked, something occurring to me. "How are they trading the minds of their husbands for everlasting life?"

"That's a trick and nothing more," Caroline answered. "It's black magic. Old. Harriet knew it when she lived in Falk. Even though she managed to live until she was a hundred and ten, she couldn't stave off death. Not really.

"They're using the souls of the men to stretch out the lives of the women," she continued. "What's left of the souls they're using to sustain Gillian, although it's not what she wants. She tries to fight them, but as long as they have the mirror, Gillian doesn't have the strength to fight."

"We'll help Gillian." I meant it. "I need to know, are all of those women coming to the circus to fight us tonight?"

"That's my understanding." Caroline nodded. "They know you have magic. They want to steal that magic."

"Do they know Gillian is responsible for the ghosts?"

"They think they forced Gillian to conjure those ghosts to keep you locked in. They don't realize that Gillian was fine with it because she thought it would protect you."

"Will they bring the mirror with them when they attack tonight?"

"Yes. They'll want to use Gillian against you if they can."

"That's good." My mind was working overtime. "That's really good. I know exactly how this is going to go."

"You do?" Kade looked more confused now than when we'd started. "How do you plan to fight all those women?"

"With a little help from our friends." I beamed at Caroline, who reluctantly returned the smile. "We need to get back to the circus and plan. You need to come with us, Caroline. We'll need your insight."

"I have no problem coming with you," Caroline said. "I don't know how much help I'll be. If you can free Gillian, even if I die, it will be worth it."

"Hopefully no one will have to die." I tapped my bottom lip with my finger. "Just one more question."

Caroline feigned patience.

"Was Gillian really a witch before all this happened? I mean, I don't think she was an evil witch, but did she have magic?"

"She did. How did you know?"

"The ghosts," Raven answered. "A normal wendigo can only be one thing. Gillian is multiple things."

"And we're going to use that to our advantage," I said. "Come on. We have a lot to do."

28

TWENTY-EIGHT

The stretch after lunch as we counted the hours before moving the patrons out was interminable. I was edgy as I breezed through readings, doing the bare minimum to satisfy customers. No one complained, and I took that as a good sign, but everything changed when a familiar woman walked through the opening.

Vivian Brooks. Troy's mother. I remembered the woman from when I walked her family to their vehicle to protect them from the ghosts. She stood in the tent opening, her eyes searching until they found me. For one brief moment my heart seized with fear. I was convinced she was going to shutter her mind and attack – that was about how my luck was going these days – but instead she broke into a broad smile and hurried to the table.

"There you are." She rummaged in her purse as she got comfortable. "The sun is bright outside and it took my eyes a moment to adjust when I came inside. I wasn't sure you were in here."

"Sometimes it feels as if I'm always here." I forced a smile for her benefit, relief washing over me when I touched her mind and found she wasn't shuttered at all. She was an open book ... and a worried one at that. "How can I help you?"

"Um ... here." She handed me twenty-five dollars – the fee I charge for a reading – and wrinkled her nose when I tried to wave it off. "No, I know that you guys have certain margins you're supposed to hit for venues like this. I want to pay."

I set the money on the middle of the table. I wasn't comfortable accepting it, mostly because I was utterly charmed by Troy. There was something different about the boy that I liked and I wanted to help him if I could. It was his face, after all, I saw reflected in his mother's head when I scanned her.

"Let's start from the beginning and we'll argue about the money later," I suggested, opting to refrain from theatrics as I regarded Vivian. "What seems to be the problem?"

"Well ... ." Vivian fidgeted in the chair, her purse clutched on her lap, and glanced around the tent as if she thought the appropriate words would somehow pop into her head.

"I can't help unless I know exactly what's going on," I pointed out quietly. "There's nothing you can say that I haven't heard before. Trust me. I want to help. I need information to help."

"Fine." Vivian looked at her lap before looking back up at me. "I think Troy is ... special."

There were so many ways I could go with that statement I didn't know where to start. "Special like he's gifted, or special like you can't leave him alone in a freshly-painted room because he might start licking the walls and poison himself?"

Despite the serious nature of the conversation, Vivian laughed. "The first one. The thing is – and I feel strange admitting this to a stranger – but Troy seems to trust you, and I hope I can as well. I think he can do things."

I was intrigued. "What kind of things?"

"I think he can see things others can't see."

I knew that was hard for Vivian to admit. No mother wanted to take ownership for a strange and peculiar child. I had to give her credit. "I think he can, too," I admitted after a beat. "I think Troy is definitely special."

Vivian looked so relieved I felt a bit of the weight lift from my shoulders. "I knew you did. That's why you were talking to him so long. Marcus, my older son, said you spent a long time talking to Troy. The only thing I could figure is that you picked up on something."

"It's not that easy," I cautioned. "I don't know what gift Troy boasts. If I had time to spend with him I might be able to identify it. If I had to guess – and don't take this as a diagnosis and run with it – I'd say he's a sensitive."

"Like ... psychic?"

"Kind of," I hedged. "I didn't see Troy exhibit the ability to read minds, if that's what you're worried about. He can't go poking around people's heads."

Vivian remained calm. "What can he do?"

"He can poke around their hearts." I was almost certain that was true. "I think he's empathic, which means he can pick up on the mood of others. He might not always understand that. It's not an easy gift."

"Are you empathic?"

"No." I shook my head. "I'm psychic. I can pick thoughts out of people's heads, occasionally feel their emotions. Troy will be better at the emotional part than I am. That might not be a good thing in the grand scheme of things."

Vivian seemed resigned that I was telling the truth even though she barely knew me. "Will this gift hurt him?"

I shrugged. "It's like anything else," I replied. "There are good and bad things associated with it."

"Do you like being psychic?"

"It's who I am. I've never known anything different. If you're worried about Troy, I think he's the same way. This is his reality. He doesn't know any different."

"I don't know what to do," Vivian admitted, chewing on her bottom lip as she squirmed. Talking to a stranger about the mental health of her son was obviously trying for the dedicated mother. "He's such a sweet boy. He's always been smart – pretty much smarter than everybody in his class – but he's also picked on quite a bit and bullied."

"That happens to all kids," I pointed out. "He'll be okay. You can't protect him from everything. My parents tried that when I was a kid. They knew I was different and wanted me to be quiet about what I could do. They were terrified someone would find out."

"And that didn't work?"

"They died when I was a teenager," I explained. "I was on my own after that. It didn't work because I wasn't protected when I was tossed into the system."

"Oh, that's awful." Vivian furrowed her brow. "Still, you managed to claw your way out. You ended up here."

"Because the owner of Mystic Caravan ran into me on the street one day and recognized that I was different," I explained. "He offered me a chance no one else was going to give me. I was lucky.

"Troy will also be lucky," I continued. "He has you. Hopefully he has other family, too. I was isolated, but most kids won't have to deal with the same set of circumstances.

"I can see Troy is loved," I said. "He's wise beyond his years and he's got a good heart. I don't think you have to worry about anything."

"But ... shouldn't I find someone who can help him with his gift?" Vivian asked, her eyes widening. "Isn't that what a good mother would do?"

"A good mother loves her child, and you do," I replied. "You wouldn't be here if you didn't love him. As for someone to help, I don't know. I don't want to make you nervous, but if Troy tells the wrong person what he can do he could be labeled a nut."

"Did that happen to you?"

"A few times," I acknowledged. "Things won't always be easy for Troy, but I think he should be okay. As for empaths in the area, I don't know where to point you. I can do a little research and see if I come up with a name. Whatever you do, though, don't volunteer that information. Make sure you research them first."

"Thanks. I will." Vivian moved to stand and then thought better of it. "One more thing. Um, Troy says that he sees ghosts hanging around, but it's okay because they're not here for him. Is that part of being an empath?"

"Not really."

"So ... he's making it up?" Vivian almost looked hopeful.

"No." I shook my head. "He's not seeing ghosts. Don't get me wrong, they look like ghosts. They're planted visions. I don't know how to explain it. He's not imagining it. That's the important thing."

"Do you see what he sees?"

"In this particular instance, yes. I see what he sees."

"So, it's real." Vivian pressed the heel of her hand to her forehead. "This all feels like so much. My husband isn't taking it well. He thinks I'm being dramatic, but I've always known Troy was different. He seemed to understand things even as a baby.

"I had a bit of post-partum after giving birth to him – that's why I don't have even more kids running around the house. I hated the feeling after – and he never cried when I was really upset or anything," she continued. "He was the calmest, sweetest baby you've ever seen."

"I think every parent wants one of those." I grinned. "As for what he's seeing now, that has nothing to do with him. It's important you're out of here before dark, though. After tonight, those things he sees should be gone."

"I don't understand."

"And I can't explain it. What's important is that those things aren't ghosts. They were created as a distraction."

"Like ... magic?"

"I guess that's as good a word as any," I answered. "You don't need to focus on that. The things he's seeing will be gone soon. We'll be gone soon, too. Troy will still be here. He'll still have the same ability. That's not a bad thing. He's merely different, and there's nothing wrong with being different."

"That's a lovely way to put it." Vivian stood on shaky legs. "He's outside. He wants to see you. I wasn't sure if that was okay."

"I'll go out to him." I grabbed the money and handed it back to Vivian, only pressing harder when she tried to beg off. "Put it in his college fund."

"Are you sure?"

"I'm positive."

Vivian accepted the money, watching as I exited the tent and closed the flap. There was no line this late in the day. Thankfully I'd worked through most of the customers in the hours after lunch. Those who remained would simply have to be disappointed. We needed to move every guest on the property out within the next hour. It wouldn't be easy.

"Here he is." Vivian beamed as she placed a hand on Troy's shoulder and eased him out from the shaded area where he tirelessly worked on eating a huge ice cream cone. "Where did your brother go?"

"He's over there." Troy offered a haphazard gesture. "He found a girl he likes, but she doesn't like him."

"How do you know that?" I asked.

Troy shrugged. "She's interested in someone else."

"Another boy?" Vivian asked.

Troy shook his head. "A girl."

"Oh." Vivian pressed her lips together and I could tell she was trying not to laugh. "Well, your brother will survive. This might be a good lesson for him to learn."

Troy fixed his inquisitive eyes on me. "You were inside with my mom for a long time."

"We had a few things to discuss." I ruffled his hair, more as a way to touch his head so I could get a quick look inside without disturbing him. He wasn't particularly bothered by anything now other than his mother's anxiety. He was especially keyed in to her emotions. "I hear you're still seeing the ghosts."

Troy widened his eyes. "Do you see them?"

"Not right at this second, but I know they're coming back." I hunkered down so we were on an even level. "Troy, I need you to listen to me. Those aren't ghosts. I know they look like ghosts, but that's not what they are."

"What are they?"

I wasn't sure how to explain the situation to an impressionable boy. "A long time ago, something very bad happened to a woman who lived close to this area."

"In Eureka?"

"No, it was a place called Falk."

Vivian furrowed her brow. "The ghost town?"

I nodded. "This is too confusing for you to understand. Suffice it to say, the woman who was hurt is still around and needs help. Some other people are hurting her. The ghosts are simply a distraction. They're not real ghosts. They're ... images that someone created and they're from a different time. Does that make sense?"

Troy solemnly shook his head. "No."

Of course it didn't make sense. It barely made sense to me. "You're going to be fine. That's the important thing. If all goes as planned, you won't ever see these particular ghosts again."

"Are you going to make them go away?"

"We're going to make sure that the person being hurt is no longer being hurt," I clarified. "That's the best we can do."

"Well, I guess that's something." Troy brightened considerably as he turned to his mother. "We're not supposed to stay here much longer. Poet is worried about getting everyone out of here before it gets dark. We should probably leave now even though it's going to crush Marcus and his plans for that pretty girl."

Vivian smiled at her son. "Well, then I guess we should get going." She extended her hand for me to shake. "Thank you so much for everything. We're going to leave now. I hope everything goes well for you tonight."

That made two of us. "It should be fine." I sounded more convinced than I felt. "As for Troy, don't worry. He'll find his own way. He has strength of character. Those who have strength of character always do well in this world."

"I'll keep that in mind." Vivian focused on her son. "Are you ready to head out?"

"Just one second." Troy held up a finger to still his mother before focusing on me. "The ghosts are whispering. Can you hear them?"

"No. What are they saying?"

"That it's almost time."

I remained calm. "Almost time for what?"

Troy shrugged. "I don't know. They just say that they're coming ... and soon."

"Well, we'll be ready for them." I mostly meant it. I touched the boy to anchor my emotions a final time before sending him on his way. "Go. You need to get out of here now. I have a lot of work to clear this place before dark."

"You'll be fine." Troy flashed a killer smile in my direction. "You know what to do."

"I hope so."

IT TOOK THE BETTER part of the hour to clear the circus grounds. Max's excuse was a generator mishap. He apologized profusely, gave everyone free return tickets for the following day, and then showed them on their way.

Thirty minutes before dark, the grounds were empty.

Max ordered the clowns and midway workers inside their trailers. Mark tried to put up a fight – he was a businessman at heart, after all – but he clearly read the determined tilt of Max's shoulders and backed off after minimal argument.

That left only members of our group to pace the dreamcatcher line as we waited for the fight to come to us.

"Max says everything is in position," Kade offered as he joined me.

I slid my hand into his and nodded. "I know. It's the waiting wearing on me. I know this will work."

"You're still upset about all of it. I can feel it."

I cocked an eyebrow as I studied the lines of his handsome face. "Are you starting to pick up on feelings and emotions?"

"I just know how your feelings and emotions go. You're worried about how this is going to end because it doesn't feel right to you. But I don't think you're going to get a better outcome than what we have planned, so you simply have to accept it."

"Yeah." I rubbed my forehead with my free hand. The building tension was giving me a headache. "It won't be long."

"It's already happening." Kade pointed to a spot over my shoulder, causing me to jerk my head in that direction. I could see a long line of women walking out of the trees together, all of them dressed in matching dresses I recognized from the night before. They were coming to war, only their battle armor left a bit to be desired.

"Well, I guess it's good that they're prompt."

"Yeah. That's exactly what I was thinking." Kade tapped my chin with his finger and gave me a heartfelt kiss, nudging a sigh out of me when he deepened it. "There's more where that came from. We just need to get through this first."

I waved off his concern with forced bravado. "Piece of cake."

"Just stay safe. That's the most important thing."

"Right back at you."

The second kiss Kade graced me with was quicker, a simple touching of lips.

"It's time," Max announced, moving next to me to take his position. He was somber, but I could feel the excitement rolling off him. "We're ready. This shouldn't take long."

I hoped he was right.

29
TWENTY-NINE

"They look like they think they're going to win, don't they?" Caroline, who laid low all afternoon and worked along trailer row, stepped closer to Max as she stared into the quickly dwindling dusk.

"I don't care what they believe," Max replied. "I care about beating them to a pulp. We only need to kill the ringleaders. The others ... well, I have a feeling the others will surrender once they realize the fight isn't going their way."

I had the same feeling. "There's Amanda Stevens." I inclined my chin in the young woman's direction. She hung back, not nearly as gung-ho as the others she walked with. Remy was ahead of her, looking eager for the fight. "I still don't understand how they snagged Amanda."

"Most of the members of their coven were enticed with the promise of eternal youth," Caroline volunteered. "That wasn't enough for some people. The others were attacked in the woods, threatened, and ultimately they signed up for the movement to save their lives. I don't know them all, but I know quite a few of them were taken into the coven against their wills."

"And that means we only have to get the main two or three, right?"

Seth asked, nervously flexing his fingers as he stared at the approaching women. "We only need to take out the leaders. That's what you said, isn't it?"

"We do." I narrowed my eyes when I thought I recognized a familiar face. "Wait a second."

"What do you see?" Kade leaned closer to me, eager to keep contact for as long as he could. "Do you see something?"

I extended my finger and pointed toward the woman in question. "Isn't that your friend from the grocery store?"

"Who? Liz?" Kade furrowed his brow. "Holy … that is her! What is she doing here?"

"Are you talking about Liz Wharton?" Caroline cast me a sidelong look. "How do you know her?"

"She was selling vegetables with another woman at the grocery store the day after we arrived. We talked to her a bit. Why? Who is she to this group?"

"She's Harriet Spencer's ancestor."

Things slipped into place. "She has the mirror."

"Yes."

"That explains the figures I saw in the parking lot."

"What figures?" Kade asked.

"I thought I saw people watching me at the shopping center. It turned out to be a glare, though there was still an image in the glare. It's hard to explain."

"Well, try," Kade prodded.

"And do it fast because we've only got a minute to spare," Luke added. "You didn't mention seeing anything that day."

"I thought I might have imagined it." In hindsight, I felt silly for believing that. "I didn't think it was important. Nothing had really happened at that point."

"Except for the chanting I'd heard in the woods," Luke argued.

"Except for finding Amanda Stevens' identification in the woods," Kade added.

"Oh, and the blood in the woods," Luke supplied.

"And the chanting in your head that first night that didn't allow you to sleep," Kade gritted out.

I held up my hands to quiet them. "Fine. I should've said something, but I wasn't sure what I was seeing."

"It's hardly important," Max interjected smoothly. "We can't go back and change things. What's done is done."

"If we had known we might have approached things differently," Luke pressed.

"Can we fix that now?"

"No."

"Let it go." Max snagged my gaze. "It seems even then Gillian was trying to warn you of danger. That's why she sent the ghosts there, as a harbinger of sorts."

"Yeah, well, I wish I would've figured it out." I rubbed my sweaty palms over my hips. "Like you said, we can't go back and change it. We have to focus on the current problem."

"Which we will." Max offered me a wink and detached from the group when the marching women came to a standstill on the other side of the dreamcatcher. It was almost completely dark, so he tossed his hand in the air and ignited sparks to illuminate the area, a smile on his face when the floating lights settled above our heads. "Hello, ladies. Welcome to Mystic Caravan Circus."

I had to bite the inside of my cheek to keep from laughing at his calm greeting to the rather odd assortment of enemies on the other side of the line.

"Do you think you're funny?" Liz asked, immediately taking a position of authority in the middle of the group. "I believe you know why we're here. You're abominations and must be cleansed. It would be easier if you gave yourselves to us willingly, but we are prepared to take you by force."

Dolph, Luke and Nellie snorted in unison at the ridiculous statement, bending their heads together to whisper something only they could hear. Liz recognized the derision, and the look she scorched them with was right out of a horror movie.

"Do you think that's funny?" she challenged.

"We think this entire thing is funny," Luke replied without hesitation. "Nellie likened it to a scene from *Lord of the Rings* being played out with Barbie dolls, and Dolph – he's not from this country originally, so you'll have to excuse him – says an army made up of women is much more terrifying when the women in question have mustaches and back hair."

I rubbed my mouth to hide my smirk and remained focused on Liz. She clearly didn't find Nellie amusing, but that wasn't exactly surprising. She was the sort of woman who perpetually appeared to be sucking on a lemon.

"And I'm done talking to you," Liz insisted, instead focusing on Kade. "I was hoping it wouldn't come to this. It seems a shame to sacrifice such a pretty face. If you want to take advantage of my generosity I'm willing to let you leave ... make an escape of sorts."

Kade opened his mouth to answer, I'm sure a scathing retort on his lips. I stepped in and did it for him, though.

"You'll let him leave for a price, right?" I challenged. "You'll let him leave if you can steal his essence and give it to one of your acolytes, leaving him a hollowed-out shell whose only purpose is to do your bidding."

"Is there something wrong with that?" Liz's smile was more of a sneer. "He won't even miss you. He'll forget you even exist. Isn't that the best thing for him? You won't survive this, but he will. As his girlfriend – he clearly has tragic taste in women, but I can fix that – you should want what's best for him."

"She is what's best for me," Kade barked, his temper on full display. "As for the rest, you're clearly full of yourself. What makes you think you can simply take us down?"

"Because I have a surprise," Liz replied, unruffled. "I have something you can't fight ... or overcome. There's a reason I have the world at my fingertips."

"It's because you eat organic, right?" I taunted.

Liz narrowed her eyes. "I wasn't lying about pesticides being bad for you. That is a proven fact. I'm also not lying about this. There's no way to escape your fate. You should give in now. We promise to take it easy on you when it's time to pass. We aren't heartless."

"No, but you are brainless," Luke shot back.

"That did it." Liz moved to storm over the dreamcatcher, but Max, ever calm, held up a hand to still her. "Wait. I'm not done asking questions yet."

Liz was obviously caught off guard by his tone. "And what makes you think I'll answer your questions?"

"Because you're a woman and all women like to talk," Max replied.

"Hey!" Raven and I were offended at the same time.

"That wasn't an insult," Max said hurriedly. "It's simply something I've witnessed over the years. I'm not an expert on women or anything, but I do know that conversation can be relaxing and cathartic."

"That doesn't mean I'll answer your questions."

"What harm can it possibly do?" Max sounded utterly reasonable. "I think we would all like to know why it's necessary that we die."

"Not all of you have to die," Liz shot back. "Only the women have to die. They're too ... different ... to fill our ranks. We're more than happy to spare the men."

"Again ... for a price," I prodded. "You want all their minds so you can feed your followers and their bodies to serve as slaves." Something horrible occurred to me. "Wait ... you're not using them as sexual slaves, are you?"

"Ugh." Luke made a disgusted face. "This is why women are gross and I don't like them."

"Yes, that's why you don't date women," Raven said dryly. "There's no other reason."

Max barreled forward, clearly intent to keep the conversation on point. "We know most of it. We only want you to fill in a few blanks for us."

"Most of it?" Liz snorted. "You don't know anything."

"You might be surprised."

"Oh, really? What do you know?"

Max inclined his head toward me, ceding the stage so I could lay it all out.

"We know about Gillian Dodd, that she was believed to be a witch and wrongfully accused of causing Falk's downfall even though circumstances and the Great Depression were the true culprits," I volunteered. "We know that the townsfolk – led by three bitter shrews – tried to cleanse her. The real goal was to kill her under the guise of cleansing her, but something else happened."

A low murmur went through the crowd.

"You turned her into a wendigo," I continued. "She's not a true wendigo, though, because you forced things upon her that she didn't willingly acquiesce to. Your ancestors shackled her in an attempt to do their bidding, but even decades after the fact you can't truly control Gillian. You can try, but you're not as strong as you think you are."

Liz turned haughty. "You throw around a lot of words – like wendigo – but I don't think you know what you're talking about."

"You're wrong," I said simply. "We've fought and destroyed a multitude of wendigos in our time."

The women surrounding Liz shifted, the news causing an undercurrent of nervous energy to flare. It made me smile.

"You've destroyed a wendigo? Ha!" Liz was smarmy smug. It was going to be a pleasure to take her down. "No one can destroy a wendigo."

"We can and have," Max said.

Liz looked to Caroline, something dark passing between them. "You shared our secrets with them. You broke the rules."

"On the contrary," Caroline countered. "They knew everything when they approached me. I think you've severely underestimated this enemy, Liz. They're stronger than you."

"You only want me to believe that," Liz shot back. "You're trying to intimidate me. That doesn't work on me. You can't win. I have the power. You're all going to boost my powerbase – and I want to thank you ahead of time for that – but I'm not afraid of you."

"Then you're dumber than you look," Raven sneered. "You have no idea what you're up against."

"Yeah," Percival chimed in, his accent all but obliterated. Whenever he was nervous, the accent seemed to be the first thing he forgot. "You have no idea." The threat didn't have as much oomph as it should have because Percival was still in his clown garb from earlier in the day, but I gave him points for trying. He didn't shrink in the face of danger.

"This talk is getting us nowhere," Liz exploded. "You're trying to distract me to save your own skin, perhaps run a con or offer something you think I can't turn down. I can't be bought."

"We don't want to buy you," Max said. "We simply want to conquer you."

"We don't even care about the people with you," I added. "If they were to turn and run right now, we would let them go. We only care about you."

This time Liz's hollow laugh, which was utterly humorless, was tinged with an air of worry. "We are one. We cannot be broken. My soldiers are loyal."

"No, your soldiers are bowed," Max corrected. "Loyalty and fear are not the same. I would suggest giving yourself time to figure out why that's true, but it would be cruel to play with you that way. You're officially out of time."

"Oh, really?" Our taunting had the desired effect. Liz dug into her pocket, returning with what looked like an antique mirror and holding it up. She'd walked right into our trap, and now it was time to spring it. "And what happens when I call my greatest warrior to smite you?"

"Then the battle will begin," Max replied simply.

"Then that's what I'll do." Liz began chanting, staring into the mirror with a smug smile. At the moment she started speaking, Naida raised her hands and started the wind churning.

It was time.

I glanced to my left and nodded at Max, readying myself for what was to come. I would have to be quick. As soon as Liz realized what was happening, she would call for Gillian. Even though the wendigo would? fight the effort, she would ultimately be forced to do Liz's bidding. I had to get the mirror before that happened.

"Now!" Max instructed, bellowing over the wind so I could hear. He joined hands with Raven, and their combined magic was enough to toss the women surrounding Liz to either side, creating a direct path for my attack.

I broke into a run, leaping over the dreamcatcher line and landing on Liz. Her face turned red when she realized she was no longer safe, although the chanting didn't cease. I dug my fingers into her wrist, determined, and ignored the way she howled as I drew blood.

"Give me that mirror," I ordered.

"No. It's mine!" Liz struggled against my strength. "I'm in charge. This is my mirror. You can't have it."

"Oh, yes she can," Kade announced, taking me by surprise when he appeared at my side. "You're going to give it to her right now."

"I'm not!" Liz jerked back and forth, the wind picking up speed. I didn't risk a glance over my shoulder to see if her followers had recovered. I had one thing to focus on, and that was getting the mirror. "You can't do this! This is mine!"

"Stop it!" Kade grabbed the woman's head to hold her still, and to my utter surprise, I found his fingers alive with magical fire the second his skin touched her thick head. He gasped when he saw it and jerked away, staring in amazement at his own hands. "What the ... ?"

"Do it again," I ordered, hoping he would be able to focus on me despite what I was sure was a deafening pounding of blood in his ears. "Do it again. Your body knows what it's doing."

"What are you?" Liz shrieked as she tried to pull away from Kade when he reached for her a second time. "What do you think you're doing?"

"Ending this." Kade was grim as he briefly met my eyes. "Let her go, Poet. I've got this."

It was a calculated risk. He'd never used magic before, never shown so much as a mild interest. Now his hands were on fire and he was asking me to have faith he knew what he was doing. I could make only one choice.

I jerked my hands away from her wrist and took a step back, watching with interest as Kade planted his hands on either side of Liz's head. "Drop. The. Mirror." He growled the order, as if something inside – some strange creature with special powers – was speaking for him.

Liz tried one more time to get Kade on her side. "I didn't know you were this powerful. Imagine what we could do together if we joined forces. Imagine what we could be."

"I'm already happy with what I am," Kade said. "As for you, I wouldn't join you if you were the last horrible wench on the planet. Now ... drop that mirror!"

Liz could no longer fight his power. She screamed and did as he commanded, her head snapping back as the wind wrapped around her, blowing so fiercely I had trouble seeing where Kade ended and she began.

I quickly grabbed the mirror, smashing it against the nearest rock and destroying it at the exact second the wendigo arrived on the battlefield.

I could see her across the way, bodies strewn left and right. Most of the women had fled when they realized we had more power than Liz, but a few stayed behind to fight. My Mystic Caravan sisters and brothers had all of them well in hand. Gillian was another story.

She didn't look like a monster. Not really. Her eyes were bigger than they should be, her back a bit hunched, but she retained most of the features I imagined she boasted during life. She saw the shattered mirror on the ground at my feet. I didn't hesitate when handing over the item in question. The mirror was scarred and broken, but it still belonged to her.

She took it, allowing me to get a glimpse of her terrible claws. She seemed surprised that I would help her without demanding something in return, but nodded when she accepted the mirror.

"It's over then," Gillian said quietly, her gaze moving to Caroline. "It's finally over."

"It is," I agreed. "Although ... I don't know what comes next for

FREAKY RITES

you. I don't think you can live out here without eventually succumbing to your baser instincts."

"That won't be a problem." Gillian insisted. "I will stay with Caroline until the end and then we will cross over together. That was always my hope."

"You want to die?" Caroline had told me that, but until this moment I couldn't be sure she had told the truth. "You're okay with that?"

"I'm okay with peace," Gillian corrected. "I will finally have it for the first time in ... well, forever. That is all I want."

"And the rest?" I gestured toward the beaten women. They were bruised and bloodied, but still alive. "Can you let the vengeance go?"

"I let the vengeance go a long time ago," Gillian replied. "I don't want vengeance. I simply want peace."

"Then take it." I stepped away from her, creating a clear path so she could escape. "Go with Caroline. Take care of each other until the end. After that ... I hope you find what you're looking for on the other side."

"Oh, I think I will." I tried not to cringe when Gillian smiled, showing off two rows of jagged teeth. "Anything is better than this."

I could definitely see how she would believe so.

30
THIRTY

I found Kade sitting at the picnic table close to trailer row when the cleanup was almost completed. He'd been quiet since it happened, his hands thankfully back to normal and resting on his knees. I decided to give him time before approaching, but ultimately I couldn't ignore my heart.

"Hi."

Kade glanced up. "Hey." He looked unbelievably weary. "Do you want to sit down?"

"Sure." He was acting a bit odd, stiff and formal. I figured he was uncomfortable talking about what had happened. He would simply have to get over that. "So ... I always knew you had magic hands, but that was pretty impressive."

Kade barked out a laugh. I'd clearly caught him off guard. "You cut right to the heart of matters, don't you?"

"That is often my plan." I grabbed one of his hands and flipped it over so I could study his palm. "Did it hurt?"

"No. Does magic often hurt?"

"Not really, but it was your first time," I replied. "Sex hurts the first time for women. I thought maybe magic might be the same in some cases."

"Ha, ha."

I smirked. "I'm glad to see your sense of humor is okay. I worried it might have been damaged during the fight."

"Yeah, well ... are you okay?" His gaze was earnest as he looked me over. "I didn't even check on you after. I'm such a selfish idiot sometimes."

"Hey, you're talking about my boyfriend. I happen to like him." I wagged a finger to let him know I was kidding. "Those are fighting words where I come from."

"Yeah." Kade looked to the sky. "I saw you talking to Gillian. I tried to come out of it long enough to help, but ... my head was kind of a blur."

"It's okay." He looked so forlorn I could do nothing but shift closer, wrapping my arm around his back and resting my head on his shoulder to share a bit of my warmth for a change. "Gillian didn't want to hurt me. I saw it the second she arrived, the way she searched the battlefield. Her soul is intact. It's ravaged and brittle, but it's still intact."

"Do you think it was wise to let her go knowing that she might kill and eat people?"

I shrugged, noncommittal. I'd worried about that very thing myself. "I don't think she will."

"You told me wendigos can't survive for more than a week without feeding," Kade pointed out. "What happens when she's starving and no longer under the thumb of a megalomaniac?"

"She wants peace. That's what she told me."

"She might not be able to fight her inner urges."

"Then she'll kill herself." Even as I said the words, I knew they were true. "Caroline is already dying. She's Gillian's last tie to this place. If Gillian can't wait it out, she'll end things on her own terms and wait for Caroline on the other side."

"How can you know that?"

I shrugged. "They love each other."

"Like ... they're girlfriends?"

I snickered at his expression. "Like there are many different kinds of soulmates. I think, in this life, Caroline ended up being more than Gillian's salvation. In essence, she was also her soulmate."

"That's a nice way of looking at it."

"Yeah, well, I'm a nice woman." I smiled when he chuckled and pressed a soft kiss to the corner of his mouth, stroking his hair as I turned serious. "Do you want to talk about what happened to Liz?"

"Not really."

"Are you sure?"

Kade sighed. "I don't know what there is to say. I killed her."

"You didn't have a choice."

"I also didn't have control," Kade argued. "At some point I realized I should stop what I was doing and managed to accomplish just that, but she was already gone by that point."

"She was going to die no matter what," I reminded him. "We talked about it over lunch. I was going to kill her. If I couldn't, it would've fallen to Max or Raven. We couldn't let her leave this place alive. She was too dangerous."

"Yeah, well, it was different when I thought someone else was going to do it," Kade admitted. "Not that I wanted you to have to do it," he added hurriedly. "I just didn't think I was going to be the one … and not in the way I did it."

"Yeah. How did that happen? All I know is that you were suddenly next to me and your hands were on fire."

"I don't know." Kade shook his head. "I was watching you fight, my heart pounding a mile a minute, and I kept thinking there had to be something I could do to help. The next thing I knew, my hands were tingling, and when I looked down I saw the flames. Somehow I simply knew what to do."

"You did the right thing." I rubbed my nose against his cheek, keeping my body flush against his. "I know you don't want to hear this, but I think it will be easier going forward. You got over the main barrier and now you'll be able to call the magic easier."

"I still don't know if I want magic."

"I don't see where you have much choice. It's a part of you. It has always been a part of you."

"But I didn't know about it. That somehow made it easier."

"Well, you know about it now." I wasn't sure if taking a pragmatic approach was the right way to go, but I committed all the same. "Max said it earlier. We can't go back in time. We can only move forward. We'll move forward with this together. I'll be right by your side when something comes up, and we'll figure it out ... because that's what we do."

Kade smiled as he slid me a sidelong look. "When did you turn into an optimist?"

That was a great question. I had pessimistic leanings. There was no doubt about that. "Maybe it happened when I realized that the wendigo wasn't the real monster in this story. Maybe it happened when a mother took time out of her day to talk to me about her special son and explain how she was worried that he would never get the life he deserved, and I found myself telling her that he would be fine as long as he kept the strong foundation he already had."

"Wow!" Kade made a hilarious face. "You've had quite the day, huh?"

"It's nowhere near the day you've had. In fact ... ." I didn't get a chance to finish because Max picked that moment to approach us. He was dirty and grimy from the fight – something I rarely saw – but he appeared otherwise happy. "Hello, Max. How are you doing?"

Max shot me a cheeky wink as he smiled and wiped his hands on the paper towel in the middle of the table. "Oh, well, I can't complain. We had a war that pretty much fizzled out. We saved a wendigo and set her free on the world with nothing but a promise that she wouldn't kill. Oh, and my son used magic for the first time. All in all, a fairly good day."

I scowled under the weight of his stare. "If you're going to give me crap for letting Gillian go ... well ... I don't care. I couldn't kill her."

"Releasing her wasn't part of the plan," Max reminded me. "We were supposed to kill her. She's still a threat to this area."

"She's not a threat. She's ... different. Not everything falls into a neat little category or box." I realized what I'd said only after it escaped my mouth, Raven's words from earlier in the week coming back to haunt me. Oh, geez. That was something to dwell on later.

"I agree she's not a threat," Max said after a beat. "Still, we should've discussed it before you cut her loose. As it stands, I believe she'll keep to herself and take care of Caroline. They seem quite devoted to each other."

"Yeah."

"As for the men, I placed a call a few minutes ago." Max smoothly changed topics. "As soon as Liz died, they returned to their former selves. It was as if a switch got thrown. They started babbling and, if what I'm hearing is true, they don't seem happy with their enslavement."

I widened my eyes. "They remember it?"

"Apparently so. They saw very little of us. Their stories will revolve around the women they married and were sacrificed for. I think that's a fitting punishment for those who ran before the fighting truly started."

"I guess." I rubbed my neck, unsure what to make of the development. "So, that's it? We're done here."

"We have another day of work, and it will be a busy one," Max corrected. "We gave out a ton of free vouchers to placate the guests earlier. We will be slammed from opening until closing tomorrow."

"Oh, yeah, I forgot about that."

"Other than that, we're done." Max focused his full attention on Kade. "Do you want to talk about what happened?"

"I just want to sleep on it right now," Kade replied, rubbing his hand over my thigh as he forced a smile for his father's benefit. "I don't know what to think about it. I'm exhausted. I really just want to throw Poet over my shoulder and hide in our new trailer until dawn."

Max chuckled. "I think you should definitely do that. We can talk about the rest during our trip to Michigan. It's going to be a long drive."

"Sounds good." Kade heaved out a sigh as he got to his feet and extended his hand. "Shall we?"

I slipped my hand in his and grinned. "Sure."

"Great." Kade took me by surprise when he grabbed me around the waist and threw me over his shoulder, causing me to squeal as he playfully patted my rear end.

"What are you doing?"

"I believe there's a saying about victors and spoils and such," Kade replied. "Well, today I'm the victor."

"Does that mean I'm the spoils?"

"That means you're the only thing I want right now."

Oh, who wouldn't melt at that? "Then let's spoil away."

"That's exactly what I plan to do."

Serious discussions could wait … at least for a few hours. For now we had each other and I recognized Kade needed quiet time. He was about to enter a new world, and there was officially no looking back.

Made in the USA
Coppell, TX
10 September 2020